HER COLTON P.I.

BY
AMELIA AUTIN

First Published in Great Britain 2016
By Mills & Boon, an imprint of HarperCollins*Publishers*
1 London Bridge Street, London, SE1 9GF

© 2016 by Harlequin Books S.A.

Special thanks and acknowledgement to Amelia Autin Lam for her contribution to *The Coltons of Texas* series.

ISBN: 978-0-263-91936-3

18-0

Our
prod
manu
the c

Print
by C

Award-winning author **Amelia Autin** is an inveterate reader who can't bear to put a good book down. . .or part with it. She's a longtime member of Romance Writers of America and served three years as its treasurer. Amelia resides with her PhD engineer husband in quiet Vail, Arizona, where they can see the stars at night and have a "million-dollar view" of the Rincon Mountains from their backyard.

For my stepmother, Mary Dorothy Callen Autin, who makes the world a special place for everyone who knows her. For my stepsister, Patti Padgett Mouton Fagan, who made my father immensely proud of the woman she became. And for Vincent. . .always.

Chapter 1

She's not going to get away with it. That was all Chris Colton could think as he listened to the tearful story Angus and Evalinda McCay unfolded before him. Holly McCay wasn't going to get away with keeping her in-laws from their beloved twin grandsons, all they had left of their son after he died.

Chris leaned back in his chair in his northwest Fort Worth, Texas, office and glanced at the pictures the McCays had handed him. One was of blond-haired, brown-eyed Holly McCay and her now-deceased husband, Grant. The other was of the McCay twins, Ian and Jamie.

"But they don't look like that anymore," Evalinda McCay said sadly. "Our grandsons weren't even a year old when that picture was taken, and that was more than six months ago. Holly won't even let us see them.

She's been like that ever since Grant…" She dabbed a tissue at her eyes.

"Don't worry, Mrs. McCay," Chris said, steel in his voice. "I'll take this job myself—I won't hand it off to an associate. I'll find your grandsons for you. And your daughter-in-law, too."

Angus McCay cleared his throat. "I don't like to speak ill of my son, Mr. Colton, because he's gone and can't defend himself. But he was blind to what his wife was really like. She trapped him into marriage—"

"They hadn't even been married seven months when Ian and Jamie were born," Evalinda McCay clarified in a shocked tone.

"Grant's will made her the trustee for their boys," Angus McCay continued, as if he hadn't been interrupted. "And…well…"

"The money is all she cares about," his wife threw in. She put her hand on her husband's arm. "I know you don't like to put it so bluntly, Angus, but you know it's true." Her gaze moved to Chris. "Holly took the boys and left town three weeks before Christmas. Right before *Christmas*…" She choked up for a moment before continuing. "Grant's fortune is tied up in a trust for Ian and Jamie, but Holly is the sole trustee. Which means she can spend the money any way she sees fit, without any real oversight."

Angus McCay added, "And since she won't tell us where she is…won't even let us *see* them…" He sighed heavily. "We don't even know if they're alive, much less healthy and happy."

"We tried to get custody of the boys through the courts right after Grant died," Evalinda McCay said, her wrinkled face lined with worry. "But grandparents don't seem to have any legal rights these days. Our lawyer said he's not optimistic—not even to force Holly to let us have some kind of visitation with Ian and Jamie."

"The police won't help us, because Holly hasn't done anything wrong," Angus McCay said gruffly.

"Except break our hearts, and Ian's and Jamie's, too, for that matter—but there's no law against that," Evalinda McCay put in.

"You don't have to say any more." Determination grew in Chris. If it was the last thing he did, he'd find Holly McCay and her eighteen-month-old sons for Mr. and Mrs. McCay. Not just because no one had the right to deprive good and decent grandparents like the McCays access to their grandchildren. But because the children deserved to know their grandparents. That was the real bottom line.

Not to mention it made him sick to think of Holly McCay isolating her children from their relatives for money. His foster parents hadn't abused him, but he'd known ever since he was placed with them when he was eleven that they were in it only for the money the state gave them.

"We tracked Holly here to Fort Worth, but then the trail went cold. That's why we decided to hire you, Mr. Colton," Angus McCay said now. "You know this part of the state—we don't." He glanced at his wife, who cleared her throat as if to remind him of something. "And there's another thing. It's all over the news here in Fort Worth about the Alphabet Killer in Granite Gulch."

Chris stiffened, wondering if the McCays knew about his family's connection to the serial killer. But Angus McCay continued without a pause and Chris relaxed. "We know Granite Gulch is forty miles away, and we know all the targets so far are women with long dark hair. But who knows? That could change at any time. And Holly...well...despite everything, she *is* our daughter-in-law. If anything happened to her..."

He trailed off and his wife picked up the thread of the story. "We heard on the news the last victim was Gwendolyn Johnson, which means the killer is up to the *H*s now. And Holly's name begins with *H*. No matter what she's done to *us*, Mr. Colton, she's Ian and Jamie's mother. They've already lost their father before they ever had a chance to know him. I shudder to think of those two innocent babies orphaned at such a young age." She turned to her husband and nodded for him to continue.

"We don't know what it will cost," Angus McCay said, "but we have some money saved. Whatever your fees are, we'll double them if you make this job your top priority. And we'll give you a bonus if you find Holly within a month. We *have* to find her, Mr. Colton. And the boys," he added hastily.

"That won't be necessary," Chris said, thinking to himself that Holly McCay didn't deserve in-laws as caring as the McCays obviously were. "I won't even take a fee for this one—just cover the expenses and we'll be square. But I'll find your daughter-in-law and your grandsons for you, Mr. and Mrs. McCay. You can take that to the bank."

Evalinda McCay unbent enough to smile at Chris with approval. "You're a good man, Mr. Colton. I knew we were doing the right thing contacting you." Her smile faded. "When you find Holly, please don't tell her anything. She might take the boys and disappear. Again.

No, I think it's better if you just let us know where she is and we'll take it from there. If we can just see her... talk to her...if she can see us with our grandsons...she can't be that hard-hearted to keep us away when she knows how much Grant's boys mean to us."

Chris nodded. "Yes, ma'am." He wasn't convinced Mrs. McCay was right, but he wasn't going to say so. If Holly McCay had fled right before Christmas, taking her twins—and their money—with her, she definitely *could* be hard-hearted enough to prevent the McCays from being a part of her sons' lives. *It's all about the money for her*, he thought cynically. *Just like my foster parents. It's all about the money.*

Holly McCay pulled up in front of her friend Peg Merrill's house, parked and turned off the engine. But she didn't get out right away. She adjusted the rear-view mirror of her small Ford SUV with one hand and tugged her dark-haired pixie-cut wig more securely into place with the other. She hated the wig, even though she'd repeatedly told herself it was a necessity. It was already too warm for comfort, and it was only the first day of May. What would she do when the north Texas heat and humidity blasted her in July?

Ian and Jamie hated the wig, too, because it confused them. Just like the other disguises she'd donned had confused them before they came to Rosewood. Her eighteen-month-old twin toddlers were too young to put their emotions into words, but Ian had started acting out recently, refusing to put away his toys or eat the food on his plate without coaxing. Even his favorite mashed potatoes—which he called "smashed 'tatoes"—didn't seem to tempt him.

And Jamie had begun clinging in a way he never had before. Almost as if he was afraid his mother would disappear from his life. He didn't even want her to leave him with Ian to play with Peg Merrill's kids while she went grocery shopping in nearby Granite Gulch— and Jamie loved playing with Peg's children. Until a month ago he'd never been the clinging type.

Holly sighed softly. *If only*, she told herself for the umpteenth time. If only Grant hadn't died. If only he hadn't left *all* his money to their twin boys in an unbreakable trust, but instead had made provision for his parents. If only Grant's parents weren't so…so mercenary.

Not just mercenary, Holly reminded herself, shivering a little even though it was a warm spring day. *Deadly*.

She gave herself a little shake. "Don't think about that now," she muttered under her breath, doing her best Scarlett O'Hara imitation. She pasted a smile on her face and glanced at the mirror again to reassure herself she presented a normal appearance. Ian and Jamie didn't need a mother who was always looking over one shoulder. Who was paranoid that somehow the McCays had tracked her down to— *Stop that!* she insisted. *You're not going to worry about that itch between your shoulder blades… Not today.*

She was going to have to worry about it soon, though. And make some hard choices. If she packed up Ian and Jamie and everything they owned—which wasn't all that much, just what would fit into her small SUV— and moved away from their temporary home in Rosewood, she'd be on her own again. No Peg to help her by watching the twins while she ran errands, like grocery shopping or driving the forty miles into Fort Worth—or the seventy-plus miles into Dallas—to withdraw cash from one of the branch banks there.

But it wasn't just Peg's help with Ian and Jamie she'd miss. Peg was like the older sister Holly had always dreamed of, and she would miss that…a lot. Besides, what would she tell Peg? She couldn't just disappear without a word, could she? Peg would worry, and it wouldn't be right to do that to her friend. Especially since the Alphabet Killer had everyone in Granite Gulch and the surrounding towns terrified.

Holly sighed deeply, gave one last tug to her wig, then scooped up her purse and headed for Peg's house.

Down the street, Chris sat slumped in the seat of his white Ford F-150 pickup truck, parked two houses away beneath the shade of a flowering catalpa tree. He watched Holly McCay walk up the driveway, skirt Peg's SUV parked there and make for the front door. The male in him noted her slender but shapely figure in jeans that lovingly hugged her curves, and her graceful, swaying walk. The PI in him ignored both—or tried to.

He shook his head softly, forcing himself to think of something other than the way Holly McCay looked. *It's a good thing she isn't a professional criminal*, he thought instead, *because she's lousy at it*.

Oh, she'd done her best to avoid detection, he'd give her that. The short dark-haired wig she was wearing was an effective disguise of sorts. And she'd paid cash for everything—there'd been no paper trail of credit or debit purchases to follow. No checks written, either. But she'd transferred a large sum of money from her bank in Clear Lake City south of Houston to the Cattleman's Bank of Fort Worth, where she'd opened a new account when she moved to the Dallas–Fort Worth area. *That* had left a paper trail she hadn't been able to avoid, since she'd used her own driver's license and social security number. That was how the McCays had tracked her this far.

True, she'd varied the bank branches she'd used to withdraw funds, so no one could stake out one branch and wait for her to show up. That showed she was smart. But she'd slipped up by withdrawing cash from the Granite Gulch branch. Yeah, she'd done it only once, but it stood out in neon letters, since it was out of the pattern—all the other branches had been in Fort Worth or Dallas. And once Chris had known that, he'd searched Granite Gulch and the surrounding area for a woman with twin toddlers who'd recently moved in. No matter what color her hair was, no matter how much she tried to fade into obscurity, everyone remembered the twins. Especially eighteen-month-old identical twin boys as cute as buttons.

And Holly McCay was still driving her Ford Escape with its original Texas license plate tags registered in her name. *Duh!* Once he'd located a woman with twins in Rosewood, the next town over from Granite Gulch, he'd staked out the Rosewood Rooming House, where by all accounts she lived, and bingo! There was her Ford SUV with those incriminating tags.

She was registered at the rooming house using her real name, too, which had made confirmation a piece of cake. He'd almost picked up the phone to call the McCays and tell them he'd located their daughter-in-law…but he hadn't. He wasn't sure why. Was it because a warning light had started blinking that very first day when they turned over everything they knew about Holly's banking transactions? Information they shouldn't have had access to...but somehow had?

Or maybe it was the self-satisfied expression on Evalinda McCay's face when she thought Chris wouldn't see it, when he'd been perusing the financial reports they'd handed him and he'd glanced up unexpectedly. The expression had been wiped away almost instantly, replaced with the look of worried concern she'd worn earlier. But Chris's instincts—which he trusted—had gone on the alert.

He'd been a private investigator for nine years, ever since he'd received his bachelor of arts degree in criminology and criminal justice from the University of Texas at Arlington. From day one he'd trusted his instincts, and they'd never steered him wrong. Only an idiot would go against his instincts in his line of work, and for all his laid-back, seemingly good-old-Texas-boy persona, Chris wasn't an idiot.

He'd also run a credit check on the McCays the same day they'd come to see him—standard procedure for all his clients these days. He never took anyone's word they had the wherewithal to pay him—he'd been burned once early in his career and had learned a hard lesson. The credit report on the McCays had come back with some troubling red flags. They were living beyond their means. Way beyond their means, and had done so for years, despite Angus McCay's well-paying job as a bank president down in Houston. Even though Chris was taking this case pro bono and wouldn't be paid except for expenses, that credit report had given him pause.

Now he was glad he hadn't called the McCays for several reasons, not the least of which was that he knew

Peg Merrill, had known her all his life. If she and Holly were friends, then Holly *couldn't* be the woman the Mc-Cays had made her out to be. Peg had an unerring BS meter—she'd nailed Chris on a few things over the years—which meant Holly couldn't have fooled Peg about the kind of woman she was. To top it off, Peg reigned supreme in one area in particular—motherhood. The worst insult in her book was to call someone a bad mother. No way would she be friends with a woman who was a bad mother.

Besides, Peg was his sister-in-law. Former sister-in-law, really, since Laura was dead. But he wasn't going there. Not now. Sister-in-law or not, Chris didn't want to be on Peg's bad side. Especially not on a pro bono case he'd already been having second thoughts about.

Chris waited until Holly McCay strapped her twins into their car seats and drove away before he got out of his truck. He shrugged on his blazer to hide his shoulder holster, then settled his black Stetson on his head and ambled toward Peg's house, determined to find out whatever he could about Holly McCay from Peg.

"Chris!" Peg exclaimed when she opened the door. "This is a surprise. Come on in."

"Unca Chris!" Peg's two-year-old daughter, Susan, made a beeline for Chris when he stepped inside, and he bent over to swing her up into his arms. A cacophony of barking from three dogs—one of which had been Chris's gift to Laura not long before she died—prevented anyone from being heard for a couple of minutes, but eventually Peg's two dogs subsided back to their rug in front of the fireplace in the family room.

Chris settled into one of the oversize recliners, still

cuddling Susan against his shoulder while his other hand ruffled Wally's fur. "Hey, boy," he murmured, gazing down at the golden retriever Laura had adored. If his heart hadn't already been broken when Laura died, it would have broken at losing Wally, too. Chris had given Laura the puppy thinking they'd soon be moving from their apartment into a house with a large fenced yard. But that dream house sat vacant now—Chris couldn't bear to live there without Laura. And an apartment was no place for a growing dog, especially since Chris was rarely home. So when Peg and her husband, Joe, volunteered to adopt Wally, Chris had reluctantly accepted their offer. At least he'd still get to see Wally, he'd reasoned at the time—he was always welcome at the Merrill house.

Chris and Peg chatted about nothing much for a few minutes. About Bobby, Peg's napping one-year-old son, who was already starting to walk. About Joe's thriving gardening center in Granite Gulch, the Green and Grow. About Chris's highly successful private investigation business—which he'd thrown himself into even more thoroughly after Laura's death—and the fourth office he'd nearly decided to add in Arlington.

When Susan's eyelids began fluttering, Peg reached to take her daughter from Chris, but he forestalled her. "I'll put her down for her nap," he told Peg, doing just that. When he came back, Peg handed him a frosty glass of iced tea prepared the way he preferred it, with two lemon wedges, not just one.

They'd just settled back into their spots in the family room, Wally at Chris's feet, when Peg put her own glass of iced tea down on a coaster on the end table and said, "So what's wrong?" She didn't give Chris a chance to answer before she continued, "I didn't want to say anything in front of Susan—you would *not* believe how much she understands already. I told Joe he needed to watch his language now that Susan is so aware—and she mimics everything he says... *especially* the bad words." Chris laughed, and Peg said, "But something's up. You wouldn't be here in the middle of the week, in the middle of the afternoon, if something wasn't wrong."

Chris shook his head and smiled wryly. "You must have second sight or something." He hesitated, considering and then discarding his original idea of pumping Peg for info about Holly McCay on the sly. "The woman who was here a little while ago—"

"Holly?" Peg's surprise was obvious.

"Yeah. Holly McCay. I've been hired by her in-laws to find her."

Chapter 2

Two days later Holly drove away from Peg's house with her vision blurred from unshed tears. She'd left the twins in her friend's care one last time, but that wasn't why she was practically crying. She hadn't told Peg—she'd chickened out at the last minute—but she wasn't going to do errands. She'd wanted Ian and Jamie to have one last opportunity to play with Susan and Bobby…while she packed up the contents of their room in the Rosewood Rooming House and loaded everything into her SUV. Then she would pick up her boys, hand Peg the note she was trying to compose in her mind so Peg wouldn't worry about them…and they'd be gone.

Chris followed Holly away from Peg's house, keeping enough distance between his truck and her little

SUV so she wouldn't spot the tail. He was surprised when she didn't stop at any of the stores in Granite Gulch but kept driving. She kept driving even after she reached the state highway that was the boundary between Granite Gulch and Rosewood. Puzzled but not really worried, Chris let the distance between their two vehicles increase, because there weren't any cars out this way to hide the fact that he was following her.

When Holly pulled into the Rosewood Rooming House parking lot, Chris was faced with a dilemma. He drove past, then doubled back as soon as he could, just in time to see Holly entering the rooming house's front door.

"What the hell is she doing?" he muttered to himself, wondering if she'd forgotten something and would be back outside soon. He made a U-turn a hundred yards down, parked close enough so he could watch the front door and Holly's SUV, but far enough away from the rooming house so he wouldn't be spotted, and waited. And waited.

A fleeting thought crossed his mind that the Rosewood Rooming House wasn't really the safest place for a woman on her own with two young children. Not only was the rooming house full of transients, but Regina Willard—whom law enforcement had pretty much identified as the Alphabet Killer—was known to have roomed here not that long ago. *Not* his baby sister, Josie, thank God. The Alphabet Killer hadn't been caught yet, but at least now everyone in town knew it wasn't Josie.

Thoughts of Josie reminded Chris that she was still missing, even after all these years he'd been searching for her. His two most spectacular failures as a PI both had their roots in his family history—Josie…and his mother's burial place. He touched his heart in an automatic gesture. The pain he felt over those failures ranked right up there with Laura's death and his guilt over that.

If his serial-killer father could be believed, however, his mother's burial place might at last be discovered, something all the Colton children devoutly wished for. When their father had killed their mother, he'd hidden her body. She'd never been found, not in twenty years. But Matthew Colton had provided four clues to where Saralee Colton's body was buried. Not that the clues made any real sense…so far. But they were clues. He'd promised one clue for every child who visited him in prison. Annabel had been the last to visit their father, and her clue—Peaches—had been just as enigmatic as the first three: Texas, Hill and *B*. The siblings had theorized that maybe—*maybe*—the clues were pointing to their maternal grandparents' home in Bearson, Texas. But that house sat on acres of land. Even if their mother was buried somewhere on her parents' property, they weren't really much better off than they'd been when they started this sorry mess.

Chris sighed. This month was his turn to visit their father in prison. He didn't know why Matthew was putting his children through this torture—other than the fact that he could because they were all desperate to locate their mother's body and give her a decent burial—but it almost seemed as if their father was getting a perverse pleasure out of it. "The serial killer's last revenge," he murmured. Matthew Colton was dying. Everyone knew it, especially Matthew himself. "It would be just like that bastard to torture us with these disparate clues…then die. Taking his secret to the grave." He relieved his anger and frustration with a few choice curse words...until he remembered he was supposed to be giving them up. He'd resolved two days earlier that he was going to clean up his language for Susan Merrill's sake, and Bobby's, just as Joe Merrill was supposed to do.

"Heck and damnation," Chris said now. It didn't have the same impact.

Regina Willard groaned as she rolled out of her un-comfortable sleeping bag and staggered outside to re-lieve herself. She hated this hideout, hated being forced by the Granite Gulch Police Department and the FBI to hurriedly leave the Rosewood Rooming House. Her place there hadn't been luxurious by any means, but at least she'd had a comfortable bed and civilized facili-ties at her disposal. Not this hole-in-the-ground living quarters without any running water.

She thought fleetingly of her half brother, Jesse Wil-lard, and his thriving farm. The last time she'd talked to him, years ago, he'd tried to encourage her to move on. To stop grieving for her lòst fiancé. Jesse didn't understand. That bitch had stolen the only man Re-gina could ever love, and she'd had to pay. No matter how the woman disguised herself, no matter how many times she changed her name, Regina recognized her... and made her pay.

Regina shook her head. She kept killing that woman, but the bitch refused to stay dead. So Regina had to keep killing her again and again. If she killed her enough times, eventually she would *stay* dead. Then she could relax, move away from this area and try to forget.

She blinked, then rubbed her eyes, trying to focus. How many times had it been altogether? She ticked them off on her fingers. "Seven," she said at last. She chuckled to herself. Yes, she'd been forced into hiding out in this shelter in the middle of nowhere, but not even the vaunted FBI had been able to stop her. She was on a mission, and no one would stop her until the bitch was dead. Permanently.

Holly packed swiftly. While her hands were performing that mindless task, she tried to make plans. *Where to go?* she thought. *New Mexico? Arizona?* Or should she just keep driving until she'd put thousands of miles between herself and the McCays? She'd never lived in the United States outside Texas, and a little niggling fear of the unknown made her heart skip a beat as she envisioned going to a completely strange place. Not just the difference between Houston and Fort Worth, but *completely* different. Yes, she'd visited South America as a young child with her missionary parents, but that was a long time ago—Texas had been her home ever since she'd started school.

Leaving again hadn't been an easy decision for Holly to make—she didn't want to leave. Not just for her own sake but for her boys, too, who had reached the age where they noticed changes in their lives. But the time had come to move on.

She wasn't really concerned about the Alphabet Killer, despite the fact that the killer was up to the *H*s now. All seven of the killer's victims had long dark hair, and while Holly's wig was dark, it was very short. Not that she was careless of her safety—she wasn't going to risk being the exception to the killer's rule.

But she wasn't running from the Alphabet Killer. She was running from the McCays. The McCays...and their attempts on her life.

She hadn't wanted to admit it at first. But when one near miss had led to a second, then a third, she'd been forced to look at the McCays with suspicious eyes. *Someone* wanted her dead. Who else could it be? She didn't have an enemy in the world. But she *was* the trustee for the twins' inheritance from Grant. Which meant she controlled the income earned on nearly twenty million dollars. Over and above the cash invested conservatively, the trust also owned stock in Grant's software company—now being run by others, but still doing well. So the trust had unlimited growth potential.

She'd always known Grant's parents—especially his mother—were cold and calculating. Grant had known it, too, although they'd never really discussed it—not when they were kids, and not after they were married. It was one of those things they'd just taken for granted. Was that why he hadn't left them anything in his will? Because he knew they were more interested in the fortune he'd earned from his breakthrough software design than they were in him or their grandsons?

She had no proof the McCays were trying to kill her, though. Nothing to take to the police except a growing certainty it couldn't be anyone else. Especially after the McCays tried to gain custody of the twins through the courts and had lied about Holly in their depositions—warning bells had gone off loud and clear. But even if she'd gone to the police, what would they have said? Those near misses could have been a coincidence. Accidents. The McCays were solid, middle-class, upstanding, churchgoing citizens. The salt of the earth. Or at least that was the image they projected. How could she even think of making a slanderous accusation against them...especially for such a heinous crime as attempted murder?

Which was why she'd packed up the bare necessities three weeks before Christmas, buckled her sons into their baby car seats and headed north toward the Dallas–Fort Worth metroplex with fierce determination. She hadn't really had a plan—plans could wait, she'd told herself—but she knew she had to put herself out of reach of her in-laws until she had time to think things through. She'd thought she could lose herself in Texas's second-largest metropolitan area.

But she wasn't a criminal on the lam, and she had no idea how to go about getting a fake ID. Not to mention she couldn't carry huge wads of cash with her in lieu of using her credit and debit cards. She had to withdraw money from the bank periodically—a bank account she'd opened with her real social security number and driver's license.

She'd moved a week after she'd opened the new bank account—as she'd moved every time she got the feeling the McCays were getting close. But she hadn't switched banks. She'd picked the Cattleman's Bank of Fort Worth precisely because it had hundreds of branches throughout the DFW area, including small branches in grocery stores. And Holly had used many of them to throw the McCays off the scent...assuming they were still trying to track her down. But she had to assume that. She didn't dare assume otherwise.

Which meant her time in tiny Rosewood, right next door to Granite Gulch, where Peg lived, had finally come to an end. Rosewood was so small she'd thought the McCays would never find her in this out-of-the-way place, since she was still paying cash for everything and varying which bank branches she was using to withdraw that cash.

She loved the small-town atmosphere here, and after she'd made friends with Peg at the Laundromat—*thank God Peg's washing machine broke down that day!*—she'd started to feel at home. So she'd convinced herself she was safe. But for the past three days she'd had... well...*the willies*, she told herself, for lack of a better term. A feeling she was being watched. Followed.

It *could* be the Alphabet Killer, she supposed. But she didn't think so. Either way was a disaster in the making, and she wasn't going to stick around to find out for sure one way or the other.

Holly stashed two suitcases into the rear of her SUV, then headed back to the rooming house for another load.

She held the door to her room open with one foot as she picked up a box of toys and books, then tried to scream and dropped the box when a tall blond man in a black Stetson loomed in the doorway.

A large hand covered her mouth, stifling her voice, and all Holly could think of in that instant was *No!* No, she wasn't going to be a victim. She wasn't going to let herself be raped or murdered or—

She tore at the hand covering her mouth, but the man plastered her against the wall inside her room and kicked the door shut behind him. Then just held her prisoner with his body as she desperately tried to free herself. She gave up trying to fight the hand that muzzled her and went for his eyes instead. But he ducked his head, placing his mouth against her ear as he said in a deep undertone, "Stop it, Holly! I'm not going to hurt you—I'm trying to save your life. Peg Merrill's my sister-in-law."

She froze. Her heart was still beating like a snare drum, but she stopped fighting at Peg's name. And when she did that, she realized the stranger wasn't using her immobility to his advantage. She tried to ask a question, but the hand over her mouth prevented her.

"If I take my hand away, are you going to scream?" he asked, still in that same deep undertone. Holly shook her head slightly and was surprised, yet not surprised, when he did just that—he removed his hand. But it hovered near her face, as if he'd clamp it back in place if she screamed.

She swallowed against the dry throat, which terror had induced, then whispered, "Who are you?"

"Chris Colton. And yes," he answered before she could ask, "Peg's really my sister-in-law."

"I don't understand. Why are you here? Why did you force your way into my room?"

An enigmatic expression crossed his face, and he looked as if he was of two minds about answering those questions. "If I let you go, are you going to run for it? Or are you going to give me a chance to explain?"

A tiny dart of humor speared through her, despite the dregs of terror that still clung to her body. "You'd catch me before I ran three steps," she said drily. "So I guess I have no choice but to listen to what you have to say."

He surprised her again by laughing softly, but "Smart woman" was all he said. He took a step backward, then another and another, slowly. As if he was expecting her to make a break for it. But Holly wasn't stupid. If he was there to kill her, she'd be dead already—her strength was no match for his. And if he was there to rape her, he'd never have let her go.

Besides, she'd felt the bulge of his gun in its shoulder holster when he held her pinioned against the wall, but he hadn't drawn his weapon and used it against her. This meant he was probably telling the truth. Probably.

"I don't understand," she said again. "If Peg sent you, why didn't she tell me she was going to? I was just there, and she didn't say a wor—"

"She didn't send me. Not exactly. And I know you were just at her house. I followed you there...and back. I've been following you for days."

"Why?" She managed to tamp down the sudden fear his revelation triggered. So she *wasn't* crazy. She *had* been followed.

He removed his Stetson as if he'd just realized he was still wearing it. Then ran his fingers through the hair the hat had flattened. "Because the McCays hired me to find you."

"What?" She barely breathed the word.

His face took on a grim cast. "I'm a private investigator, Holly. The McCays came to my office a week ago. They spun me a cock-and-bull story about you, which I almost swallowed hook, line and sinker. Almost." He looked as if he were going to add something to that statement, but didn't.

"Let me guess. I'm an abusive mother, and they want to rescue Ian and Jamie from my clutches."

"No."

A wry chuckle was forced out of her. "Well, that's a change. That's the story they told the court when they tried to wrest custody of my boys from me after Grant died." Curious, she asked, "So what was their story this time?"

Chris glanced down at the Stetson in his hand and ran his fingers along the brim. "You're the trustee for the boys' inheritance from their dad," he said when he raised his eyes to meet hers again. "You wanted to use the money on yourself instead of for the boys' benefit, and you took Ian and Jamie away from their loving grandparents so no one could call you to account. And you won't let the McCays even know where you are...where the boys are. Won't let them be a part of your children's lives."

Holly closed her eyes for a second, laughed again without humor and shook her head. "All of that is true, except for one thing," she admitted. "I *am* the sole trustee. And I *did* run with Ian and Jamie—three weeks before Christmas, did they mention that?" Chris nodded. "And I *haven't* told the McCays where we are... for a perfectly good reason. Because—"

"Because they're trying to kill you."

Stunned, Holly asked in a breathless whisper, "How did you know that?"

One corner of Chris's mouth twitched up into a half smile. "Because I'm damned good at what I do, Holly. Because the minute I found out you were friends with Peg, I knew the McCays were lying through their teeth, and I wanted to know why. I hate lies and I hate liars. But even more than that, I hate being taken for a sucker. So I did a little more digging...on them. And found out a hell of a lot more than they want the world to know."

"I can't believe you believe me."

"It's not so much a matter of believing *you*, it's

putting the facts together and believing the story they tell—no matter what that story is. No matter if the story seems incredible on the face of it."

Holly buried her face in her hands as emotion welled up in her. For months she'd had no one she could confide in about her suspicions. No one she could share her worry with. She hadn't even told Peg. And this man, this *stranger*, was telling her she'd been right all along.

When she finally raised her face to his, her eyes were dry. She wasn't going to cry about this, not now. She'd cried enough tears over the McCays, almost as many tears as she'd cried over Grant's death. Her lips tightened. "That means I'm doing the right thing taking the boys and leaving town."

Chris shook his head. "I didn't tell them I located you. And I won't."

"But don't you see? Even if you don't tell them where I am, if they hired you they know I'm in this area. And the next PI they hire might not... What I mean is, not everyone will suspect their motives. Not everyone will believe the truth."

Chris stared thoughtfully, then nodded. "You're right. But I can't let you run away again. Not knowing what I know. I'd never be able to forgive myself if..." He seemed to reach a decision. "I think the best thing would be for you and your boys to check out of this rooming house...but stay where I can keep an eye on you until we can set a trap for the McCays."

Holly shook her head vehemently. "I can't do that to you and your wife—put you in danger that way."

All expression was wiped from Chris's face in a heartbeat. "My wife is dead."

She gasped and covered her mouth with her hand.

"I'm so sorry," she whispered eventually. "I didn't know. You said Peg's your sister-in-law, and since you and she don't have the same name, I assumed..." Her words trailed off miserably.

"Peg never mentioned her younger sister, Laura?" Holly shook her head again. "I guess I shouldn't be surprised," Chris said. "Peg and Laura were particularly close. She took Laura's death hard." He didn't say it, but Holly could see Peg wasn't the only one who'd taken Laura's death hard. But that closed-off expression also told her this wasn't a topic of conversation Chris wanted to pursue.

Is that why Peg bonded with me so quickly? Holly wondered abstractedly. *Because she saw in me the little sister she'd lost?*

"So you're not putting my wife in danger," Chris said, drawing her attention back to the here and now. "Most of my family is in some kind of law enforcement, too, and I can recruit them to help me set a trap for the McCays. Of course, everyone's focused on capturing the Alphabet Killer right now, so the McCays aren't going to be a top priority. Especially since there's no concrete evidence against them. In the meantime, though, I want you and your boys in safekeeping."

"Ian and Jamie aren't in danger," she was quick to point out. "Just me."

"Are you so sure?" Chris's eyes in that moment were the hardest, coldest blue eyes she'd ever seen. "If the McCays are willing to kill you to gain custody, who's to say they wouldn't eventually arrange 'accidents' for the boys, too, once they had them in their control?"

"Their own grandchildren? I can't believe—"

Chris cut her off. "Believe it. Once you've taken the

first life, the next one is easier to justify in your mind. And the next." A bark of humorless laughter escaped him. "I should know. My father is Matthew Colton."

Holly's brows drew together in a frown. "I don't think I—"

"Mathew Colton, the original bull's-eye serial killer. He was infamous in his day. The Alphabet Killer is a copycat of sorts, marking her victims the way he did." His face hardened into a grim mask. "My father killed ten people twenty years ago. Including his last victim—my mother."

Chapter 3

"Oh, my God!"

Shock was obvious on Holly's face, followed quickly by the emotion Chris hated the most—pity. He'd had a bellyful of pity in his life—from the time he was eleven and became a quasi-orphan, right up through Laura's death almost two years ago. He didn't want pity and he didn't need it.

"My father killed nine men who reminded him of his hated brother, Big J Colton," he said brusquely, "before he killed my mother…whose only crime was that she loved him. So don't tell me the McCays couldn't possibly kill their innocent grandchildren."

"I…won't." The fear in Holly's eyes surprised Chris, because it wasn't fear of him. It wasn't even fear for herself as a target of the McCays. No, the fear was for her children. Then her face changed, and the fear morphed into fierce determination to protect her children at all costs, no matter what. If Chris had needed one more bit of proof Holly McCay was a good mother, he'd just received it.

"They're not getting anywhere near Ian and Jamie," Holly stated unequivocally. "What do you want me to do?"

He glanced away and thought for a moment, then nodded to himself. His eyes met Holly's. "I've got a house on the outskirts of Granite Gulch. No one lives there, but Peg looks after it for me, so it's not… abandoned." A wave of pain went through him and his right eye twitched as he remembered this was Laura's dream house, the one he'd built for her right before she died. The house she'd never had a chance to live in. The house he couldn't bear to occupy after her death. "It stands all by itself on several acres, and it's up on a ridge—you can easily spot someone coming almost a mile away. I can't think of a safer place for you and the boys to hide out."

"Just us?"

"And me. Until we can set a trap for the McCays, I don't want you out of my sight if I can help it."

"What about your job? You can't just—"

Chris's jaw set tightly. "I run my own business. I haven't taken a day off since Laura's funeral, so I think I can manage this. Besides, I do a lot of my work over the phone or on the computer. I can work from the office in the house. We designed the house—" *...with that in mind*, he started to say, but his throat closed before he could get the words out.

Holly didn't respond at first, just assessed him with an enigmatic expression on her face. The silence stretched from ten seconds to twenty, to thirty. Nearly a minute had passed before she said, "Okay. I appreciate the offer. And I'll accept it on my children's behalf. If it was just me...that would be a different story, but it's not."

A half hour later everything Holly and the twins had with them was loaded into her SUV, with the exception of the two fold-a-cribs she'd bought when she moved to Rosewood. Chris stashed those in the back of his truck, and Holly realized if she'd taken Ian and Jamie and run, she would have had to leave the twins' cribs behind—they just wouldn't fit.

"I'll follow you to Peg's," Chris said as he raised the hatch and clicked it firmly closed. "But first, we'd better stop in town and get some groceries. The utilities at the house are on—so we'll have water and electricity—but there's no food."

Holly nodded. "Sounds good."

"And while I'm at it, I'd better stop off and pack a suitcase, and pick up my laptop from my apartment. I live above the Double G Cakes and Pies."

"Oh, I love that place!" she exclaimed. "Mia—the woman who runs it—she always gives Ian and Jamie special cookies she makes just for them."

Chris smiled. "Sounds like Mia. She and my sister Annabel are best friends—they were foster sisters together." His smile faded, replaced by the closed expression that was becoming familiar to Holly, and she knew instinctively this was another topic of conversation he'd never intended to bring up. Foster care joined the growing list of subjects to avoid...unless Chris brought it up himself.

As they drove the short distance to Granite Gulch, Holly wondered about Chris. About his motives for doing this—protecting her boys and her. She also couldn't help wondering about his wife, Laura, and what had happened to her. Car accident? Some kind of illness, like cancer? Peg had never mentioned Laura that she could recall. But it wasn't just idle curiosity. She really wanted to know, because it was obvious Chris had been in love with his wife.

Holly glanced in the rearview mirror at the man in the truck behind her and sighed. If only Grant had loved her the way Chris had loved his wife. If only...

She couldn't help feeling a dart of envy comparing Chris to Grant. Not that Grant hadn't been a good man—he had been. So very different from his parents. No, the problem was that Grant had been her best friend growing up, and while he'd loved her, he hadn't been *in love* with her. Not the way she'd been in love with him.

She'd grieved for Grant. Those first few months after his death she'd been devastated...but she hadn't been able to grieve for long. The McCays had seen to that.

Was that why I recovered from Grant's death so quickly? she asked herself now. *Because Grant's parents tried to gain custody of Ian and Jamie and that took all my energy and concentration? Because when that didn't work they tried to have me killed, forcing me to take my babies and flee?*

The first time a car unexpectedly swerved into her lane on the expressway just as she was approaching an overpass, Holly had dismissed it as merely poor driving on someone's part. The second similar attempt only two weeks later had raised her suspicions, especially since she thought she recognized the car. But the third try on her life had been the clincher—someone had deliberately attempted to run her down in the grocery store parking lot, and she'd escaped with her life only by diving between two parked cars as the vehicle in question sped away without stopping.

Holly glanced in the rearview mirror again. *Or is the reason I'm not still grieving because Grant never loved me the way I wanted him to love me? The way I loved him.*

She would never know. All she knew was that not quite a year after Grant's death she was ready to move on with her life…if the McCays would let her.

Holly buckled Ian into one car seat while Chris buckled Jamie into the other. She'd been surprised at first at how baby-knowledgeable Chris was, but she quickly realized she shouldn't be—Peg's kids adored their "Unca Chris," as Susan called him. Which meant even though she'd never met Chris at Peg's house in the three months the two women had been friends, he had to be a fairly frequent visitor.

Holly turned back to thank Peg just as the other woman came out of the house with a bag of dog food balanced on one hip, a bag of doggy treats perched precariously on top and a leashed Wally dancing joyously beside her.

"What the—" Chris began, but Peg cut him off.

"Holly's kids adore Wally, and he's attached to them, so that will help the kids acclimate faster. Besides, it won't hurt to have a guard dog out there, Chris. You know that. It's why you got Wally for Laura in the first place."

Chris's slow smile did something to Holly's heart. She wasn't sure what it meant, but she wouldn't have minded having that smile aimed at her.

"Thanks," Chris said, relieving Peg of the dog, the dog food and the doggy treats before planting a kiss on her cheek. "Come on, boy," he said, opening the door of his F-150 and letting Wally scramble up onto the front seat as Chris plopped the dog food on the floor.

Holly turned to Peg. "Thanks for watching the boys for me," she said softly. "I wasn't going to leave without telling you—please believe that."

Peg smiled and hugged her. "I do." She stepped back and her smile faded. "But you can't run forever, Holly. I know it's not easy, but sometimes you just have to face up to the truth and take a stand. Chris's idea is better any way you look at it. You owe it to your boys to have the McCays put away so y'all can stop running."

"I know."

The two women embraced once more, and Peg whispered in her ear, "Chris needs to do this, Holly. I can't explain, but he needs to do this. So just let him take care of you and your boys."

Chris drove at a sedate pace—unlike his usual hell-bent-for-leather style—watching Holly's SUV in his rearview mirror, making sure he didn't lose her. And as he drove he wondered about her. Not the facts and figures he'd uncovered in his investigation—he already knew far too much about her past, much more than most people would find out in a year of knowing her.

He knew where she'd grown up, what had happened

to her parents, where she'd gone to college and where she'd worked after graduation. He knew she'd been a stay-at-home mom when her husband had been side-swiped on the I-45 in Houston, triggering a massive pileup that had killed three people...but not the drunk who'd instigated the accident—a driver who'd been using a revoked license, and who now resided in the state prison. He knew how much Holly had received from her husband's insurance, and he knew how much her twins had inherited from their father in the trust the McCays had told him about—just about the only truth in their pack of lies.

But he didn't care about all that. What he wanted to know was what made her tick. She obviously loved her sons. Had she loved their father? His investigation hadn't uncovered any men in her life other than her now-deceased husband, which put her head and shoulders above most of the women he'd been hired to investigate. While the bulk of his work was doing background checks for a couple of major defense contractors in the Dallas–Fort Worth area, as well as extensive white-collar-crime investigation, no PI could completely avoid divorce work. Infidelities were profitable.

But the cases that eviscerated him were the non-custodial kidnappings. He'd had half a dozen of those cases in his career, three of which he'd taken pro bono, the same way he'd taken the McCays' case. What he wouldn't accept—could *never* accept—were people who deliberately separated children from the rest of their family for no real reason except selfishness. Not just parent and child, but also brothers and sisters.

His foster parents had done that. They'd deliberately

isolated him from most of his siblings growing up. They hadn't been able to keep Chris away from his twin sister, Annabel—Granite Gulch had only one high school, and they'd had classes together from day one.

But his foster parents had done their best to keep them apart anyway—even grounding him on the slightest of pretexts and piling him with a heap of after-school chores in addition to his homework—but Annabel had needed him. And beneath his laid-back exterior, Chris had always been something of a white knight. His twin had come first…even if it meant being perpetually grounded.

Chris had managed to reconnect with the rest of his siblings once he was an adult—all except his baby sister, Josie—but he could never get back those growing-up years he'd spent without his four brothers. Without those close familial bonds brothers often formed. That could have made a difference in all their lives, especially given their tragic family history.

That was why he'd taken those pro bono cases in the first place, one of which had come early in his career, when he'd been struggling to make ends meet. But he couldn't turn down a case involving children. Which was why he'd almost fallen for the McCays' sob story. Which was also why he was taking on the toughest case of his career to date—protecting Holly, Ian and Jamie McCay.

"Four bedrooms, Holly," Chris said as he shifted Ian into his left arm and unlocked the front door, then keyed in the code to disengage the alarm system. "Take your pick. Let me know which one you want for the twins, and I'll set up their fold-a-cribs. One of the bedrooms is—"

He broke off for a heartbeat, then attempted to finish his sentence, but Holly said quickly, "I want them with me." She cuddled Jamie, who was starting to fret. "I know all the baby books say it's a bad idea, but ever since…well, ever since we left Clear Lake City, Ian and Jamie have stayed in the same room with me. First in the motels and then in the Rosewood Rooming House. I'm afraid they'll be scared if I try to change that tonight, especially since this is a new place to them and all." She smiled down at the toddler in her arms. "Yes, Jamie, I know you're hungry. Give Mommy a few minutes, please. Okay, sweetie?"

"If that's what works," Chris said, "then it'd probably be best if you took the master bedroom. It's a lot bigger than the others, more room for both cribs."

"But that's *your* bedroom," she protested. "I don't want to put you out of—"

Chris shook his head. "I've never lived here. Never slept a night in that room. So you wouldn't be putting me out."

I did it again, Holly thought as that closed expression replaced Chris's smiling demeanor. She put Jamie down, and he clung to her leg. "I'm sorry." Her voice was quiet. "You're going out of your way to help us, and I…I keep saying the wrong thing."

Chris lowered Ian to the floor but kept a wary eye on him so the toddler didn't wander off. "Not your fault," he said gruffly. He herded Ian toward Holly with a gentle foot. "Why don't you give these two some lunch while I get everything unloaded? I'll bring in the groceries and the high chairs first."

* * *

Chris set up the fold-a-cribs in the master bedroom while Holly fed the twins. As he'd told Holly, the master bedroom held no memories for him, except...Laura had picked out the furniture. She'd picked out everything in the house...without him. Her dream house, she'd laughingly called it. But he'd been too busy to go with her, so she'd gone without him. She'd driven into Fort Worth with her sister, armed with the platinum credit card Chris had given her, and she'd furnished the house, room by room.

That was where she'd been exposed to viral meningitis. Somewhere in Fort Worth she'd come into contact with a carrier of the disease. Much later the Center for Disease Control had reported a mini outbreak of viral meningitis in Fort Worth—too late. Laura had never mentioned the subsequent symptoms she'd experienced to Chris—the severe headache, fever and neck stiffness—and he hadn't noticed. He'd been too busy to—

His cell phone rang abruptly, startling him out of his sad reverie. "Chris Colton," he answered, recognizing the phone number.

The voice of one of the administrative assistants in his Fort Worth office sounded in his ear. "Chris? It's Teri. Angus McCay just called. He wants to know the status on his case. I told him you'd call him. Do you need the number?"

"No, I've got it, thanks. Oh, and, Teri, I'll send an email, but can you let everyone in all three offices know I won't be in for the next few days? Something personal has come up I need to take care of. They can reach me by phone or email if it's urgent. And if any other client calls come in, have Zach or Jimmy deal with them."

"Sure thing, Chris."

He sensed the question Teri wanted to ask but wouldn't. His staff knew not to ask because that's the kind of manager he was—he kept his personal life and his business life completely separate. Chris disconnected, then thumbed through his phone book until he found the listing for Angus McCay and picked the office number. The phone rang only twice before it was answered.

"Angus McCay."

"Chris Colton here. You called me?"

Angus McCay cleared his throat. "I know you told us you'd let us know if you found Holly, Mr. Colton, but…it's been a week and we haven't heard from you. My wife…well, she wanted me to call you and see if you've made any progress."

"Not to worry, Mr. McCay," Chris assured him, his mind working swiftly. "I tracked Holly to Grand Prairie, but she gave me the slip." He deliberately named Grand Prairie because Holly *had* stayed there…just not recently. And Grand Prairie was southeast of Fort Worth, nowhere near Granite Gulch. "I'm hot on her trail, though. I think she might have moved northeast to Irving." Another place Holly really had stayed… briefly. "Just sit tight, and I'll let you know as soon as I have something concrete."

"It's not just our grandchildren at stake, you know. They still haven't caught the Alphabet Killer and… well…you see how it is. Holly's name begins with *H*."

Yeah, Chris thought. *Keep beating that drum. How stupid do you take me for?* "I don't think you have to worry about that, Mr. McCay. Both Grand Prairie and Irving are closer to Dallas than to Fort Worth, and the Alphabet Killer isn't striking anywhere near there."

"Okay, well…just remember, if you find Holly, we don't want you to do anything to scare her off. Just let us know and we'll fly up from Houston immediately. If we can just see that the boys are okay…if we can just talk to Holly…"

"You bet," Chris told him. "I'll keep you posted. And don't worry, Mr. McCay. Holly won't slip through my fingers next time." He disconnected just as a sound from the doorway made him swing around. Holly stood there, white as a ghost, a twin balanced on each hip.

Chapter 4

"You...you said you believed me about the McCays," Holly managed, despite the way her heart was pounding so hard she could barely breathe.

Chris tucked his phone back in his pocket. "I do."

"Then why... What were you telling my father-in-law? It sounded like you—"

He cut her off. "Just throwing him off the scent, Holly. I had to tell him something, and part of the truth is better than an outright lie—I *did* track you to Grand Prairie...after I'd already located you in Rosewood. And I wasn't lying...you *did* move on to Irving after you left Grand Prairie. But you only stayed there two weeks, too."

"How do know that?" Her voice was barely above a whisper.

One corner of his mouth curved upward in a half

smile. "I told you, I'm damned good at what I do. After Irving you moved to Mansfield, then Arlington. After Arlington you stayed almost a month in Lake Worth before you moved here."

He walked toward her as he said this, and she backed away on trembling legs, clutching Ian and Jamie as if they were talismans. *I was so careful*, she thought feverishly. *How could he know all that?*

She hadn't realized she'd spoken aloud until Chris gave her an "are you kidding me?" look and said, "You make a lousy criminal, Holly. But that's a compliment, not an insult."

When Holly bumped into the hallway wall outside the bedroom doorway, she realized she was trapped. But all Chris did was take Ian from her, hefting him under one arm like a football and gently swinging him until Ian laughed at the game. "Time for your nap, bud," Chris told him. "You and your brother." His blue eyes met Holly's brown ones, and there was a gentleness in his face. An honesty she couldn't help but believe. "I'm not going to hurt you, Holly. Ever. And I'd never do anything to hurt your sons."

Holly was so mentally exhausted and emotionally drained that after she read the twins a story, sang them two songs and tucked them up in their cribs, she lay down on the bed, telling herself she'd rest for just a moment. Then she'd unpack their suitcases, wash the lunch dishes, put away the dry-goods groceries she and Chris had bought and decide what to make for dinner. But before she realized it, she was out like a light.

At first her dreams were of happier times, when the twins were newborns and Grant was there. He'd been so proud and nervous at the same time, like most new fathers. Then her dreams segued into nightmares, starting with the devastating news of Grant's death...the lawyers trying to probate Grant's will and the McCays attempting to contest it...followed swiftly by the Mc-Cays trying to seize custody of the twins, along with control of the trust Grant had set up for his sons. A dazed and bereft Holly had been forced to fight, not only for custody and to carry out Grant's last wishes but for her good name, too.

That time in her life had been a waking nightmare. She'd won the preliminary battles in the courts and thought she was finally on firm ground...until those three close calls. Any one of them could have been an accident, but three? After the last one, when she'd shown up at the McCays' house shaken and trembling to pick up the twins, she'd sensed the McCays' surprise... that she was still alive. And she'd known in that instant they were trying to kill her.

In the way of dreams, Holly suddenly found herself at the Rosewood Rooming House with Chris. He was holding her, but not the way he had in real life. This time his strong arms were surrounding her in comforting fashion as he pressed her head against the solid wall of his oh-so-warm chest and promised her she was safe. "I won't let them hurt you," he said, referring to her in-laws. "And I won't let them get custody of Ian and Jamie."

The sense of relief she felt was incredible, and all out of proportion to her real life. Holly didn't subscribe to the theory that a woman couldn't take care of herself, that she needed a man to look after her. She was a software engineer, for goodness' sake! She'd supported

herself after her missionary parents had been killed in
one of their trips to South America—leaving very little in the way of life insurance—and had put herself
through college. After graduation she'd held down a
challenging job for NASA at the Johnson Space Center
in Clear Lake City, Texas, before she'd taken maternity leave when the twins were born. She didn't need
"rescuing" from her life...as a general rule.

But that was before the McCays had tried to kill her.
The situation she found herself in now was so totally
outside her experience, so much like one of the thrill-
ers Grant had loved to read but that Holly had always
avoided, that she recognized she couldn't do it all on
her own. Single mother? Check. Guardian of her children's financial future? Check. Putting attempted murderers behind bars? Not so much.

Maybe that was why when Chris had held Holly in
the shelter of his arms in her dream and promised she
and the boys were safe, she'd believed him...because
she *wanted* to believe him. Because she *needed* to believe him.

Then he'd kissed her.

No one had ever kissed her that way, with an intensity that shattered everything she'd thought she knew
about men and women. Chris's kiss exploded through
her body, as if she were gunpowder and he were a
lighted match. He was hard everywhere she was soft,
and it made her want to get closer...impossibly closer.
Her nipples tightened and her insides melted as Chris
tilted her head back and his lips trailed down, down,
to brush against the incredibly sensitive hollow of her
throat. Then lower.

Holly moaned in her sleep and curled onto her side,

pressing her legs together against the throbbing she felt there. And the dream suddenly vanished.

She woke to the mouthwatering aroma of baked chicken, Ian and Jamie's chorus of "Ma-ma-ma-ma-ma" as they stood and banged on the sides of their cribs to get her attention and the guilty memory of Chris's dream kiss. Not the kiss so much as her reaction to it, she acknowledged as a flush of warmth swept through her body. As if…

A tap on the door frame drew her attention, and there stood Chris in the doorway, almost as if she'd dreamed him into existence. Holly quickly hid her face with her hands and rubbed at her eyes, pretending she needed to wake up that way. She didn't—she just didn't want Chris to see her flaming cheeks.

"Dinner's ready" was all Chris said, and as he walked farther into the room, Holly scrambled off the bed. "I'll take Ian for you," he said, lifting the older of the twins—older by three minutes—out of his crib.

"How do you know that's Ian?" she asked, moving to grab Jamie. "They're identical. Most people can't tell the difference. Peg can, but it took her a week."

The intimate smile Chris gave her curled her toes. "Ian looks up when he sees me. Jamie looks away."

"That's it? That's how you can tell them apart?"

"Well…that and the fact that Ian's ears stick out just a little more than Jamie's, and Jamie's hair is just a shade lighter than Ian's."

Holly stopped short, glancing from the toddler in Chris's arms to the one in her own arms. "You're right," she said after a minute. "I never realized about the ears…but you're right."

"So how do you tell them apart? Motherly instinct?"

She adjusted Jamie to balance him against her hip and popped a kiss on his rosebud mouth. "I can't really tell you," she confessed. "I just know."

Chris nodded as if she'd given him the answer he expected. "Motherly instinct," he repeated, but this time it wasn't a question. He turned toward the doorway. "Come on, dinner will be getting cold."

"I was going to make dinner," she protested as she followed Chris into the kitchen, feeling guilty.

"You were fast asleep every time I came to check on you, and I didn't have the heart to wake you." Chris settled Ian in one of the two high chairs he'd pulled up beside the kitchen table and strapped him in. "Hang tight, buddy," he told the boy as Ian began banging on the tray and shouting, "Din-din-din-din-din!"

Jamie took up the chant as Holly got him settled. "Sorry," she told Chris over the boys' urgent demands. "I usually feed them a little earlier. I must have been more exhausted than I thought."

"Adrenaline will do that to you," Chris said as he grabbed two child-sized plates that were sitting in the microwave, added the baby cutlery she'd used at lunch from the rack on the drain board—*he must have washed the lunch dishes*, Holly realized with another little dart of guilt—and whisked the plates in front of Ian and Jamie. Baked chicken, cut into baby-sized bites, sat next to miniature mounds of mashed potatoes. Peas with a tiny dollop of melted butter rounded out the servings.

"Are you sure you're not a nanny in disguise?" Holly joked as the twins' eyes lit up and they dug in, soon making a mess out of feeding themselves. "How do you know—"

"Don't even *think* about finishing that sentence," Chris told her in a stern voice, but the twinkle in his eyes gave the lie to his tone. "I'm the second oldest of seven. That many kids in a family—you need a lot of hands to get all the work done. My twin sister, Annabel, and I used to help Mama with the younger kids, especially my baby sister, Josie."

He turned away to take the rest of the chicken out of the oven, but not before Holly saw a troubled expression slide over his face. *More land mines*, she warned herself. *He doesn't want to talk about his childhood*. That made sense given what he'd told her this morning—that his father was a notorious serial killer who'd killed Chris's mother, too.

She cast about in her mind for a safe topic of conversation as she filled a plate for herself from the chicken pan and the pots on the stove, and Chris filled Wally's bowl with fresh water. "I didn't realize you're a twin," she said as she seated herself at the table.

Chris started to respond, but Holly leaned over to Jamie, who was rolling his peas across his highchair tray and then smashing them flat with the tip of one chubby pointer finger. "You're going to eat those, mister," she told him in a no-nonsense voice. "So you just peel them up and pop them into your mouth." She waited until Jamie obediently scooped up two peas and ate them before she glanced up at Chris. "Sorry. It's a constant battle with boys this young. They want to feed themselves, but… What were you going to say?"

"I was just about to say that yeah, I'm a twin myself. Not identical, of course, but there *is* an unbreakable bond."

"I've seen that with Ian and Jamie already."

"Not surprised. It starts early."

"What does your sister do? Is she a PI like you?"

Chris shook his head. "She's a cop." He hesitated. "My brothers and I—we didn't want that for her. I know it's chauvinistic in this day and age, but this is Texas. We wanted her to be safe, you know? I had a big argument about it with her. And—" he had the grace to look ashamed "—none of us except Sam attended her graduation from the police academy. She graduated top of her class, too." He took his plate and settled in a chair at the other end of the table.

They ate in silence for a minute, then Chris said roughly, "I know how it sounds, but we've already lost one sister. Josie. We don't want to lose the only one we have left."

Treading cautiously, Holly asked, "What happened to Josie?"

"No one knows. We haven't heard from her in six years." His brows drew together in a troubled frown. "And even before that she practically refused to have anything to do with us for years." He thought for a moment. "I guess she was about twelve when she told the social worker she didn't want us visiting her anymore."

"How old were you?"

"Twenty. The summer before my junior year in college." He sighed. "But even before that she... When Trevor turned eighteen—Trevor's the oldest, three years older than me—when he turned eighteen, he tried to get custody of Josie, take her out of foster care. But she refused. We figured it had something to do with her foster sister, Lizzie. They were particularly close. And Lizzie says they were both attached to their foster parents."

He sighed again. "I also tried to get custody when I turned eighteen and graduated from high school. I'd have passed on college if that's what it took—scholarship be damned. But I didn't have any more luck than Trevor." He looked down at his plate, forked a bite of chicken and swirled it in the mashed potatoes, then ate it.

Holly pried peas off Jamie's tray, piled them on his plate and tapped an imperious finger. "Eat those, mister." She glanced over at Ian to make sure he was eating what was set before him without difficulty, then looked up at Chris. "What happened then?"

"Even with the scholarship it wasn't easy, but I managed. I worked to put myself through school, and when I graduated, I came back here to Granite Gulch. Laura was waiting for me—we'd been engaged since my junior year in college—but I told her I needed to try one more time with Josie...who turned me down flat."

That hurt him. Chris didn't have to say it; Holly just knew. "Josie didn't say why?"

"Nope. Basically her message was 'Leave me alone.'" He paused. "I don't blame her in one way. She was only three when our father murdered our mother—I doubt she even remembers her or us as a family."

But you do, Holly thought. *You remember...and it hurts you to remember.*

"So it only makes sense she didn't want to have anything to do with her brothers and sisters—we're not her family anymore. Then six years ago..." Chris began, but when he stopped, Holly raised her eyebrows in a question, so he continued. "Josie ran away six years ago. At least that's the best we can figure. I've been searching for her off and on ever since."

Now Holly thought she understood what Peg had

meant when she said Chris needed to do this, needed to shelter Holly and her boys from the McCays. Chris carried a load of guilt over his missing sister. *Probably some guilt over his mother, too.*

"You said there were seven of you, and that Trevor's the oldest. What does he do?"

"FBI profiler."

"Wow. Impressive."

Chris nodded, but Holly got the impression there were some unresolved issues between Chris and his older brother. *I wonder what that's about.* She wasn't going to ask, of course. But maybe he would volunteer something later on. "After Trevor it's you and Annabel, right? And Josie's the baby. Who else?"

"Ridge. He's two years younger than me."

"Unusual name."

Chris laughed. "It suits him. He's in search and rescue. He's big and bad and nobody messes with Ridge."

Kind of like you, Holly thought, but she kept it to herself. "And after Ridge?"

"Ethan. He's twenty-seven, and he is *intense*. He kind of keeps himself to himself, if you know what I mean." Holly nodded. "He's a rancher. His ranch is… oh, about ten miles from here. The isolation suits him, but he's going to have to get accustomed to having more people around—his wife, Lizzie, is expecting a baby any day now."

"Oh, that's nice. You'll be an uncle again." She counted up in her mind, then said, "One more. Another brother, right?"

"Yeah. Sam. He's a police detective, right here on the Granite Gulch police force, just like Annabel. He's twenty-five, and he just got engaged in January to the sweetest woman, Zoe. You'd like her."

"Wait. Zoe Robison? The librarian?"

Ian piped up, "Zo-ee, Zo-ee!" and Jamie copied him. Holly quickly looked over at her boys and realized they were pretty much done. They'd left a disaster that would need hosing down to clean up, but at least they'd managed to eat most of what was on their plates. What hadn't been eaten was now adorning them. She shuddered at the mashed potatoes Ian had massaged into his eyebrows.

"You know Zoe?" Chris asked.

Holly jumped up and grabbed the washcloth from the sink. "She runs the Mommy and Me reading program at the library," she explained as she wiped Jamie's hands and face, then did the same for Ian. "Ian and Jamie adore her, and yes, she's really sweet."

Chris waited until Jamie was clean, then he unstrapped the boy and lifted him out of the high chair, setting him on his feet. When Ian was ready, he got the same treatment.

"Leave this," Chris told Holly. "I'll clean up and put the dishes in the dishwasher."

"I should do it," she protested. "Ian and Jamie are the ones who made such a mess." She grimaced as she took in the condition of the floor, which had a few peas scattered beneath the high chairs—the ones Wally hadn't gobbled up—not to mention a couple of gooey globs that looked like mashed potatoes.

"You probably want to give the boys a bath before too long."

"You mean before they track the mess into the rest of the house?"

Chris grinned. "Yeah, that's exactly what I mean."

"You really don't mind cleaning up in here? I feel awful leaving this for you."

"Don't sweat it." He was already swiping a damp paper towel over the mashed potatoes and picking the remaining peas up off the floor as she spoke. Chris's cell phone rang at that moment, and he threw the peas into the garbage disposal before he checked the caller ID. "Annabel," he told Holly. "I should take this. Excuse me." He pressed a button. "Hey, Bella, what's up?"

He stiffened almost immediately, and Holly watched his lighthearted expression fade away as he listened to his sister on the other end. Two minutes passed, then three, before Chris said, "I'm sorry to hear it. What does Trevor say?" He made a sound of impatience, then nodded as if Annabel could see him. "Okay. I understand. Besides Trevor and Sam, who else knows?" He listened for a minute, then said, "Nothing I can do, but thanks for letting me know. Watch yourself, okay?"

He disconnected but didn't put the phone away. He hit speed dial, waited a few seconds, then said, "Peg? It's Chris. Have you been watching the local news?" Apparently the answer was no, because he added, "Turn it on. Now. Annabel just called me. They found another body with the bull's-eye marking. Yeah, number eight—Helena Tucker."

Chapter 5

Chris hung up with Peg, then glanced at Holly. She was kneeling on the floor, an arm around each twin, clutching them tightly. "Sorry," Chris said, thinking she was trying to keep the boys from hearing his side of the conversation. "I forgot there were little ears around." The face Holly raised to his was ashen, and guilty. "What?" he asked.

"It's terrible," she whispered. "I should be praying for that poor woman. But all I could think about when I heard her name was that I could stop worrying."

Chris shook his head. "You didn't really think you were in danger, did you? Yeah, your name begins with *H*, but hell—" He caught himself up short, remembering too late his vow to watch his language. "Heck," he amended, "you don't have long dark hair. Your hair isn't even really dark—I have the pictures to prove it."

"I know. I wasn't *really* worried, but…fear isn't always logical. It was just there in the back of my mind, you know? And the newspaper reported that the woman who's suspected of being the Alphabet Killer—I forget her name—"

"Regina Willard."

"Right. She once stayed at the Rosewood Rooming House, same as me."

"I know." Chris suddenly thought of something. "Before I forget, I wanted to tell you there's no internet service here at the house yet. And no cable. Water, gas, electricity and phone—yeah. I couldn't turn the water off—unless I wanted to let the landscaping shrivel up and die. Not to mention Peg needs water when she comes out here to take care of the place. And electricity and phone service are necessary for the alarm system. But no cable or internet landline. I called to get them turned on when we were at Peg's, but it'll be a few days."

"That's okay," Holly informed him. "I haven't watched TV since I left Clear Lake City. And I only browse the internet at the library anyway, so it's not a hardship to do without. But what about you?"

"I can survive without cable for a few days. And I've got mobile internet access for my laptop and smartphone—I need it for my PI business. So, I'm good."

Ian and Jamie both squirmed to get free at that moment, and Chris said, "Better get them their baths. Go on," he insisted. "It won't take me more than a few minutes to clean up in here. Then I have some work to catch up on. I'll be in the office."

A half hour later Holly ruefully fished her dark pixie-cut wig out of the tub in the master bathroom, where Ian had dunked it after he tugged it off her head. She rolled the wig in a towel to dry it as much as she could, then hung it on a hook over the shower. "Laugh," she told Ian in a mock-threatening tone as she lifted him out of the tub and wrapped his wriggling body in a towel. "You just wait until you grow up. I'm going to take delight in embarrassing you by telling your friends all the things you did to me.

"No, Jamie, we don't eat soap," she said, changing subjects, quickly removing the bar of soap from his vicinity. She scooped him out of the tub and wrapped him in a towel, too. She played peekaboo with both boys and their towels for a couple of minutes, then gathered them close as intense motherly love for her babies washed through her. "You're little monsters—you know that—but I love you madly," she told them. "And I wouldn't trade you for anything in the world."

Clean, Ian and Jamie looked like little angels, their golden curls fluffed into tiny halos. Holly brushed their barely damp hair, ruthlessly suppressing the curls, before using the brush on her own head when she caught sight of herself in the mirror. She wasn't vain about her appearance—well, not much—but she didn't want anyone seeing her with her hair a flattened mess. She refused to acknowledge who she meant by "anyone," but in the back of her mind lurked the memory of her dream that afternoon. The dream, and the kiss. Not to mention her erotic reaction to it.

Holly let the twins run naked into the bedroom, dabbing futilely at the large, damp patch on her pale blue T-shirt where Jamie had—deliberately, she was sure—splashed her with soapy bathwater. Then she followed her sons into the other room.

She dressed them in the pull-ups they still wore at night because they weren't *quite* potty trained yet, then in their nightclothes. "Come on," she told them, taking their hands in hers. "Let's go say good-night to Mr. Colton. Pretend you're really as angelic as you look so he won't mind sharing a house with us."

Chris leaned back in his leather desk chair and absently fondled Wally's head as the dog lay quietly beside him. "Look at this, boy," he murmured. "You think…?" *This* was a news article on his laptop's computer screen—a story about the daring capture of a fugitive on the FBI's Ten Most Wanted list. A dangerous man who was an alleged associate of a drug lord who'd been dead for six years—Desmond Carlton. The name Carlton was enough like Colton for the story to have caught Chris's eye, and he shook his head at a vague memory. Then he picked up his smartphone and hit speed dial.

"Hi, Chris," Annabel said when she answered. "What's up?"

"Carlton," he said abruptly. "Wasn't that the last name of Josie's foster parents?"

"Um…I think so. Yes, it was. Why?"

"I was just reading something on *Yahoo News* about a man who ran with Desmond Carlton six years ago."

"The guy who was on the Ten Most Wanted list? The one the FBI just captured?"

"Yeah, him."

"Why is that important? Other than someone else will be promoted to the list tomorrow, now that he's in prison where he belongs, the creep."

"I don't know," Chris said slowly. "But as I was

reading the story the name Carlton rang a bell. That, and the fact that Desmond Carlton has been dead for six years. Six years, Bella. Think about it."

"You don't mean… Josie? It's got to be a coincidence."

"I don't like coincidences. And I don't trust them. Especially two coincidences together." He thought a minute. "Do me a favor, will you? Find out what prison this guy is in. I might want to have a little chat with him."

Annabel's soft drawl took on a hard edge. "You don't want to ask Trevor? He's FBI. He could probably get in to see this perp whether or not he wants visitors." When Chris didn't respond, his sister said, "Are you still holding a grudge against Trevor? I thought you agreed it wasn't fair to him."

"Trevor's got enough on his plate right now," he pointed out, "what with trying to find Regina Willard. Especially now that she just added number eight to her victim list—the pressure to catch her has got to be intense."

"It's not just the FBI, you know," Annabel said drily. "The Granite Gulch Police Department is involved in this case, too."

Chris winced. His sister didn't say it, but it had been Annabel's solid police work that had identified Regina Willard as the Alphabet Killer. The woman hadn't been caught yet, though not for lack of trying on Annabel's part.

But the real reason Chris didn't want to ask for Trevor's help wasn't that his older brother was too busy—that had just been an excuse. Chris *was* still holding a grudge…but he wasn't going to admit it to Annabel. Okay, it was an old wound from his childhood that he should have gotten over long since—he knew that. The adult in him knew that. And yeah, it wasn't fair to Trevor—Annabel was right about that. And true, he and Trevor had finally reconnected years back…mostly.

But deep inside him resided that eleven-year-old boy who'd idolized his older brother, who'd felt betrayed when the family was split up and Trevor made no attempt to maintain the connection with him when they all went into foster care. Yeah, they'd seen each other a few times a year at the home of Josie's foster parents— court-mandated visits—but that wasn't the same thing at all. Chris had pretended it hadn't hurt…but it had. Badly. He was still trying to excise the scar tissue that had left on his psyche, but he wasn't there yet.

Then there was the whole Josie thing. When Trevor turned eighteen, he'd tried to get custody of Josie…or at least that was the story. But how hard had he tried, really? Chris didn't know, and the uncertainty of that ate at him. Josie would have been only seven back then. She'd turned Chris's offer down when *he* turned eighteen, but by that time it was already too late—she'd been ten, and had spent seven years with the Carltons. Maybe it was unreasonable, but Chris laid the blame for losing Josie squarely on Trevor's shoulders.

"But you're right," Annabel said, breaking into his thoughts. "Trevor's got enough to worry about. I'll see what I can find out."

"Thanks, Bella."

"No problem." Silence hummed between them, until Annabel said out of the blue, "I can't stop thinking about the day I saw her."

"Josie?"

"Mmm-hmm. I can't *swear* it was her, but—"

"But that gold charm you found clinches it," he finished for her.

"Yeah." She sighed. "Ridge and Lizzie believed it was her when they had their own Josie sightings."

"I know. At least she's alive. For the longest time I…" Chris's throat closed as he thought of how he'd imagined the worst. Young women disappeared all the time. Murdered. Their bodies disposed of in the most callous ways. It had killed him to imagine that was Josie's fate.

Annabel seemed to understand Chris couldn't talk about it, and she changed the subject. "Speaking of sightings, Mia told me she spotted you coming out of your apartment this morning carrying a suitcase and your laptop bag. You taking a trip? Something to do with your work?"

Chris hesitated, then remembered his heart-to-heart conversation with Annabel last month and his promise that he would take her seriously as a police officer going forward. She'd earned that right and then some. "No," he told her. "Remember that missing-person case I mentioned the other day? The one I was taking pro bono?"

"The widow who ran off with her twin sons? The one the in-laws are trying to track down?"

"Yeah, her. Turns out I was way off base."

His sister snorted. "Told you there was more to the story."

"Don't rub it in." Chris massaged the furrow he could feel forming between his eyebrows. "Anyway, long story short, I found her. But she had a damned good reason for running—her in-laws tried to kill her."

Annabel gasped. "Are you kidding me?"

"Nope. She's been living in the Rosewood Rooming House with her boys for the past three months, but she was just about to run again." He took a deep breath. "So I convinced her it would be safer for the three of them to live in my house for the time being...with me."

"Your house? You mean the one you built for Laura?"

"Yeah. I couldn't let her run, Bella. I wasn't going to tell the in-laws I found her, but I couldn't let her run. If she did and the in-laws hired someone else..." He knew he didn't have to draw his twin a picture.

"So you're living there with her?"

"And her sons," he was quick to point out. "Just until we can set a trap for her in-laws."

"We?"

"I was thinking Sam, you and me. Unless you don't want to." He knew when he said it what Annabel's answer would be. Set a trap for would-be murderers? If they pulled it off, it would be another professional coup for his sister.

"Count me in."

Annabel's enthusiastic response made Chris smile to himself. "I haven't asked Sam," he told her, "so don't say anything to him yet, okay? This all just happened this morning."

"No problem. Just let me know when and where. So, what's her name?"

"Holly. Holly McCay. And her boys are Ian and Jamie."

"Cute names. What's she like?"

Chris smiled again. Knowing his sister, he'd known

the question—or one very similar—was coming. "You'd
like her. She's very down-to-earth. Very unassuming.
And a good mother. You're not going to believe this, but
Holly and Peg are friends," he said, knowing the message that would convey. "Other than Peg and me, you're
the only one who knows where Holly is right now, and
until we can prove anything against her in-laws, that's
the way I want to keep it."

"Works for me. When do I get to meet her?"

Children's voices from the hallway outside his office
alerted Chris that Holly and her boys were approaching, so he cut off his conversation with Annabel. "I'll
let you know," he told her quickly and disconnected.
He swung his chair around and stood up, but Wally
was faster. The dog bounded across the room toward
the hallway, tongue lolling out, tail wagging.

"Holly, I—" Chris began but stopped as if he'd
been poleaxed when a blonde woman appeared in the
doorway with Ian and Jamie. Long blond hair that
owed nothing to artifice. Long blond hair that shim-
mered under the lights with a hundred different lay-
ered shades of gold. Long blond hair parted slightly
off center, paired—unusually—with pale brown eyes.
The eyes he'd seen before, but not with the blond hair.
Holy crap, he thought as desire unexpectedly slashed
through him, but all he said was, "What happened to
the dark-haired wig?"

Holly laughed ruefully. "Ian thought it was funny
to pull it off and dunk it in the tub."

He didn't mean to say it, but the words just popped
out. "Your pictures don't do you justice."

She laughed again, but this time a slight tinge of

color stained her cheeks. "Thank you... I think." She stood there for a minute staring at Chris as if caught in the same trance as he was, and her not-quite-steady breathing drew attention to her breasts rising and falling beneath her damp T-shirt. But when the twins tugged free of her hold to play with Wally, the spell—or whatever it was—was broken. "We came to tell you good-night," she explained, the color in her cheeks deepening.

"Oh. Right," Chris said, forcing his eyes away from Holly and down to the toddlers and the dog. Their well-scrubbed cherubic faces were misleading, he knew—if they were like most boys, Holly's twins were no angels. But they were all boy, just as Wally was all dog. Boys and dogs went together like...well... like boys and dogs. And Chris had a sudden memory of his younger brothers Ridge and Ethan—four and two to Chris's six—and his dog back then, Bouncer, a golden retriever, just like Wally. It was a memory from his early years that didn't stab at his heart for once, a memory that made him smile for a change. He glanced at the clock on the wall and said, "Kind of early for bedtime, isn't it?"

"I start early," Holly explained. "I read them stories, then they get lullabies, and..." She smiled. "All of that can take an hour or more before they finally settle down and go to sleep."

He didn't know what made him make the offer, but he said, "How about I read them their bedtime stories?" When Holly looked doubtful, he added, "I'm a pretty good bedtime-story reader. Peg's daughter, Susan, would vouch for me if she was here."

Holly chuckled. "Okay," she agreed. "I wouldn't

mind a few minutes to myself for a change. Let me get the books. We have a ton of library books—I was going to return them on my way out of town today," she rushed to explain, as if she didn't want him to think of her as a library thief. "And we have some books I bought for the boys. I let them pick the books they want me to read."

She was back in no time, carrying a stack of books that Chris quickly relieved her of. "Their favorites are on top," Holly told him. "But I usually just spread the books out and they choose based on the cover."

"Fly," Jamie said. "Want fly."

"A Fly Went By?" Chris asked him, juggling the stack until he found the Mike McClintock title three books down from the top. He handed it to Jamie, who hugged it.

"You remember that book?" Holly asked, surprised.

"Hell—heck, yeah," he amended. "That was one of Josie's favorites. I read it to her so many times I think I have it memorized."

"Me, too." Holly smiled at Chris, a somehow intimate smile, and something he hadn't felt in forever tugged at his heart. Holly's smile made him realize there was more to life than merely putting one foot in front of the other. More to life than the work he'd thrown himself into with even more dedication after Laura's death. Except for his relationship with Peg, Joe and their kids, except for his relationship with his sister and brothers, his life revolved around his work. Work that gave meaning to a life that held little else.

But Holly's smile reminded him he was a man, first and foremost. A man who hadn't made love to a woman in close to two years, who hadn't even given it serious thought in all that time.

He was thinking of it now, though. He was definitely thinking of it now. In spades.

Chapter 6

Holly escaped to her bedroom, her cheeks burning. The intently male look Chris had given her the moment before was branded into her memory. *He wants you*, she told herself as she quickly stripped and stepped into the shower. *Just as you want him.*

The hot water pummeled her body, which had become hypersensitized merely from that one look from Chris, and felt like a man's caress. Which was *crazy*! She didn't react to a sexy man that way. Yes, she'd been physically attracted to Grant—far more than he'd been physically attracted to her, since Grant had looked on Holly more as a sister than anything else—but she'd been in love with Grant. She couldn't have carnal urges like this for a man she'd just met that morning… Only, she did. *Don't lie to yourself, Holly*, she warned. *You want him. Admit it.*

"Okay," she muttered, soaping her body and rinsing off quickly. "Okay, so I'm a normal woman with normal needs and it's been more than a year since I…"

Not just a year since she'd made love. It had been a lot longer than a year since a man had looked at her with that burning intensity in his eyes, his face. An expression that conveyed how unutterably desirable she was to him, and at the same time triggered those same needs in her.

Holly washed her hair just as quickly as she'd washed her body. *No one's* ever *looked at you like that*, she admitted to herself as she rinsed, and the memory made her nipples tighten into tiny buds that ached beneath the warm spray.

She wasn't afraid Chris would do anything she didn't want him to do…but that was the problem. She wanted him to do things to her she'd never imagined having a man do to her. And she wanted to do things to him she'd never believed in her heart women really wanted to do for men. And that was a *huge* problem.

She'd been nothing but Mommy for so long she'd thought she was immune to men. She'd thought wrong.

Chris knew Peg didn't allow her dogs on the furniture—not a dictum he would have made, but Wally wasn't really his dog, so he enforced the rule anyway. Since the twins wanted Wally close enough to pet while Chris read to them, he solved the dilemma by plopping down on the floor in his office with his back to the sofa. Wally lay across his legs and a boy sat on either side of him as he read. He'd finished *A Fly Went By* and had nearly reached the end of Dr. Seuss's *Green Eggs and Ham* when Holly returned.

Her long blond hair was damp and had been sleeked back away from a face that held not a vestige of makeup that he could see, not even lip gloss. But the minute she walked into the room the temperature rose to an uncomfortable level.

Holy crap, he thought as he read aloud the last two sentences, then closed the book and said, "The end."

He'd thought his sudden attraction to Holly had been nothing more than an aberration, the normal reaction of a man who'd gone too long without receiving an attractive woman's smile. He'd been way off base.

But there was something inherently…unsavory… about lusting after a woman when her eighteen-month-old sons were cuddled on either side of him, enthralled by his renditions of children's stories. So Chris tamped down his desire and smiled up at Holly without letting her see how much she affected him. "You're just in time," he told her. "We're done here."

Jamie scrambled to his feet, tripped over Wally's thumping tail and picked himself up again, patting Wally's backside as apology. "Sor-ry, Wally, sor-ry." Then he turned to his mother and demanded, "Ma-ma sing now."

"Later," she replied, bending over and picking him up, settling him against her hip. "Did you thank Mr. Colton for reading to you?"

Ian piped up, "Unca Cwis." He patted Chris's arm, and repeated, "Unca Cwis."

"Sorry," Chris said swiftly. "I told them to call me that. That's what Susan calls me, and I figured it was easier than saying 'Mr. Colton.'"

"Not a problem," Holly replied, then asked her boys, "Did you thank Uncle Chris?" A chorus of childish thank-yous followed her pointed question before she explained to Chris, "They don't have any real uncles. No aunts, either. Grant was an only child, and so was I." She sighed and added wistfully, "I always wanted a brother or a sister. So did Grant. I think that's one of the reasons we were such good friends growing up."

"You can have one of mine," Chris joked. "I've got plenty." He paused for a second. "Not Annabel. Not my twin. But you can have one of my brothers." He tilted his head to one side and thought about it for a moment, as if seriously considering his offer. "Not Sam, either. Or Ethan. They're too young—you don't want a younger brother. How about Ridge? He's twenty-nine, same age as you."

"Ridge, as in 'big and bad and nobody messes with Ridge'? That brother?"

"Yeah, him."

Holly shifted Jamie to her other hip. "I'm not sure I want a brother who will scare away all my dates," she teased, getting into the game. "I'll bet you heard that same line from Annabel. Am I right?"

Chris winced and held up both hands in mock surrender. "Guilty as charged," he admitted. "But it was for her own good. Honest. And I didn't scare away *all* her dates, just the ones who had something nefarious in mind."

"Mmm-hmm." She nodded. "I'll bet. What would Annabel say, though, if I asked her?"

He chuckled softly. "Funny you should ask me that. My sister just got engaged last month, so I guess I didn't scare them all away. Her engagement was kind of late in the game, though, especially since that's all my brothers and I wanted for her—that she find Mr. Right and settle down."

"Finding Mr. Right doesn't happen for all women." The suddenly serious way she said this made Chris wonder. "I should get these two down for the night. Come on, Ian. Say good-night to Mr.—to Uncle Chris, and let's go."

Ian patted Chris's arm to get his attention and in a plaintive tone asked, "Cawwy me?"

"Carry," Holly corrected automatically. "And you don't need to be carried, Ian. You're a big boy."

Before she could put Jamie down and make him walk, too, the same as Ian, Chris stood and swept Ian into his arms. Then he effortlessly lifted the toddler up onto his shoulder. "Hang on, buddy," he told Ian as the boy chortled with glee at being so high up.

"Me too, me too!" Jamie pleaded, holding his arms out to Chris, and Holly was so startled she almost dropped him. Jamie never voluntarily went to *anyone* other than her, so for him to want Chris to carry him was a shock.

"You don't have to," she protested in an undertone as Chris took Jamie from her arms.

"Fair's fair," Chris retorted, hefting Jamie onto his other shoulder. "Nobody wiggle," he told both boys. "And watch your heads as we go through the doorway."

Holly followed Chris through the hallway to the master bedroom, sighing a little at how easily he carried the twins. Ian and Jamie were off the charts for eighteen months, and it was getting harder and harder for her to carry one boy, much less two. But it wasn't just that. She also ruthlessly suppressed the little pang of motherly jealousy that her twins preferred Chris over her, even in something as simple as this. *If Chris was their father it would be different*, she reasoned. *I wouldn't be jealous. Would I?*

She wasn't quite sure, and that bothered her. She wanted so badly to be a good mother, wanted to raise strong, independent boys who would become strong, independent men. She didn't want to be one of those mothers who spoiled her children but kept them emotionally dependent on her, tied to her apron strings. *Not that you wear an apron*, she thought with a flash of humor. But that phrase perfectly described what she *didn't* want for her boys.

So this is a good thing for Ian and Jamie, she reasoned. A little masculine attention from a man she already knew would be a good role model…after knowing him for only a day. She stopped short at the realization that, yes, she'd known Chris for only a day. Not even an entire day at that.

Chris and the twins disappeared into the master bedroom, and she hurried after them. She was just in time to see Chris swing each boy down from his shoulders into his crib and was surprised he got them right. Jamie was in his crib, the one with baby pandas adorning the sheets, and Ian was in the crib with dolphins on the sheets. *He doesn't miss a thing*, she realized. *He notices…and he remembers.*

There was something very appealing in that revelation.

Chris had started down the hallway back to his office when he heard a warm, sweet contralto voice coming from the master bedroom, singing a lullaby he recognized with a sense of shock. And though he told himself not to, that he had no business intruding on Holly's private time with her children, he was drawn back to the doorway.

The room was dark, but the light was on in the master bathroom and the door was cracked open—a makeshift night-light for the twins. Chris could make out Wally's shape on the floor—the twins had begged to be allowed to have Wally sleep with them, and Chris hadn't been able to refuse. Neither had Holly. So Chris had used a folded-up blanket as a dog bed for Wally and had placed it meticulously equidistant between the two cribs.

But he wasn't really looking at the dog. And he wasn't really looking at the twins. All he really had eyes for was Holly, her back to him as she sang the haunting cowboy ballad he knew as "Utah Carl."

Chris closed his eyes, and in his mind he was four years old, listening to his mother, Saralee, singing that very same song to a two-year-old Ridge as she rocked him to sleep. She'd been almost nine months pregnant at the time—*that would have been Ethan*, he realized now—but despite her financial worries and her constant pregnancies, his mother had never let her children know her life was hard. The love she'd felt for each and all of them had shielded them from the knowledge of the trials she faced on a daily basis, not the least of which was loving Matthew Colton and standing by him through thick and thin.

There hadn't been a lot of money in the Colton household, but none of the children had known it at the time. There had always been enough money for the important things—school clothes, books, birthdays and Christmases. And Saralee had made sure all her children knew they were loved, from Trevor right down to baby Josie.

The ballad came to an end, but Holly barely skipped a beat, moving right into another song Chris also remembered from his childhood. A desolate ache for that long-ago time and for the mother he still mourned ripped through him, and his face contracted in pain. His eyes were damp when the song ended, and he quickly rubbed his fingers over his eyelids to remove that betraying moisture.

Then, before Holly could start another song, he slipped noiselessly away from the doorway. He went into his office and shut the door behind him. Firmly. As if he could shut the door on his memories the same way.

It was almost midnight and the house was shrouded in darkness when Holly turned over restlessly in bed. Ian and Jamie were fast asleep—she could hear their rhythmic breathing—and she envied them. If only she could sleep with that same innocent abandon. If only she could sleep believing all was right with the world.

"Shouldn't have had that nap this afternoon," she whispered to herself, although she knew it was a lie. It wasn't the nap preventing her from sleeping, it was her conscience.

Holly's missionary parents had raised her to know right from wrong. And to believe that actions have consequences. Which meant that sometimes—like now— her conscience uncomfortably reminded her that if she hadn't done what she'd done…maybe things would have been different. Maybe she wouldn't be running for her life.

Grant's death wasn't her fault. No way was she responsible for that. But the McCays? If she'd never gotten pregnant, if she'd never married Grant, then the McCays would have inherited Grant's wealth when he died, and they would have no reason to want her out of the picture.

"That's stupid," she told herself sternly. "You're not responsible because they're so mercenary they're willing to kill to get you out of the way."

But...

Friends to lovers was a popular theme in romance novels, but it didn't always work out that way in real life. Best friends Holly and Grant had attended the University of Texas at Austin together and had both earned software engineering degrees. Then Holly had landed that plum job at NASA, while Grant—always more adventuresome than she—went out on his own, starting his own software company.

They'd seen each other often, at least once a week. Holly had known about the women Grant was dating but had consoled herself that as long as he was playing the field she didn't really have to worry he was getting serious about any one woman, the same way he'd been in high school and college. And she'd done everything she could to remain a key part of his life.

One mistake on Grant's part on a night when he'd had too much to drink, and Holly had soon discovered to her secret joy she was pregnant. Grant had done the honorable thing and proposed when she'd told him. After all, he'd reasoned, they'd been best friends forever, so what better basis for a strong marriage? Especially since they'd eventually learned Holly was expecting not one but two babies.

I should have known better, Holly told herself now. Loving Grant secretly the way she had, she'd agreed to his proposal, hoping their babies would bring them together. Hoping that someday he'd realize he loved her, too, the way she loved him.

It hadn't happened. And while they'd both loved Ian and Jamie, their marriage had been…shaky… threatening to destroy their lifelong friendship. *My fault*, she acknowledged now. *I thought I could make Grant love me. But you can't* make *someone love you. Either they do, or they don't.*

Grant's breakthrough software design had hit the market at just the right time, and suddenly his company was raking in millions when Holly took a maternity leave of absence from her job. Holly had intended to return to work when the twins were three months old, but found she just couldn't leave them when the time came. And since Grant had certainly been able to afford it, Grant and Holly had decided she would be a stay-at-home mom until the boys were older.

Then Grant was killed in a car crash when the twins were six months old, leaving Holly mourning what had never come to be, and now never would.

Grant had left Holly comfortably well-off but had left the bulk of his estate in a trust for his sons—something Holly had known about and approved of when they'd both made their wills a month after the babies were born. No provision had been made for Grant's parents, who had first fought the will, then fought to gain custody of the twins from Holly so they could get their hands on the income from the trust. But Holly's in-laws hadn't been willing to wait for the court's final ruling…

Holly sighed and turned over again. Rehashing old

history in her mind was no way to fall asleep. She could never resolve the past. Couldn't change it, either. She just had to live with it, accept that she'd made mistakes and move on.

But thinking about moving on was dangerous, too, especially when the man she was interested in moving on with was Chris Colton. *So much emotional baggage*, Holly thought. *Holy cow, I thought* my *past was troubled.*

She started listing all the reasons getting involved with Chris was a bad, bad idea, but soon gave up… because she didn't care. Because the reasons *for* getting involved with him far outweighed the reasons not to, starting with the way he was with her boys. Not to mention the way he'd looked at her when he'd seen her without the wig for the first time…and her reaction.

Holly sighed again as she saw him in her mind's eye—so tall and impressively male, with muscles that rippled beneath the black T-shirt that fit him like a glove, the same way his jeans did. "Not helping," she muttered.

After ten more sleepless minutes she gave up. She tossed off the covers and rose from the bed, wrapped her robe around her and belted it tightly, then crept barefoot out of the bedroom and headed quietly for the kitchen. She'd tossed a box of her favorite herbal tea with oranges and lemons in their shopping cart this morning, and if that didn't help her sleep nothing would.

The tea bags and a mug were easy to find. Holly thought she might have to boil water in a pot—she didn't care for microwaved tea—but when she looked for a pot in the cabinet beside the stove, there was a brand-new teakettle. As she filled it with water and put it on the stove to boil, she couldn't help wondering about this house furnished with everything anyone could reasonably want…standing vacant. Uninhabited. Chris had told her Peg looked after it for him, so she wasn't surprised everything was spotless—as if the house's loving owners had merely stepped out and would return momentarily.

But it wasn't just that the house was well tended. Someone *had* loved this house once, even if Chris had never lived here. And it didn't take a genius to figure out that someone had to be Chris's deceased wife, Laura. But if Chris had never lived here, that meant Laura probably hadn't, either. And Holly's heart ached for the woman she never knew, the woman who had put so much time and effort into creating a home for the man she loved…and then died. A home her husband couldn't bear to live in without her…but couldn't bear to get rid of, either, because it had been *hers*.

Tears sprang to Holly's eyes as empathy and a kind of envy converged in her heart. *What would it be like to be loved that much?* she wondered with bittersweet intensity. And she knew in that instant she would sacrifice anything except Ian and Jamie to be loved like that.

The teakettle chose that moment to start whistling, and Holly dashed the tears from her eyes. Then she turned the flame off, grabbed a pot holder and poured hot water over the tea bag in her mug.

A deep voice from the doorway said, "Holly?" and she whirled around, almost dropping the teakettle in startled panic.

Chapter 7

Chris hadn't been to bed yet. After he'd left Holly singing her sons to sleep, he'd tried to do some work, but the memories evoked by Holly's lullabies were too sharp, too poignant. Though he tried to focus, his mind kept sliding back to his childhood. To his mother, of course. But also to his father.

Saralee had been a near-perfect mother, but Matthew hadn't been a bad father. Stern. Harsh on occasion. Busy, as a man would be trying to support such a large family on what a handyman could earn, and trying to keep the ramshackle Colton farmhouse from falling to pieces around them. But…he'd taken Chris fishing sometimes, had taught him how to ride a bike. Had even taught him how to handle a rifle and a shotgun and not blow his own damn fool head off.

Chris would also never forget the day he'd turned six

and Matthew had given him the best birthday present a boy could ever have—his golden retriever, Bouncer. Chris hadn't known then that Bouncer was the partial payoff Matthew had received for a job he'd done for a rancher who couldn't pay him in cash. Chris also hadn't known money was so tight for the Coltons that year that Saralee had despaired of where the money would come from for birthday presents for Chris and Annabel. All Chris knew back then was that Bouncer was *his*, and he'd loved that dog almost as much as he'd loved Saralee and Annabel. Almost as much as he'd loved Trevor.

Bouncer had been his constant companion for more than five years. Losing his dog had cut a gaping hole in Chris's heart. If he'd had Bouncer, the other losses—his mother, his father, his brothers and sisters—wouldn't have hit him so hard. But the foster parents who'd taken Chris into their home for the money the state paid them weren't willing to take on a dog as well—not without compensation. Bouncer had been sent to an animal shelter...and euthanized.

The boy he'd been had never recovered.

Now Chris stood in the kitchen, staring at the woman who'd opened the door to so many painful memories from his past he almost resented her for it. But then he realized she wasn't to blame—it wasn't her fault his father was a serial killer, had made Chris's mother his last victim and set in motion a chain of events no one could have predicted. And he couldn't blame Holly for being a good mother to her sons, either, for singing the bedtime songs Saralee had sung to her own children more than twenty years ago.

No, the only one to blame in all of this was Matthew Colton...whose murderous blood ran in Chris's veins.

"Sorry," he told Holly. "I didn't mean to startle you."

She shook her head. "You don't have to apologize. It's my own fault—I shouldn't be so jumpy. It's just that I wasn't paying attention, because I was thinking about—" She stopped abruptly.

"Thinking about the McCays?"

She shook her head again, then turned and put the teakettle down. "No. I was thinking about this house. About..." She hesitated. "About Laura. About how much you must have loved her. And I was thinking I would give anything to be loved that much."

Chris moved into the room until he stood right in front of Holly, staring down at her. So clean and wholesome. So sweet and desirable. "Yes, I loved Laura... but not enough," he said roughly. Holly's face took on a questioning mien, but all he said was "You don't want to know, Holly. But don't have any illusions about me. Laura wasn't a saint, but she was far and away too good for the likes of me."

The ache in Chris's heart grew until it threatened to overwhelm him. The urge to touch Holly, to kiss her, to lose himself in her arms was so great he almost did just that. And something in her soft brown eyes—a yearning empathy—told him she wouldn't stop him if he *did* try to kiss her. But if he touched her, it wouldn't end with kisses. It wouldn't end until he'd disillusioned her, until he'd proved to her she'd been wrong to trust him. Because he *would* hurt her...just as he'd hurt Laura. Not physically—he would never do that—but emotionally. And hurting Holly...hurting *any* woman ever again...would destroy him.

He took a step backward, putting distance between himself and temptation. "Don't look at me like that. And for God's sake, don't pity me." It hadn't been pity he'd seen in her eyes, but…

"Not pity," she told him quietly. "You're wrong if you think that. And you're wrong if you think anything your father did is a reflection on you, or that you could turn out like him," she added, unerringly going right to the heart of Chris's deepest fear. "Grant was a wonderful man—*nothing* like his parents. Should I not have loved Grant because his parents are the way they are?" Her voice dropped a notch. "Ian and Jamie are McCays, too. Should I blame them because their grandparents tried to kill me?"

Holly turned around and picked up her mug. She fished the tea bag out of it with a spoon, threw the tea bag in the trash, then turned back to Chris. "Think about it," she said. "Good night, Chris."

Chris stared at the doorway through which Holly had disappeared as he acknowledged she was right—his father's sins were his alone. Chris didn't need to atone for them. Just because a killer's blood ran through his veins didn't mean he was a killer. Chris had always known that deep down, but…but what? He'd let society's scorn for a serial killer's son color his perception of himself? He'd let the people of his hometown judge him for actions not his own?

Saralee's blood also ran through his veins, and she'd never hurt anyone. The people of Granite Gulch hadn't focused on that, though, just on what Matthew had done, and all the Colton children had paid the price to a greater or lesser extent. But Chris wasn't Saralee any more than he was Matthew. He was his own person.

His character had been forged by the life he'd lived, and the sense of right and wrong his mother had inculcated in him.

A few people in Granite Gulch outside his family had seen beyond the stigma he'd carried. Laura and Peg, of course. Peg's husband, Joe, who'd been Chris's best friend in high school. And when Chris had escaped Granite Gulch, when he'd gone to college in Arlington, no one had known who he was. No one had judged him except by his own actions. It had been a refreshing change, so refreshing he'd been tempted not to return to Granite Gulch after graduation.

But Laura had persuaded him to come back. Laura hadn't wanted to move to Fort Worth, even though that was where Chris had started his PI business, using connections he'd made in college. Laura had wanted to stay in Granite Gulch, near her parents and her sister. And because he'd loved her, Chris had compromised. He and Laura had lived in Granite Gulch and he'd commuted the forty miles each way to and from Fort Worth. But there'd been a price to pay for that compromise, a price Laura had increasingly resented. She'd never voiced that resentment to Chris...but deep down he'd known. He just hadn't been able to—

Chris stopped himself. He wasn't going there. Not tonight. Too many painful memories had already been dragged out into the light from the dark place Chris had stored them, and it was after midnight. He was going to have enough trouble sleeping without adding any more.

Holly woke to the smell of frying bacon. She hadn't had bacon in forever—it wasn't all that healthy for you, especially the kind sold in the United States—but she hadn't stopped Chris when he'd added a package to their grocery cart yesterday, because she secretly loved it. Bacon, eggs, toast and grits had been a Sunday-morning staple in her home growing up.

She glanced at the clock and realized it was early, just past six, which was why Ian and Jamie hadn't been what woke her up. If Holly slept past seven, the twins invariably woke her by banging on the sides of their cribs and calling "Ma-ma-ma-ma-ma!"

She dressed swiftly, brushed her teeth and washed her face, then decided to dispense with the wig. She wasn't planning to go anywhere, and besides, Chris had seen her without it. *And liked what he saw*, said a little voice in her head she tried to ignore.

Holly checked that the twins were still soundly sleeping before she headed for the kitchen, where she knew she'd find Chris. She'd thought about him last night as she'd drunk her tea, replaying that scene in the kitchen in her mind. Each time she'd thought of something different to say to him. Each time she'd wished she hadn't made it so obvious she was attracted to him. *But he was attracted to you, too*, her secret self reminded her now. And that gave her courage to face him without the shield of her twins.

"Good morning," she said as she walked into the sunny kitchen and saw the table set for two adults, with the two high chairs also set up.

Chris turned around from the stove. "Morning." He brought his attention back to his task and stirred something in a pot. "I should have asked you yesterday, but what do Ian and Jamie have for breakfast? I've got oatmeal here, do they eat that?"

Holly laughed. "They eat anything I'll let them eat, but they love oatmeal with a little milk."

"No sugar?"

She shook her head. "I'm trying to keep them from getting my sweet tooth," she confessed. "So no added sugar, no processed cereal except plain Cheerios."

"Good for you." He turned the stove off. "How do you feel about bacon and eggs?"

"I love them." She grimaced. "I shouldn't, I know. Nitrites and cholesterol."

Chris shook his head, his lips quirking into a grin as he leaned one jeans-clad hip against the counter. "Guess you haven't read the latest studies. The cholesterol in eggs is the good kind of cholesterol, not the bad. As for nitrites in bacon being bad for you, that myth has been debunked. The vast majority of the scientific studies suggest that not only are nitrates and nitrites not bad for you, but they may even be beneficial to your health."

"Really?" Holly could hardly believe it.

"Yeah. Doesn't mean you should eat them every day, but a couple times a week won't hurt you." He took a carton of eggs out of the fridge as he said this. "Bacon's already cooked—it's in the oven keeping warm. So how do you like your eggs?"

"I prefer them over easy, but salmonella is an issue." Her eyes sought his. "Or am I wrong about that, too?"

"No, it's a concern. I'm like you—I prefer them over easy, but I fry them hard for that reason."

"Then fry mine hard, too."

Chris's smile deepened, and all at once Holly couldn't breathe. She couldn't tear her eyes away from his face, either. Just like last night, sexual attraction tugged at her. Chris was so uncompromisingly *male* standing there in jeans and a white T-shirt, with a day's scruff on his chin—he practically oozed testosterone. And yet, he was comfortable in his masculinity. He didn't need to thump his chest in the "me Tarzan, you Jane" approach so many men thought made them seem more macho. There was something particularly appealing about a Texan who didn't think cooking was women's work. Who didn't look on child rearing as women's work, too.

But it wasn't just that. What Holly couldn't reconcile in her mind was her reaction to him on a sexual level. Just like last night, he made her think of things she had no business thinking about. Of cool sheets and hot kisses. Very hot kisses.

A plaintive wail floated into the kitchen, breaking the spell. "That's Jamie," she managed from a throat that had gone uncustomarily dry.

"I'll get breakfast on the table," Chris told her, turning back to the stove. "You go take care of your boys."

Evalinda McCay folded her lips together and stared at her husband over the breakfast table. "I don't like it, Angus."

"I told you what Mr. Colton said."

"Yes, but I don't like it. When we spoke with him last week, he didn't think it would take very long. Now it sounds as if he's not even *trying* to find Holly."

"It's not as if we're paying him by the hour, Eva," Angus McCay was quick to point out as he swallowed the last of his coffee. "He's not even charging us at all, except for expenses, so what's the complaint? Besides," he said, "*you* were the one who was so sure he was the perfect PI for the job, what with his father being a serial killer. And he didn't seem all that smart to me—he bought the story we told him."

"Maybe," Evalinda McCay said. "But now that I think of it, I wish we hadn't mentioned the Alphabet Killer angle. Too far-fetched. That might have made him suspicious."

"I don't think so. If Mr. Colton believes the idea that Holly was ever in danger from the Alphabet Killer is ludicrous, I'm sure he'd chalk it down to us being loving in-laws, overly concerned about Holly's safety." He cleared his throat. "Either way, it's no longer a concern now that the Alphabet Killer's eighth victim has been found—Helena what's-her-name."

"That's good," Evalinda McCay said. "Just be sure you don't mention anything about the Alphabet Killer the next time you talk to Mr. Colton."

"Yes, dear. Of course." Angus McCay winced inwardly. He wasn't about to tell his wife he'd brought up the Alphabet Killer only the day before, when he'd discussed the progress in the investigation with Chris Colton. It wasn't important, and she didn't need to know.

He wiped his mouth on his napkin and rose from the table. "I'd better be getting to the bank. I'll call you if I hear from Mr. Colton."

Chris put out two fires at work via phone and made a judgment call to trim the bill on the case of a man who'd been desperately searching for his teenage daughter—*it'll barely cover expenses*, his office manager had protested, but the man had cried when his daughter had finally been located. *It's not always about money*, Chris thought as he dashed off an email to his office manager. Business was booming, especially since so many companies were implementing preemployment background checks on their new hires, and employing firms like Chris's to do the work rather than relying on in-house human resource departments. He could afford to take the hit financially. He could still remember the way the man had wrung his hands when Chris had escorted the onetime runaway through her father's front door. Could still see the heartfelt tears in the man's eyes.

Happy endings didn't always happen in his line of work. The joy on that father's face when he was reunited with his missing daughter was priceless.

Chris rose and stretched, then moved to the other end of his L-shaped office, to the window there. He stared out into the fenced yard, where Holly, her twins and Wally were playing Wiffle ball. The twins were—understandably—not very good yet. But Wally chased down every ball that got past the boys and herded it back to them or carried it back in his mouth. Then, his tail wagging cheerfully, did it again and again.

Chris smiled, remembering playing ball with his younger brothers and Bouncer the same way. For the first time in a long time, thinking about Bouncer didn't hurt. "I must have been eight," he thought out loud. "Yeah, because Sam was about two, which meant Ridge was six and Ethan four." Stair steps, his father had dubbed them. "Stair steps," he whispered now, wondering how he'd forgotten that nickname. Trevor had been three years older, and somehow hadn't been included—only Chris, Ridge, Ethan and Sam. Annabel hadn't counted in his father's eyes; neither had a soon-to-be-born Josie.

Thinking of his father reminded Chris that this was his month to visit Matthew Colton in prison. His month to obtain the next clue to his mother's resting place. He didn't want to go. Unlike his brother Trevor, an FBI profiler who'd visited their father in prison regularly as part of his job, Chris had never gone, despite Matthew's requests some years back. From the time Matthew had been arrested for murder twenty years ago, from the time a trembling and tearful seven-year-old Ethan had confessed to an eleven-year-old Chris how he'd found their mother lying in her own blood, he'd had no desire to see his father ever again. But he couldn't *not* go. Not when everyone was counting on him for that next clue.

Chapter 8

Fifteen minutes passed before Chris went back to his laptop. Fifteen minutes spent watching Holly, the twins and Wally, torn between getting back to work and going out to join in the innocent play. But then he remembered that moment in the kitchen this morning with Holly, and the similar instances last night, and he told himself discretion was the better part of valor. The more time he spent in her company, the more he would want her. The more he wanted her, the more difficult it would be not to touch, not to taste. Not to run his fingers through the spun gold that was her hair and drown in those soft brown eyes. Not to carry her to his bed that had been empty and lonely for so long.

Just thinking about doing those things to Holly made him hard. Made him ache the way he hadn't ached for a woman since Laura. Not just an ache. More like a hunger, really. And he wondered about that. What was it about Holly that pierced the iron shell he'd built around his body...not to mention his heart?

It wasn't just that she was a good mother, as his mother had been, although that played into it, sure. And it wasn't just that she was quietly lovely in a whole-some, All-American, girl-next-door way, although that was part of it, too. At first he couldn't figure it out. Then it hit him. Holly trusted him. What had she said late last night? *You're wrong if you think anything your father did is a reflection on you, or that you could turn out like him...*

Very few women who knew about Chris's serial-killer father had ever looked beyond that fact enough to trust him. Really trust him. Laura had. Peg, too. And now Holly. Somehow she'd sensed that he didn't have it in him to kill as his father had killed. That whatever had been missing in Matthew wasn't missing in his son. She'd known Chris just a little over a day, and yet she trusted him with herself and her sons. Implicitly.

Which was another reason to keep his distance from Holly. Because even if she trusted him, he didn't trust himself.

When Chris finally dragged himself away from the window, he sat down and began Googling for more information related to the article he'd read last night on Yahoo, the one he'd discussed with Annabel. As he'd told his sister, he didn't believe in coincidences. Six years ago Josie had disappeared. At first every-one thought she'd run away because her boyfriend had dumped her. Then there'd been that period of time when Chris had feared Josie had been murdered, her body hidden in a remote location. But after the supposed sightings of Josie, he'd reverted back to thinking she'd run away for some reason. But what if she hadn't just run away? Could her disappearance have anything to do with the death of the drug lord with the same last name as her foster parents?

But the more he dug, the more questions he had... because he couldn't find *anything* on the death of Desmond Carlton. Not a single story. Not even a reference to Desmond Carlton in a related story *before* his death six years ago. The only mention of the man Chris could find anywhere was in the article from the day before.

That could mean only one thing. Someone—or a group of someones—had gone to a lot of trouble to erase Desmond Carlton's existence.

Chris picked up his smartphone and hit speed dial. "Brad?" he said when a voice answered. "It's Chris. I need you to run a trace for me. And this one's not going to be easy. I need you to track down any references you can find to a Desmond Carlton." He spelled the name carefully. "Or to a couple who may be related, Roy and Rhonda Carlton... Yeah, same last name. All I know about Desmond Carlton is he was a drug lord who was killed six years ago. As for Roy and Rhonda, they used to be foster parents, so there's got to be some kind of record of them with the state—criminal background checks, home inspections, the works. Oh, yeah, and they died in a car crash about five years ago."

He listened for a minute, then said, "No, there's no case to charge this to, but I'll clear it with payroll. Oh, and, Brad, when I said this one wasn't going to be easy, I meant it. You're not going to find anything on Desmond Carlton on the internet—I already looked.

You're going to have to hit the main libraries in Fort Worth and Dallas, see if you can turn something up the old-fashioned way. And if that doesn't work, try the offices of the *Star-Telegram* or the *Morning News*. I'm betting there will be articles in their morgues," he said, referring to the newspapers' private archives.

He listened for another minute, then laughed. "Yeah, that's why I called you. The younger guys wouldn't even know where to begin if they couldn't Google the name." His laugh trailed away. "Call me the minute you find out anything. And, Brad? Watch yourself, okay?... No, no, this isn't like the Winthrop case. But no one knows I'm looking for this info. Someone whitewashed the search engines, and until I know why...Yeah, exactly. Thanks, Brad."

Chris disconnected. His fingers flew over his laptop's keyboard and he pulled up the article he'd been reading the night before. He quickly skimmed through it again, noted the originating newspaper was the *Dallas Morning News* and jotted down the byline. "The guy must have dug deep to get as much as he got," he murmured to himself. "Good thing I told Brad to check those newspaper morgues—I'll bet a dollar to a doughnut that's where this guy found the link."

He thumbed through his smartphone's contacts until he found the number he wanted and hit the dial key. It rang three times before it was answered.

"Hey, Taylor, Chris Colton here...Yeah, long time." He shot the breeze with his old college buddy for a few minutes, then said, "I need to talk with one of your fellow reporters...No," he added drily at a question from the other end. "No, I'm not planning to give a scoop to a rival—any scoops I have go to you, you know that."

Chris rolled his eyes, glad Taylor couldn't see him. "I just need to ask a few questions about an article this guy wrote, so I need his direct line." He gave Taylor the reporter's name and jotted down the phone number he was given. "Thanks, Taylor, I owe you one."

Never one to let grass grow under his feet, Chris had no sooner hung up than he was dialing the new number. But all he got was the reporter's voice mail. He thought about it for a few seconds, and before the recorded message finished Chris decided not to leave a callback number and disconnected.

He drummed his fingers on his desk for a moment, then called Taylor back. "Hey, buddy, it's Chris again. I need another favor. Can you set up a one-on-one for me with your colleague?...Yeah, him. ASAP." After a few seconds he said, "No, nothing like that." Realizing he'd need to reveal a few more details to convince Taylor, but not wanting to say anything about the possible connection to Josie, he dangled a carrot. "I might know something about a perp in a story your colleague wrote that he would find very interesting." *It's not a lie*, Chris reminded himself. *If the two cases are connected...*

"Okay, thanks. Call me when you set something up. You've got my number."

Chris checked his work email again while he waited to hear back from Taylor, scrolling through quickly, skimming and scanning as was normal for him. Three cases had been successfully resolved during his brief absence from the office, and he answered with "Attaboy!" messages, CCing the entire staff. It never hurt and cost him only a minute or two of his time. He paid all his staff well, especially his investigators—anyone who wasn't worth the salary Chris paid didn't last long at Colton Investigations. But money wasn't the best motivator—recognition was. Chris had learned that early on in his career. He'd just clicked Send on the last email when his cell phone rang.

"Hey, Taylor," he answered. After a minute he asked, "Where?" followed by "When?" He wrote swiftly. "Okay," he agreed. "I'll be there."

As soon as he hung up he hit speed dial. "Bella?" he said when his sister answered. "You're off today, aren't you? I need a big favor."

"I don't need a babysitter," Holly said furiously when Chris told her he was going out but that Annabel was coming over to watch her. "If that's what you think, you'd better think again."

"Not a babysitter," Chris explained patiently. "A bodyguard."

"Same thing."

"No, it's not." There was something implacable in his face, in his voice, and Holly knew she wasn't going to win this argument...unless she took her boys and stormed out of the house. Which would be a stupid "cutting off your nose to spite your face" kind of thing to do.

"Look," she began, but Chris stopped her.

"No, *you* look. Do I think the McCays will find you here while I'm gone? No. But am I willing to take that chance? No." His blue eyes had gone cold, but there was something fierce in their depths that reminded Holly of an eagle's basilisk stare. "*No one* is dying on my watch ever again, you got that? I made myself responsible for you—and you agreed to it." He was breathing heavily now, as if he'd been running… or as if deep-rooted emotions were taking their toll on his body. "I've already lost—" He broke off, as if the rest of that sentence would reveal more than he wanted. "You agreed to let me protect you and your sons, Holly," he said after a minute, a little calmer now. "You have to let me do it my way."

"But—"

"No buts. My way, Holly."

She was going to keep arguing, but then she heard Peg's voice in her mind. *Chris needs to do this, Holly. I can't explain, but he needs to do this. So just let him take care of you and your boys.*

She breathed deeply once, then again, and pushed her independent spirit aside for now at the sudden reminder. She wouldn't always knuckle under to Chris—it wasn't her nature and it wouldn't be good for him anyway. But in this instance, maybe he was right. There was only a chance in a thousand something could happen to her or the boys while Chris was gone, but that was a risk he wasn't willing to take. She wasn't willing to risk it, either, not when it came to Ian and Jamie.

"Okay." She held up one hand before he could say anything. "Okay, this time. When are you going? And when will your sister arrive?"

Chris glanced at his wristwatch. "Annabel will be here in about fifteen minutes. I'm not leaving until she gets here."

Holly let the tension drain out of her muscles. "I'd better check on the boys—they've been quiet too long. Then I'll make lunch."

* * *

Chris was long gone. They'd eaten lunch, after which Chris had left and Holly had taken the twins to the master bedroom for their nap. Then, with Wally at her heels, she returned to the family room, where Annabel was reading a magazine she'd brought with her, *Law Enforcement Technology*. Holly had given Annabel the silent treatment during lunch but realized with a touch of remorse it wasn't fair—Annabel was just doing her brother a favor, and giving up her free time to do it.

Before she could speak, though, Annabel said, "Your kids are really cute."

"Oh. Thanks." Holly chuckled, taking a seat at the other end of the sofa. Wally plopped himself at Holly's feet, and she reached down to ruffle his fur before saying, "You've only seen them after they're worn-out playing ball with Wally. Wait until you see them after their nap, when they're reenergized. The word *rambunctious* was created with Ian and Jamie in mind."

Annabel laughed. "Kids are like that. All kids. But women still keep having them anyway." A wistful expression crossed her face. "I wouldn't mind…" She didn't finish that sentence, just tossed her magazine to one side and asked, "How old are Ian and Jamie?"

"Eighteen months."

"Identical twins? They look like it, but have they been tested to know for sure?"

Holly nodded. "Identical. Even so, Chris can already tell them apart."

"Really." There was something in the way Annabel said that one word, something meaningful. Not a question, just an acknowledgment of what that said about Chris.

Holly nodded again. "He's incredibly observant." She started to say "for a man" but realized that wasn't true. Chris was incredibly observant, period.

"That's what makes him such a good PI," Annabel stated. Then she laughed softly. "Of course, that wasn't always such a great thing when I was in high school."

"Chris admitted he scared away a few of your boyfriends."

"That's an understatement!" Annabel's laughter softened into a reminiscent smile. "I tease him, I know, but he's a great brother in most ways. When we finally reconnected in high school—"

"Reconnected?" Holly's eyebrows drew together. "What do you mean, reconnected?"

Annabel looked surprised. "Didn't you know? We were all sent to different—" Then she stopped. "You *do* know about our father…and our mother…don't you?"

Holly nodded. "Chris told me the first time we met."

"Hmm. Doesn't sound like Chris. He doesn't tell many people."

"He was trying to make a point," Holly said. "I think he wanted to shock me."

"Now, that *does* sound like Chris," Annabel replied. Her expression turned somber. "And it's not like it's a secret—just about everyone in Granite Gulch knows." She was silent for a moment. "Well, if you know what happened, then I would have thought you'd know when our mother was killed and our father went to prison, the whole family was split up. We were all sent to different foster homes."

"Oh, Annabel…" Holly tried to imagine someone doing that to Ian and Jamie, and could hardly fathom it.

Annabel sighed, then continued. "That's what I meant when I said Chris and I reconnected in high school. We were eleven when we were separated. We didn't meet again until then."

Holly didn't know any way of expressing the pain that speared through her for the brother and sister who'd been so ruthlessly torn apart. All she could say was "Oh, Annabel" again.

"Chris and I were close growing up. I was a bit of a tomboy—do they even use that word anymore? But we did nearly everything together. He was always protective—not just toward me, but toward our younger brothers and sister, too. Our mother's death and the separation only exaggerated that trait in Chris. So when we reconnected in high school…" She shrugged. "There were some bullies who tried to pick on me because of…well, because of our serial-killer father. Chris helped me put a stop to it."

"It sounds like him." After she said it Holly was struck with the realization that she'd known Chris less than two days, but she already knew this much about him. It didn't seem possible…but it was true.

Holly still had questions about Chris, however, questions she didn't really want to ask him, and this seemed like the golden opportunity. She looked at Annabel and blurted out, "What was Laura like?"

Chris's sister thought for a moment. "Sweet. Pretty. And she had a gentleness about her that was very appealing, especially to a man like Chris." She hesitated, then added, "Chris was her world, and whatever he did

was right. Good in some ways, not so good in others."
Annabel looked as if she could say more, but wouldn't.

Holly digested this, then asked, "How did she die?"

"Viral meningitis."

"Oh." Holly stared blankly at Annabel. "I thought
that was treatable."

"It is…if you treat it in time. There was an outbreak
in Fort Worth, and somehow Laura was exposed. She
had all the classic symptoms—headache, stiff neck,
fever. But she never mentioned it to Chris. By the time
she called her sister, Peg—you know Peg, right?" Annabel said in an aside. "Isn't that what Chris said?"
Holly nodded and Annabel continued. "By the time
Peg rushed her to the doctor she was in a really bad
way. She was airlifted to Baylor Medical Center in
Fort Worth, but she didn't make it—she died en route."

A wave of empathy for Chris enveloped Holly, because she could relate. Grant had been airlifted from
the scene of the traffic accident that had taken his life,
but he hadn't made it to the hospital, either. "How hor-
rible for Chris," she whispered.

"He took it hard," Annabel confirmed. "Especially
since he blamed himself."

"What do you mean? How could he— If Laura
didn't tell him she was feeling bad, how could he have
known?"

"That's something you're going to have to ask him,"
Annabel said with a guilty expression. "I probably
shouldn't have told you that much." She sighed suddenly. "But here's something maybe you should know,
something Peg could tell you but probably didn't. Laura
was four months pregnant when she died."

"Oh, my God." Holly covered her mouth with one

hand. Suddenly the statement Peg had made about Chris the last time she'd seen her friend made complete sense. "Peg told me—she said she couldn't really explain, but she said Chris needed to take care of the twins and me. And I should let him. This must have been what she meant."

"Probably." Annabel's blue eyes—so like her brother's—held Holly's gaze. "You haven't known Chris very long, so you might not understand. Chris has a very stern conscience. He would never admit it, but he fervently believes in atonement. He knows you can't change the past, no matter how much you might want to. But he *does* believe you can make up for it—if you're willing to pay the price. And he is."

Chapter 9

Chris drove the roughly seventy miles to Dallas in just over fifty minutes, with his foot on the accelerator of his F-150 and one eye on the rearview mirror, watching for the highway patrol. He'd gotten a couple of speeding tickets in his lifetime, but nothing that appeared on his driving record, and he wanted to keep it that way. Not enough to slow down—this was Texas after all—but enough to be semicautious.

He was pretty sure he remembered where the sports bar he was heading to was located, but he had his GPS on anyway, and he followed the directions. His tires squealed only slightly when he pulled into the parking lot, stopped the truck and got out.

Chris was accosted by a wall of television sets, all tuned to different sports channels, when he walked into the otherwise dimly lit sports bar. He glanced around, looking for the clothing Taylor had described the reporter would be wearing, but realized he didn't need that help after all. Taylor was standing at the bar with the other man, both of them nursing beers and munching on bar snacks, when Taylor spotted Chris and waved him over.

The introductions were made swiftly, after which Chris murmured to his friend, "Afraid of being scooped?"

Taylor laughed. "No, but whatever you have to say to Roger, I want to know. Just in case."

Chris ordered a longneck and a plate of nachos—he'd yet to meet a reporter who wasn't hungry, literally as well as figuratively—then said, "Let's get a booth. More privacy."

Chris sipped his beer as the other two men dug into the nachos, then put the bottle down in front of him and abruptly said to Roger, "What do you know about Desmond Carlton?"

Roger swallowed. "Uh-uh. That's not how this works. Taylor said you might have information for me related to the article I wrote on the man who was captured, one of the FBI's Ten Most Wanted."

Chris shook his head and moved his beer bottle infinitesimally. "Quid pro quo," he said. "Give and take. You tell me what you know, and I'll tell you what I know. *That's* how this works."

Roger glanced at Taylor, who said, "I vouch for him, Roger. He's never lied to me yet."

Roger nodded thoughtfully. "Okay," he told Chris. "What do you want to know?"

"Desmond Carlton."

Roger shook his head. "I don't know all that much. I'd been working on a story for a while, gathering whatever bits and pieces I could find on *all* the men on the FBI's Ten Most Wanted list." He grimaced. "Okay, so the angle was how long each man had been on the list, and why the FBI wasn't making progress in catching them."

Chris pursed his lips. "And?" he prompted.

"And then, boom! The FBI arrests one, and that angle kinda sorta went out the window. But my supervising editor said we could salvage at least part of the work I'd done by publishing what I'd uncovered on the guy, including his past history, the creeps he ran with, everything."

Chris took another sip of his beer. "So how did Desmond Carlton's name come into it?"

"He was collaterally associated with the perp the FBI arrested. But Carlton's been dead for six years. Now that this guy's finally been arrested, everybody associated with Carlton is either dead or behind bars. End of story."

Chris mulled this over for a minute. "Not quite," he told Roger. "Are you aware there's not a single mention of Desmond Carlton on any search engine?"

Roger's face betrayed him. "Yeah," he said slowly, "I didn't really focus on it, but now that you mention it, you're right."

"How did you find out the facts about him you included in your story?"

"The morgue had a few articles on Desmond Carlton," Roger said, confirming Chris's hunch. "Including one on his death six years ago. But remember," he was quick to justify himself, "Carlton wasn't the main focus of the story. So it never occurred to me…"

Taylor spoke up finally. "Are you saying someone

wiped Desmond Carlton's name out of every database?" He glanced at Roger. "Now, *that's* a story."

"I don't know who, and I don't know why," Chris admitted, "but yeah. Electronically Desmond Carlton is a ghost." He slid his beer bottle back and forth between his hands, considering what more—if anything—he should reveal. Finally he reached a decision.

"Deep background, guys," he said, his voice rough. His eyes met Roger's, then Taylor's. "Deal?"

Chris knew what he was asking. If Taylor and Roger agreed, they could never quote him on what he was about to disclose. They could only use his information if they could confirm it with other sources, sources willing to go on the record.

"Deal," said Taylor, and Roger echoed, "Deal."

Chris fixed his eyes on Roger. "In all your research, did the name Josie Colton ever come up in connection with Desmond Carlton in *any* way?"

Taylor blurted out, "Josie? You mean—" Chris kicked Taylor under the table, and his friend fell silent.

Roger thought a minute. "Josie Colton?" He shook his head regretfully. "Not that I recall, and I looked under every rock I could find." Then he made the connection. "Wait a sec. Josie Colton. Wasn't the FBI looking at her for the Alphabet Killer murders?"

Chris held back his sudden spurt of anger. "Not anymore." He didn't trust himself to say anything else at that moment.

Taylor, after one glance at Chris's suddenly closed face, said, "That's right. They've pretty much narrowed it down to Regina Willard, haven't they?"

Chris nodded, hoping that was the end of the questioning, but Roger said, "Colton, huh? Any relation of yours?"

"My youngest sister," he admitted reluctantly. But that was all he was going to say about Josie. No way was he going to mention her foster parents had the same last name as Desmond Carlton. No way was he going to reveal she'd been missing for six years, either—the same amount of time Desmond Carlton had been dead. If there was a connection…if Josie was somehow involved…

"You said you found an article in the morgue about Carlton's death," Chris said suddenly. "How did he die?"

"Shot to death. But there were no shell casings and someone even dug the bullets out of him, so there was very little to go on."

"Was anyone ever arrested for it?"

"Nope," Roger said. "The case is cold…not that anyone in the police department is losing sleep over it. Drug lord shot to death? A man who'd been a suspect in several murders but never arrested for any of them? The police probably figured whoever offed him was doing the public a favor taking him off the streets."

Taylor elbowed Roger in the ribs. "What?" Roger exclaimed. "I'm not saying anything other people haven't thought."

"Yeah," Taylor said. "But still…someone getting away with murder…it's not right. Whoever killed Desmond Carlton is probably still out there. And if he killed once, he could kill again. And the next time it might not be someone who deserved to die."

"Was there any mention of reprisals?" Chris asked.

"Could Carlton's murder have been the result of some kind of rivalry between drug cartels?"

"I never uncovered anything about that. Doesn't mean it wasn't drug related, but there was no mention of any kind of drug war in the newspapers in the months following Carlton's death. I couldn't find anything indicating he'd been killed in a coup within his own organization, either."

Which brings me right back to Josie and her possible involvement, Chris thought but didn't voice. He couldn't imagine his baby sister killing anyone—he'd never really bought into the idea that Josie might be the Alphabet Killer, but he'd sure been glad when the finger of suspicion had finally pointed away from her. He also couldn't imagine what connection Josie could have to a slain drug lord…except the coincidences of the time frame of her disappearance and her foster parents' last name. Coincidences he didn't trust.

Chris rubbed a hand over his jaw, then asked Roger one last question. "Are you planning any follow-up articles?"

"Nothing about Desmond Carlton, if that's what you're asking."

He smiled briefly. "Yeah, that's what I'm asking. Just wondered if you were holding anything back." *The way I am,* he finished in his mind.

"Nope, not this time. But—" Roger held up one hand, palm outward "—if I find anything from other sources that ties Josie Colton to Desmond Carlton's murder…all deals are off."

"Understood." Chris finished the dregs of his beer and stood. "Thanks, Roger. I owe you one."

"Hey, what about me?" Taylor asked in a mock-serious tone.

"I bought you the nachos," Chris said with a sudden grin. "We're even."

Evalinda McCay hummed to herself as she ruthlessly pruned the hydrangea bushes on either side of her front door. But she wasn't really giving as much attention to her gardening as she usually did; she was thinking about Holly. *Snip!* went the shears, slicing effortlessly through the branches the way she could easily have sliced through her daughter-in-law's throat.

I should have taken care of Holly myself, she acknowledged privately. She could have done it, too—no qualms assailed her about the course of action she'd decided on to get custody of the twins...and their all-too-tempting trust fund. Angus had protested at first, but he hadn't been difficult to persuade—she'd been unilaterally making their major decisions for all the years they'd been married...and even before then.

If I had killed Holly, she'd be dead now, and all that money would already be mine.

But Angus had insisted they insulate themselves, make it appear to be an accident. Even more, he'd shrunk from having a direct hand in eliminating Holly, as if that made it less of a sin somehow.

Evalinda wasn't worried about sin any more than she was worried about divine retribution. All she cared about was the money that would preserve their standing in the community. The income from the trust fund would eliminate their debt, would remove the sword of Damocles hanging over their heads and allow them to continue to live lavishly...the way she deserved.

It wasn't just the income from the trust she intended to have, however—the principal was also in her long-range plans, although she hadn't mentioned that to Angus yet. But first things first. Custody of the twins was the primary step. Everything else would follow from that. Which meant one way or another, Holly had to die. And soon.

That night, after the twins were in bed, Holly sought out Chris in his office. She tapped on the open door and said, "Knock, knock," before she realized he was on the phone. Chris swung around in his chair, cell phone to his ear, and held up a finger to indicate his call was almost finished. "Thanks, Sam," he said. "I appreciate it." Then he disconnected.

"Hey," he said to Holly. "What's up?"

"I wanted to talk to you about the McCays," she said, leaning against the doorjamb. "You said yesterday you wanted to set a trap for them, and I... Not that I'm not grateful for your hospitality," she rushed to add. "I am. It's a lovely house, and Ian and Jamie had a blast playing with Wally in the yard this morning." One corner of her mouth quirked into a half smile. "Peg was right to insist we bring him. He has helped the boys adjust to this new place better than anything I could have thought of."

"Boys and dogs," Chris said softly. "Nothing like the bond that develops between boys and dogs."

"Girls, too," Holly was quick to point out. "I had a dog myself growing up, a cocker spaniel I named Chocolate Bar because she was such a rich brown color. I called her Chox for short. I got her for Christmas in first grade. She died when I was fifteen and I wept buckets."

Chris's eyes crinkled at the corners for just a moment, and though he didn't say anything, Holly sensed there was a very sad story somewhere in Chris's past about a dog. She hurried to get back to her original subject. "Anyway," she said, "I wanted to discuss that trap you mentioned."

He leaned back in his chair with a creak of leather and indicated the sofa. "Have a seat," he said. "It just so happens I was talking with my brother about this when you walked in."

Holly sat. "You were?"

"Mmm-hmm. Sam agrees you can't keep running. He also agrees setting a trap for the McCays is the way to go, but we have to be careful about entrapment. Which means—"

"We can't entice them into committing an illegal act," Holly said before he could. "I understand."

A flash of admiration crossed Chris's face. "Exactly. We can do this, but we have to plan it carefully. And of course, Sam's concerned about using real bait."

"You mean me."

"Yeah. But I don't think we have a choice. You're the only way to draw them out into the open."

Holly nodded. "Makes sense."

"Sam's also worried about the twins. No matter what kind of trap we set, there's going to be some danger involved. He doesn't want the twins around when we spring the trap. I don't think you do, either."

"Of course not."

"So that means we need to stash them somewhere safe for the time being."

Holly stared blankly at Chris. "You mean…turn my children over to a stranger?"

Chris shook his head. "No," he said gently, and Holly realized despite his big, tough exterior, he really was a gentle man. "I'd never suggest that. But what about Peg? She'd do it for you, don't you think? The boys know her and her kids. And Peg told me you and she have traded off babysitting for the past three months."

"A few hours at a time," Holly said faintly as a sense of suffocation overwhelmed her. "And never overnight."

"If you've got a better idea, I'd like to hear it."

If she hadn't already been sitting down, she would have fallen, because her legs were suddenly weak and trembling. Leave her babies? Not just for a few hours, but for however long it took to set and spring a trap? She hadn't been able to go back to work after her maternity leave ended. How was she expected to spend nights away from them?

Holly's lips moved, but no words came out, and she forced herself to focus on Chris's face. "You want me to leave Ian and Jamie with Peg…indefinitely."

He shook his head again. "Not indefinitely. A few days, a week at the most."

Could she do it? She wasn't sure. But did she really have a choice? Chris and his brother were right—she couldn't keep on running. Not just because the McCays might eventually run her to ground, but also because the constant moving was too hard on Ian and Jamie, especially now that they were getting old enough to notice the change in their environment. She had to close that chapter in her life, and the only way to do it…the only *safe* way to do it…was to settle with the McCays once and for all. To get them arrested, tried and convicted. To get them locked away where they would no longer be a threat. Not to her, and not to her sons.

"Could I…could I at least talk to them every day?"

"Nobody's trying to stop you from being a good mother, Holly…except the McCays." That gentleness was back in Chris's voice. "But I don't want you to visit Ian and Jamie at Peg's, because once we set the trap the McCays will know where you are…and instead of going after the bait and trying to kill you, they could track you to Peg's house. Secretly. We'd have no way of knowing. And that would put the boys in danger. I know you don't want that."

"Of course not," Holly repeated.

"You can talk to Ian and Jamie several times a day, for however long you and they need. A week, max, I promise. Hard on you. Hard on them. But it'll be worth it if we catch the McCays in the act."

"Okay." She didn't want to do it, but Chris's points were irrefutable. She suddenly realized her palms were damp, and she rubbed them nervously on the sides of her jeans. "So when do we start?"

"As soon as I can coordinate things with Sam and Annabel—tomorrow or the next day. And I've got to get Jim Murray's blessing, too." She raised her brows in a question, and he added, "He's the Granite Gulch police chief. Sam and Annabel answer to him, so we can't do this without him giving it the green light. But I don't see Jim saying no."

"Can he be trusted?" Holly blurted out.

Chris smiled faintly. "He's honest as the day is long.

I've known him since I was a kid, and I would trust him to do the right thing. Always."

"Okay," she said again. She didn't say anything more, but she didn't leave, either. She knew she should—that would be the safe thing. The smart thing. But suddenly all she could think of was the kiss in her dream yesterday. The kiss that had devastated her with how much she wanted this man she barely knew. And then there was the kiss that wasn't. The almost-kiss in the kitchen last night. She'd seen it in his eyes—he'd wanted to kiss her. Why hadn't he?

Then she realized he was looking at her the same way he had last night, as if he was a little boy standing on the sidewalk outside a store window gazing longingly at something he wanted but knew he couldn't have because he couldn't afford it. As if—

"Go to bed, Holly," he told her, his voice suddenly harsh. But she couldn't seem to make her feet move. "This isn't what you want." Oh, but it was, it *was*.

So when her feet finally did move it wasn't to leave. Six steps was all it took to bring her right up to Chris, right up to his rock-hard body that exuded unbelievable warmth, just like her dream. She reached up and brushed a lock of hair from his forehead, then let her fingers trail down his temple, his cheek. The slight scruff of his unshaven chin made her shiver with sudden longing, and her nipples tightened until they ached.

Then he pulled her flush against his body, and she wrapped her arms around his waist, holding on for dear life. She raised her face to his, her eyes mutely asking, and he kissed her.

Kissed? If she could think, she'd find a better word for what his lips were doing to hers, but every thought flew out of her head and all she could do was kiss him back. All she could do was match the hunger in him. The need. The frantic longing for something just out of reach, which they both knew could be theirs, if only…

She heard a whimper and realized it was coming from her throat. Heard a moan and realized that was hers, too. She couldn't seem to get close enough, even though he was holding her in his powerful embrace as if he would never let her go. *Don't let me go* reverberated in her brain, and if she'd had the breath she would have said the words out loud. But she couldn't, because he'd stolen her breath. Stolen her sanity.

He was hot and hard, but not where she wanted him to be—he was too tall…or she was too short. Then his hands grasped her hips and lifted her with unbelievable strength. She wrapped her arms around his neck and her legs around his hips, gasping with relief as she rocked up against the hardness she yearned for.

He was still kissing her and—oh, God!—just like her dream, she couldn't get enough of him. She was burning up from the inside out, and if he didn't make love to her in the next sixty seconds she would go crazy, she would—

A sudden wailing from the master bedroom brought everything to a crashing halt.

Chapter 10

Letting Holly go ranked right up there in the top ten most difficult things Chris had ever done, but he did it. He reluctantly let her slide down his body until her feet touched the floor. Compelled his lips to release hers. Forced his arms to set her free. Her breasts were rising and falling as if she was having the same difficulty he was having breathing, and there was a dazed expression in her eyes...one that quickly changed to mortification.

"I...I... That's Jamie," Holly stammered, practically running from the study.

Chris followed her, turning on the light in the hallway so she didn't have to feel her way in the darkness. She disappeared into the master bedroom before he could catch up, and when he turned the corner, she was already lifting a weeping Jamie from his crib.

"It's okay, sweetie," she soothed. "Mommy's here."

Ian, woken from a sound sleep by his brother's sobs, started fussing, his face crumpling as if he was going to cry, too. But Chris wouldn't let him. He lifted the boy out of the crib and propped him up against his shoulder. "Hey, buddy, don't you start." He chucked the boy under the chin. "Come on now. You're okay."

He glanced over at Holly cuddling Jamie in her arms, his face pressed against her shoulder as she rocked him back and forth. "Bad dream, you think?"

"Probably."

Holly's eyes wouldn't meet his, and disappointment slashed through him as he figured she was already regretting what they'd done. The best thing that had happened to him since Laura died...and Holly was regretting it.

Should have known better, he berated himself. *Should never have touched her. You knew that, so why...?*

He didn't want to address that question, but the answer refused to be silenced. He'd touched Holly... kissed her...caressed her...damn near made love to her...because he had to. Because the yearning in her eyes had aroused an ache in him he hadn't been able to suppress. Because the need to hold her had swept everything aside like a force of nature, the way a river in flood swept away everything in its path.

And now she wouldn't even look at him. As if she was ashamed.

That was the most hurtful thing of all.

Chris sat in his study a half hour later. Staring at his laptop, but not really seeing the web page he'd opened. Work, which had been his saving grace after Laura's death, couldn't hold his interest. He kept reliving the scene of Holly and him in this very room tonight. Only this time when he told her to go to bed and she refused to go…this time when she walked toward him and touched his face…this time when she raised her face to his asking for his kiss…this time he didn't touch her.

Which was what he should have done in the first place.

"Chris?"

He whirled around in his chair when a hesitant voice from the doorway said his name. Then he stood, needing to be on his feet to offer Holly the apology she deserved. In one way he wasn't sorry—he'd wanted to kiss her since the first time he'd seen her walking up the driveway of Peg's house, and now he had. And it had been like nothing he'd ever experienced in his life. But in another way he regretted it…because now he *knew* what it would be like with Holly…and he couldn't have it. Couldn't have *her*.

"I'm sorry."

"I'm sorry."

Chris spoke first, but Holly's apology was only a half second behind his. He shook his head. "You don't have anything to apologize for," he told her. "I should never have touched you."

Holly blinked, then her eyes creased at the corners. "I started it," she said quietly. "I'm not one of those women who blame the man for losing control when—" She broke off and breathed deeply. "You didn't do anything I didn't want you to do."

"That doesn't absolve me of blame." Chris tucked

his hands in his back pockets to keep himself from reaching for her. "You're under my protection, Holly. And you're feeling vulnerable—I knew that. I shouldn't have taken advantage."

A fierce expression swept over her face. "You shouldn't have taken *advantage*?" Her voice held that same fierceness. "What is this, the eighteen hundreds? If one of us took advantage of the other, it was me. *I* took advantage of *you*. I wanted you, and I—" She stopped, then continued bravely. "I wanted you, Chris. I've never wanted that way in my entire life, not even with Grant."

His brain tried to process her words, but they didn't jive with— "You ran out of the room," he grated. "You were mortified—no, don't deny it," he interjected when she tried to speak. "And in the bedroom you wouldn't even meet my eyes. You were *ashamed*."

"Not for the reason you apparently think," she said, a tinge of color in her cheeks. "When I heard Jamie crying, I...I didn't want to stop. Didn't want to go see what was wrong with him. *That's* why I was mortified," she explained. "Because I wanted you so much that for an instant I actually resented Jamie for interrupting." Her lips curved up slightly at the corners in a rueful smile. "I didn't want to be a mother at the moment, Chris. I just wanted to be a woman. A woman you wanted as much as I wanted you."

He could have sworn he didn't move, but suddenly he found himself standing right in front of Holly. "I wanted you," he said in his deepest voice. "I wanted you like I wanted my next breath." He raised a hand to her cheek and admitted, "I still do." He let that confession hang there for a couple of seconds before adding,

"And when Jamie cried?" His rueful smile matched hers. "I wished him in perdition."

Suddenly they were both laughing softly, and Chris lowered his forehead to Holly's. "That doesn't make us bad people," he told her, unutterably relieved she hadn't been ashamed of what they'd done after all. "It just means we're human."

"So I'm not a bad mother because I didn't immediately switch off the woman gene and switch on the mother gene?" she whispered, but in a tone that told him she was teasing.

"Hell—I mean, heck no," he teased back.

Holly touched her lips to his. "Glad to hear it," she murmured.

Desire zinged through his veins, but this time he had enough self-control not to follow through on it. "Don't start something we can't finish," he warned lightly.

"We can't?"

"Holly…" he began, then realized she was teasing again.

"It's going to happen, Chris," she told him, all teasing aside. "Not tonight. Maybe not even tomorrow night. But it's going to happen." Despite her brazen words, the little flags of color in her cheeks, the not-so-sure-of-herself expression in her eyes and the almost defiant way she said it told Chris this wasn't normal behavior for Holly. *She's probably never made the first move in her life*, he thought. And that turned him on no end. The idea that Holly—sweet, innocent Holly—wanted him that much was incredibly arousing.

But he wasn't taking any chances. Not tonight. "Go to bed, Holly," he told her, gently this time. "But I won't be upset if you dream about me, 'cause I'll be dreaming about you." He laughed deep in his throat, and it felt good to laugh, even though he knew he'd go to bed hard and aching and wake up the same way. "Oh, yeah, I'll be dreaming about you."

Holly woke before the twins again and lay there for a moment, enjoying the peace and quiet. Then she remembered how she'd brazenly told Chris last night they would eventually become lovers. Just *thinking* about it made her cheeks warm—she'd never been that bold with a man. Even when she'd made up her mind to do whatever she could to entice Grant into loving her, she'd never come right out and said it.

But then she'd never felt for Grant what she felt for Chris. Yes, she'd loved her husband, but…she'd never hungered for him. She'd never *craved*. And that was a revelation. She just wasn't sure what it meant.

She wasn't merely drawn to Chris physically, though. He tugged at her heart, too, now more than ever. Her conversation with Annabel yesterday afternoon had explained a lot about his behavior, and she believed she knew him better. But it wasn't just that. Watching him with her sons—could there exist a man more destined to be a father than Chris? He was a natural, his father instincts always on target. Like last night, for instance, when he'd stopped Ian from crying. How did he *know*? How did he unerringly know just what to do, what to say in every interaction with Ian and Jamie?

Holly turned over and tucked her hand beneath her cheek. Chris was a triple threat—hotter than sin, a perfect dad in the making and a man whose emotions ran so deep any woman would be drawn to him.

She sighed. Problem was…she was starting to fall

for him. Which had epic disaster written all over it, because she wasn't the kind of woman men fell in love with. Okay, yes, Chris wanted her. She was pretty enough, sexy enough, and other men had wanted her before. Not Grant, though. Except for the night Ian and Jamie had been conceived—and it had taken a few drinks more than he normally allowed himself before he'd seen her as a sexy, desirable woman—Grant's lovemaking had been...restrained. Good enough in its way, but...restrained. They'd tried hard to make a go of their marriage for the twins' sake. But Grant had never been in love with her...because she wasn't the lovable kind.

Chris told Holly at breakfast, "I called Peg this morning. She agreed to take Ian and Jamie for as long as you need."

She stopped supervising Jamie's attempts to feed himself and darted a dismayed look at him. "So soon?"

"The sooner we start, the sooner it will be over," he said patiently. "But actually, I have something I need to get out of the way first." She raised her eyebrows in a question and he hesitated, then realized there really wasn't any reason not to tell her. "I have to visit my father in prison."

"Visit your father?" The faint way she asked told him he'd surprised her.

"He's dying," he said abruptly. "Back in January he promised Sam that if each of his children visited him, he'd give us clues as to where he buried our mother."

"I don't understand."

Chris glanced at Ian and Jamie, but they were completely occupied with eating and weren't paying the least bit of attention to the adult conversation. "I told you what he did to our mother," he explained, masking his words for the twins' benefit. "But I never said that when he did it he took her away and buried her somewhere. Law enforcement searched at the time, but they never found her." Chris couldn't keep the hard edge out of his tone. "My brothers and I, and Annabel, too—we've been searching for years."

"But no luck," Holly stated.

"No luck," he agreed. "We've all been taking turns visiting my father since January. Annabel went last month. Now it's my turn." He breathed deeply, trying to tamp down his emotions, then added in a low voice, "We just want to give her a decent burial, Holly. Is that too much to ask?" She shook her head. "I haven't seen him in nearly twenty years. I never wanted to. But I can't pass up the chance to find out where my mother is."

"Of course you can't," she said stoutly. Her lovely brown eyes were filled with empathy. "I understand. When my parents were killed in South America—they were missionaries," she explained, and Chris didn't bother to tell her he already knew. "I…I was only a teenager. But I knew I had to bring their bodies home. It was a nightmare of frustration and paperwork, but I finally did it. They're buried together in a cemetery not far from their old church, so their close friends can visit their graves." She paused, then added softly, "Grant's buried right next to them."

Chris saw the tears in her eyes she was struggling to hold back. "Grant's parents—they wanted him buried in a more fashionable cemetery, but…he loved my parents and they loved him. I wanted them all together, you know?"

He cleared his throat. "Yeah, I do." The silence was broken when Ian accidentally knocked his sippy cup off his high-chair tray. The lid was securely fastened, so only a small amount of milk leaked onto the floor. But Holly jumped up, retrieved the cup, then grabbed a paper towel to wipe up the spilled milk.

After she rinsed off the cup and gave it back to Ian, she resumed her seat, and Chris said, "Anyway, I have to visit the prison today. I was thinking...if you wouldn't mind...I could take you and the twins to Peg's this morning. You could stay there until I come back to pick you up. I think you'll be safe there."

Holly's mouth twitched into a faint smile. "Let me guess—you already suggested this to Peg, right?" Chris had the grace to look abashed, and she chuckled. "Why am I not surprised?"

The independent woman in Holly knew she should be insulted, the same way she'd been insulted yesterday when she'd told Chris she didn't need a babysitter. Nevertheless there was something appealing about Chris's protectiveness that spoke to a more primitive aspect of her nature. Grant had never been protective of her—not that way. They'd grown up together, so he knew Holly could take care of herself. Still...she couldn't really fault Chris for wanting to make sure she and the boys were safe in his absence. Especially since he'd told her, *No one is dying on my watch ever again...*

She needed to ask Chris what he meant by that statement. Based on what Annabel had recounted about Laura, she had a pretty good idea it had something to do with his dead wife...and their unborn child.

But before she could ask him, Chris rose and put his breakfast dishes in the dishwasher. "I'll load the cribs and high chairs in the back of my truck. You'd better pack enough clothes and things for the twins to last a week. And maybe their favorite books and toys. Susan and Bobby have plenty, but those little bunnies the boys sleep with? Don't want to leave them behind." Then he was gone.

Matthew Colton looked smaller than Chris remembered. *Only to be expected*, he thought after the first shock of seeing his father sitting at the table, behind the glass separating the prisoners from the visitors. Chris had been eleven back then—nearly twenty years had passed. And his father was sick…dying. Which would account for his frail appearance that made him seem…a pathetic old man. *He murdered your mother*, Chris had to remind himself, steeling against the sudden wave of good memories. *Not to mention all the others he killed.*

And yet…there were a lot of worse fathers than Matthew Colton had been. How to reconcile the two pictures of Matthew? *Remember the bad times*, he told himself. *Remember Ethan finding Mama's body with the bull's-eye on her forehead. Remember your family being torn apart. Remember Bouncer being sent to the pound. That's all on him. That's all Matthew's doing.*

Chris sat at the table across from his father, removed his Stetson and placed it on the table in front of him, then ran a hand through his hair, which the Stetson had flattened. Then and only then did he pick up the phone. He had no idea what he would say, but Matthew spoke first.

"You look like your mother." If Matthew had stabbed him, Chris couldn't have been more surprised, but Matthew wasn't done. "Not your coloring, of course. Saralee's hair was long and dark, not blond." There was a wistful intonation to his words. "But you and Annabel look like her in every other way."

Chris cleared his throat against the wave of emotion that rose in him. "Yeah," he agreed. "Everyone who remembers her says we look like Mama." He'd thought he could do this, but now that he was here… "So you wanted to see each of us. And you bribed us here by promising a clue to where Mama's buried. Piss-poor clues, but then you knew that, didn't you?" Matthew's eyes turned crafty, and Chris nodded. "Okay, I'm here. You've got your pound of flesh from me. So what's my clue?"

"No 'Hello, Daddy'? No 'How are you doing, Daddy'? Just 'What's my clue?'"

Chris drew a deep breath and held it, holding his anger in at the same time. "What do you want from me?" When Matthew didn't respond, Chris reluctantly asked, "How are you doing?"

"I'm dying." The bald statement stood there while neither man spoke.

After a long, long time, Chris said the only thing that came to him. "I know."

Again there was silence between them, silence that was eventually broken by Matthew. "Twenty years, I've been locked away in this cage. Near twenty years, and the only one of you children to come see me was Trevor…and only because it was his job."

"What did you expect?" Chris couldn't keep the

bitter edge out of his words. "You really think any of us wanted to see you ever again?"

"Don't you sass me, boy," Matthew retorted with a spurt of anger, his free hand forming a fist. "I can still tan your hide, and don't you forget it!"

All at once Chris was eleven again, facing his father over a broken window caused by an errant baseball Annabel had thrown. Matthew yanking his belt out of its loops and fiercely demanding of his children, *Who did it? Who threw that ball?*

Chris had stepped forward immediately. Matthew wouldn't have hesitated to use the belt on eleven-year-old Annabel, and Chris was too protective of her—of all the younger children—to let her take the imminent whipping. But Annabel had piped up bravely, *I did it, Daddy.* So Matthew had whipped them both—Annabel for breaking the window, Chris for lying. For trying to take the blame, for trying to shield Annabel from Matthew's wrath.

Chris and Annabel had hidden out in their secret hideaway afterward, lying on their stomachs in the shade of a catalpa tree so as not to further exacerbate the wounds on their smarting bottoms. Annabel trying so hard to be as tough as Chris, fighting back tears. But Chris hadn't cried. Not then…and not at their mother's memorial service a few months later. He hadn't cried until Bouncer…

Then Chris's mind jumped to Laura's funeral, and he realized he hadn't cried then, either. He hadn't cried at the loss of the two most important women in his life. But he'd cried over Bouncer. He'd never thought about it before, but now he realized maybe the reason he hadn't cried for his mother and his wife was because some things went too deep for tears. Heart wounds, both of them. And one of them had been caused by the man sitting across from him.

"Whatever happened to your dog, boy?" Matthew asked abruptly. "Whatever happened to that golden retriever I gave you when you were six?"

Cold anger shook Chris. "He's dead."

"Well, hell, boy, 'course he is." Matthew smirked. "Dogs don't live as long as humans. I just wondered how he died, that's all."

Suddenly it was all too much for Chris. Suddenly the years rolled back, and he wanted to wipe that smirk off Matthew's face. Not just for Bouncer, euthanized despite Chris's tearful pleas to his foster parents, but for his mother, too. And for his brothers and sisters, orphaned yet not orphaned. Fighting the stigma of being Matthew Colton's child—a serial killer's child—to this day. He gripped the phone in a death grip and rasped, "Tell me where Mama's body is buried, Daddy. I'm begging you, damn it! Tell me!"

Chapter 11

The crafty expression returned to Matthew's face, and he shook his head. "Can't do that, boy. You get your one clue, just like the others." He waited for Chris to say something, but when Chris didn't speak, he offered, "Biff."

"Biff? That's it? Biff?"

Matthew nodded, a secretive smile forming. As if he knew what Chris was thinking. As if he knew that if Chris could have reached through the glass he would have put his hands around his father's throat and—

No! A tiny corner of Chris's brain forced him back to sanity. *You are not a killer,* he reminded himself, the words becoming his mantra. *You are not a killer. He's your father, but you are not him. And you are not a killer.*

He settled his Stetson on his head, shielding his eyes

from Matthew's searching gaze. "You are an evil man," Chris told his father evenly through the phone. "And yes, your blood flows through our veins. But Mama's blood flows through our veins, too. You killed her, but you can't kill her spirit—we're her legacy. She lives on in us."

He put the phone down and stood. Matthew was speaking—his lips were moving—but Chris didn't want to hear anything more his father had to say. He turned and walked toward the door...to freedom. Freedom his father would never know until the disease ravaging his body claimed him, and he left the prison in a hearse.

Chris would never return. Would never look on his father's face ever again, not even at his funeral...which Chris would not attend. But this visit had been necessary after all, and not just to receive his clue that was no more help than the clues the others had received. No, this visit brought closure. Chris hadn't realized he needed it, but now he finally acknowledged that the father he'd once known no longer existed. The stern father who—despite that sternness—had loved his wife and children had been a different man. This man— Matthew Colton, wife murderer and serial killer— wasn't the father of Chris's memory. Something had changed him. Twisted him. He was beyond the reach of even his children's pleading.

And knowing that, the shackles binding Chris to the past were finally broken. *I'm his son*, he acknowledged once again. *But I am not him.*

On the way back to town Chris passed the entrance to his brother Ethan's ranch. A sudden impulse to talk with Ethan made him brake sharply and swerve into the turn without signaling, earning him an angry honk from the truck behind him.

"Sorry," he muttered, glancing at his rearview mirror even though he knew the other driver couldn't hear him.

It wasn't just letting Ethan know the clue their father had given him that had made Chris turn, but also the desire to share that he finally understood Ethan's complete rejection of Matthew all these years. Ethan had been only seven to Chris's eleven when their father had murdered their mother—he didn't have the memories Chris had of the good times with their father. But that was all gone now, erased by the knowledge that the father he remembered and the man dying in prison were two different people.

Chris pulled up in front of the ranch house, parked and got out, leaving his hat on the seat and not bothering to lock his truck. *Ethan's probably out on the ranch somewhere, but Lizzie can tell me where he is.* His boots thudded as he mounted the wooden stairs and crossed the front porch, thinking about the last time he'd been out here. Ethan's ranch—Ethan and *Lizzie's* ranch, he reminded himself with a smile—had quickly become the Colton family gathering place. And soon there'd be another celebration, when Lizzie gave birth.

His smile faded as the never-to-be-forgotten sadness came to the fore. The loss of his own baby when Laura died wasn't the constant heartache it had been at first, but the pain would never go away completely. *His* baby would have been the first Colton of the next generation, not Ethan's. But that wasn't Ethan or Lizzie's fault. And he would love their baby the way he loved Susan and Bobby. The way he loved Ian and Jamie.

He stood stock-still for a moment. The way he loved Ian and Jamie?

You do, his shocked mind acknowledged. *You love them as if you were their fath—*

He chopped that thought off before he could finish it. "Don't go there," he muttered. "Don't."

He forced himself to move, to knock on the screen door. The front door was open, so he called through the screen, "Lizzie? Lizzie? It's Chris."

The only answer he got—a long, low moan—scared the hell out of him. "Lizzie!" He grabbed the handle on the screen door and pulled, but the latch was on and the door refused to budge. Another moan, and this time Chris wrenched at the screen door with all his might. With a creaking sound, the old wood gave way, the latch pulled free and Chris was inside. "Lizzie?" His gaze encompassed the neat living room, but he saw nothing, so he moved down the hallway, bellowing, "Lizzie, where the hell are you?"

"Kitchen— *Ohhh!*"

He found Lizzie there, her face drenched in sweat. She was bent over the back of a chair, gripping it tightly as the labor pain ebbed. His eyes took in everything, including the way her clothes were sopping wet and the panting sounds she was making as she breathed.

"Crap!" He lifted his sister-in-law gently into his arms and headed for the front door. *Hospital*, his frantic mind told him. "How far apart?"

"I...I couldn't time them," she gasped, "so I don't know. Four minutes maybe?"

"Your water broke already, so this didn't just start

a few minutes ago. Where the hell's Ethan?" He was already outside, maneuvering his way to his F-150 as fast as he could.

"He went into town. I didn't tell him... I've had false labor pains twice before and...and I didn't want to worry him again."

"Where's Joyce?" he asked, referring to the wife of Ethan's foreman, Bill Peabody.

"Joyce and Bill went to visit their kids. I never expected..."

He listened to her explanation with only half his attention. The rest was laser-focused on what he had to do. "Open the door, Lizzie," he told her when they reached the passenger side, and when she did, he kicked it wide-open with one booted foot. He placed her as carefully as he could on the passenger seat and fastened the seat belt around her, but when he went to close the door, she grabbed his arm.

"My things. Suitcase by the front door. Please!"

"Okay," he told her. "I'll get them. Don't go any-where."

Lizzie choked on a laugh. "Don't worry. Just hurry."

He found the suitcase right where she'd said it would be, then raced out, pulling the front door closed behind him. He wedged the suitcase behind his seat, sat down and belted himself in. As the engine roared to life he said, "Did you call Ethan?"

"I called him earlier, but...my water hadn't broken yet. He said he was on his way to get me."

Chris floored it, leaving a cloud of dust in their wake. The truck jounced and jolted until he got to the main road, and the minute he turned Lizzie clutched her stomach and started moaning again. "Crap!" he said again, glancing at his watch, then gave her his right hand, steering with the left. "Hold tight on to me," he said. "Scream if you want to—don't hold back. And aren't you supposed to be panting like a dog? Isn't that supposed to help?"

Between moans Lizzie laughed again the way he'd intended her to, but she didn't say anything, just gripped his hand in a death grip that—*holy crap!*—hurt.

When she finally let go, Chris surreptitiously wiggled his fingers to see if any bones were broken. When he figured they were still intact, he hit the Bluetooth button on his steering wheel as they barreled down the county highway.

He waded through the interminable questions the disembodied recorded voice asked him until he finally heard Ethan on the other end. "Ethan, it's Chris," he said, cutting his brother off. "I've got Lizzie and we're heading to the hospital." He darted a look at the clock on the dashboard. "I figure five to six minutes, tops." It would take longer...if he wasn't going ninety miles an hour. "Meet us there."

"Got it," Ethan replied. "Turning around now. Lizzie? Can you hear me?"

Chris glanced at Lizzie, then pointed to the speaker above his head. "Talk loud," he advised.

Lizzie laughed again. "I can hear you, Ethan," she shouted.

"Lizzie, honey, you hang in there, okay? I'll be with you before you know it."

"Okay."

"And, Lizzie?" The hesitation, Chris knew, was because he could hear every word Ethan said to her. "I love you, honey. You and the baby are the best things that ever happened to me, and I—"

"Yeah, yeah, yeah," Chris interrupted. "You love her, you need her, you can't live without her. Forget that crap and *drive*!"

He hit the disconnect button and glanced over at his sister-in-law, who was sitting there with tears in her eyes. "Now, don't *you* start," he told her in bracing tones.

"I love you, Chris," she blurted out as the tears overflowed. "I'm so lucky to have you as a brother-in-law." Then she caught her breath as another labor pain snared her in its grasp, and Chris could actually see the ripples go through her.

"Crap!" he said again and depressed the pedal until the speedometer hovered around a hundred. He offered Lizzie his right hand again, mentally girding himself against the pain he knew was forthcoming, but also knowing that whatever pain Lizzie inflicted on him was nothing compared to what she was going through. "Hold on tight."

Two hours later Chris was still in the hospital waiting room. Ethan had met them at Emergency and had lifted his pregnant wife out of Chris's truck even more gently than Chris had placed her in it. Chris had parked in the visitor's lot, retrieved Ethan's truck from where he'd left it half on the driveway and half on the sidewalk—smooth talking a policeman out of a ticket in the process—then headed for the Emergency entrance with Lizzie's suitcase in hand. He'd turned the suitcase over to the admitting clerk and had followed her instructions on finding the waiting room. Where he'd waited. And waited.

He'd called Peg and told her what was happening, asking her to pass along the news to Holly and explain why he was delayed getting back. Then he'd called Annabel and Sam, who were on duty and couldn't talk for long. But they'd both spared him a moment to say Jim Murray had approved them working with Chris and Holly on setting the trap for the McCays.

Chris had forgotten about that. Well, not exactly forgotten, but Lizzie's crisis had driven everything else out of his head in the heat of the moment. He'd quickly called Ridge and Trevor after that, but both calls had gone right to voice mail. He'd left a message, though, both about Lizzie and the clue he'd obtained during his trip to the prison today—Biff. Then he'd turned his mind to the problem of how best to set a trap for the McCays.

Lost in thought, he didn't see Ethan walk into the waiting room. Not until his brother stood right in front of him did Chris realize he was there. Ethan looked wiped out. Pale beneath his tan. But happy. Ecstatically happy, and relieved.

Chris stood up. "Lizzie okay?" Ethan swallowed hard, as if he wanted to speak but couldn't. Then he nodded, and Chris asked, "And the baby? Everything okay there?"

"Yeah." The rasped word was accompanied by a sudden smile that split Ethan's face. "A boy. Eight pounds, eleven ounces. Twenty-one inches."

"Wow, big baby. Must take after his dad." Chris grinned and wrapped his brother in a bear hug. "Congratulations, little brother. You did good."

Ethan returned the hug, and when the two men finally separated, Ethan dashed a hand against his eyes, swiping away the moisture. "Got something in my eye," he muttered, turning away.

"Same here," Chris said, following suit.

But then the brothers faced each other again, smiling to beat the band. Ethan shook his head. "I can never thank you enough, Chris."

"It was nothing."

"Don't give me that BS. I should never have left Lizzie this close to her due date, especially since Joyce and Bill weren't there. But she swore to me she'd be okay, and I was only going into town." His eyes took on an expression Chris remembered from their childhood, when the two youngest boys—Sam and Ethan— had looked up to their older "stair steps" and wanted to emulate them. And all four of them had looked up to Trevor, the oldest. "If not for you," Ethan continued in a grateful voice, "I don't know what Lizzie would have done."

Chris flexed his right hand and joked, "That's some woman you've got there. She almost broke my hand twice, so I figure she's tough enough to have worked out some other solution." Ethan laughed at that, and the emotional moment passed.

The brothers collapsed into two of the waiting-room chairs. Chris dug a hand into his pocket, pulled out Ethan's keys and handed them to him, saying, "Better give you these before I forget. Your truck's in the visitor's lot. Two rows down."

"Thanks."

After a moment Chris asked, "So you got a name picked out?"

"Lizzie and I had been toying with names ahead of time, but she and I talked just now and we're changing it. James Christopher Colton." Chris got that choked-up feeling again and couldn't have spoken even if he'd wanted to. "We figured a middle name would be okay. That way if you ever have a son and want to name him after yourself—" Ethan broke off as if he'd just re-membered Chris's baby that never was, and a stricken look filled his eyes. "Sorry," he said quickly. "I didn't think… I didn't mean to…"

Chris tapped Ethan's jaw with his closed fist, but lightly. "Yeah, I know you didn't mean anything by it. Don't sweat it. And tell Lizzie I'm purely honored."

The two men were silent for a few moments, then Ethan said gravely, "You know, I never wanted to marry. Never wanted to have kids. With a serial killer for a fa-ther, I…I didn't want to pass on the Colton name, or—" repugnance was in his voice "—Matthew's blood."

"I understand." This wasn't the time to get into what he'd planned to tell Ethan earlier, that Chris had com-pletely severed any emotional bond to the father he'd once known.

"But life doesn't always work out the way you plan," Ethan continued. "I never planned on Lizzie. I never planned on a baby. But Lizzie…well…"

"Yeah, yeah, yeah," Chris teased, trying to make light of another emotionally charged moment by using the same words he'd used in his truck on the way to the hospital. "You love her, you need her, you can't live without her."

"Yeah." The fervent way Ethan said the one word told Chris that—all joking aside—his brother adored his wife. And an ache speared through him. Not because he'd loved Laura and lost her, but because he hadn't loved her as much as Ethan loved Lizzie, as if all light and hope in life emanated from her.

"Lizzie and our baby—they're everything to me now. And I wouldn't change a thing even if I could. I thought I could cut myself off from life. Lizzie proved me wrong."

Simple words. Not particularly profound. Not even the kind of words that evoked a strong emotional re-action. And yet…there was something in those sim-ple words that seemed to reverberate in Chris's mind. *I thought I could cut myself off from life.*

Wasn't that what he'd done? When Laura had died, and their baby with her, hadn't he tried to cut himself off from life, tried to build a fence around his heart? Hadn't he retreated—like Superman—into his for-tress of solitude?

Those he already loved—his sisters and brothers, Peg and Joe and their kids—he couldn't stop loving *them*. But he'd walled himself off from loving another woman, because…

Because what you don't love you can't lose.

It sounded like a quotation from something. If it was, he couldn't place it, but it seemed singularly appropriate.

Only…he hadn't really been able to do it. Holly's boys had crept into his heart in just three short days. Identical twins be damned—he could tell them apart, and not by their tiny physical disparities. Ian, the out-going one, with his "damn the torpedoes" outlook on life. Jamie, the shy one, with that "don't hurt me" look in his eyes. Holly's eyes.

That was when it hit him. Ian and Jamie weren't the only ones who'd slipped beneath his emotional fences. Holly had, too.

Chris stayed to keep his brother company at the hospital until Ethan went up to visit Lizzie again, in her room this time with the baby, dragging Chris along. Lizzie looked a thousand times better than the last time Chris had seen her, and baby James looked so much like Ethan it was almost comical. Chris knew you couldn't tell what color a newborn's eyes were going to be, but between Lizzie's green eyes and Ethan's hazel ones, he figured the odds were good his nephew's eyes would at least be hazel.

He kissed his sister-in-law's cheek and told her he'd back her in an arm wrestling competition anytime—making both Lizzie and Ethan laugh. He admired the baby, marveling that something so tiny could have such powerful lungs. "Just like you, Lizzie," he said, again making them laugh. Then he left the three of them to have some family time alone together and headed out.

It was after dark by the time Chris finally reached the Merrill house. His stomach was rumbling—he'd skipped lunch, and breakfast was a distant memory, but even if Peg asked him to stay for dinner he couldn't. He'd left Wally at his house, not realizing he'd be gone all day. Although Wally was outside in the fenced yard with a food bowl and a water dish, the food was probably long gone, and maybe the water, too.

Peg answered the door, Susan at her heels, and the minute he walked in Susan grabbed his knee. "Pick me up, Unca Chris." He obliged, heading for the family room with her propped on his left shoulder.

"Everything okay?" Peg asked, trailing behind him.

Chris waited until he reached the family room to make the announcement. "A boy," he told Joe and Peg. "James Christopher Colton. Mother and baby are doing great. Ethan I'm not so sure about—he looked pretty shaky to me."

The Merrills laughed. "Yeah, Peg wanted me in the delivery room when that one was born," Joe said, pointing at his daughter cuddled in Chris's arms. "But I nearly passed out. Remember, Peg?"

She snorted. "Yes, but I wasn't about to let you off the hook when Bobby was born." She didn't say it— *little pitchers have big ears*, he thought with an inward smile—but he knew Peg well enough to know what she was thinking. *If you're there for the conception, you damn well better be there for the delivery.*

Joe said something in reply, but Chris wasn't really listening because just then Holly walked into the room and took a seat near the twins. This was the first time he'd seen her since that morning, and now, after his startling revelation in the hospital…now he couldn't seem to look away. Her long blond hair was clipped neatly away from her face on one side—she'd ditched the dark-haired wig, and Chris couldn't be sorry. Not when she looked like this. He remembered the cornsilk feel of her hair between his fingers last night when he'd—

He put a clamp on that memory. But then he heard Holly saying in his mind, *It's going to happen, Chris. Not tonight. Maybe not even tomorrow night. But it's going to happen.*

Which was why he'd stopped off at the pharmacy in the hospital before he left. That package was hidden in the armrest of his truck, tucked there so Holly wouldn't see it and think he was assuming…well…what he was assuming.

"Staying for dinner?" Peg asked.

"What? Oh. No, we can't," Chris replied. "Wally's been home alone since this morning. Outside," he clarified. "But I'm sure he's as hungry as I am." He looked at Holly again. "You about ready to go?"

A stricken expression fleetingly crossed her face, then she pasted a smile in its place. She knelt between Ian and Jamie, who were arguing over who deserved the bigger truck, and tugged them into one last embrace. "Mommy has to go now. You be good for Ms. Peg and Mr. Joe, okay?"

"'Kay," Ian said, and Jamie echoed, "'Kay."

She kissed them both, then stood, stony-eyed, as if she refused to let herself cry in front of her sons. "Say goodbye to Uncle Chris."

Chris handed Susan to her father, then picked his way through the toys scattered across the rug. He leaned over, curled an arm around each boy and lifted them simultaneously, tickling their tummies with his fingers. "You be good for Ms. Peg and Mr. Joe," he reiterated and was rewarded with the same chorus of *'kays*, giggling ones this time.

He didn't know what made him do it—well, yes, he did—but he popped a kiss on Jamie's nose, then on Ian's, before he set them down. Then he grabbed Holly's hand and tugged her toward the doorway. "Come on," he muttered. "Let's get out of here before the waterworks begin."

They were already out the door before Holly gulped air and said, "I didn't think Ian and Jamie were going to cry. I've left them with Peg before, and they—"

"I wasn't talking about the twins. I was talking about you."

Chapter 12

"I wasn't going to cry," Holly insisted as Chris held the passenger door of his truck for her.

"Weren't you?" His voice held tenderness and understanding.

"Well…" She gave a little huff of semitearful laughter as she buckled her seat belt. "Not where the boys could see me anyway." Then she realized something. "Wait. My SUV is here."

"Yeah, I know. Give me the keys." When she did, he closed the door and left, but was back a minute later, climbing into the driver's seat. "I gave Joe your keys. I think it's best for now we leave your SUV here, rather than at my house."

He was already putting the truck into gear as he said it, and Holly asked, "Why?" Wanting an answer before they got too far away.

"Because I don't want the McCays to know you're at my house, not until we're ready to spring the trap. Do I think they suspect anything yet? No. Am I willing to risk it? No. I told Joe to park your SUV in their garage so no one can see the license plates." He glanced at her. "We're not that far away. If we need it, we can get it. But I don't think we will."

She didn't know why a little dart of panic went through her. She was so used to having the freedom of her own wheels—was that it?

"Besides," Chris said drily, breaking into her thoughts, "this way you can't sneak off to visit the twins when my back is turned."

That made her laugh for some reason. "I wouldn't do that," she protested. "I already agreed it would be safer—"

He reached across the seat and clasped her hand for a moment. "I know you did. But this way you won't be tempted." Then he let her hand go so he could shift gears, saying softly, "You're a good mother, Holly."

"I try to be."

"You remind me of my own mother."

When he said that, she remembered Chris had been eleven when his mother died. Old enough to have vivid memories of her. "What was she like?"

He didn't answer right away. Then he said slowly, "Beautiful…to me. Now when I look at old photos, I realize she wasn't really beautiful. Not classically beautiful. But if ever a woman's heart reflected in her face, hers did."

She gathered her courage and asked, "Why did your father kill her?"

At first she thought he wasn't going to answer at all.

Then he said, "No one can really answer that except him. She loved him through everything—the loss of his ranch, financial hardship, seven children. And for the longest time no one had a clue why he did it, because he refused to say. Not even when he was convicted of her murder. He finally told Ethan back in February— Ethan was the one who found her dead—that she figured out he was the bull's-eye serial killer.

"That's how my father used to mark all his victims," he explained, "with a red bull's-eye drawn on their foreheads." She heard him breathe deeply in the darkness. "She caught him in bloody clothes one day, which he tried to explain away. But then she found the permanent red marker in his pocket. And she saw something on the news the next day that made her put all the pieces together. She confronted him, told him what she knew and insisted he turn himself in. In a—I guess you could say a fit of rage...or fear...or both—he killed her. Before he knew what he was doing, he'd marked her forehead the way he'd marked his other victims."

"Oh, God," she whispered helplessly, her heart aching for him.

"Then he panicked," Chris continued, still in that deliberate way. "He realized he had to get rid of her body somehow, so he went to the garage...for a big trash bag."

She couldn't help her soft gasp of dismay. "Oh, Chris, no."

"Yeah...a trash bag. He killed her, and then he— Like she was garbage." This time she reached across the distance and touched his arm in empathy. He downshifted and turned a corner before adding, "He didn't know that in the few minutes he was gone, Ethan had come home from school—I told you Ethan found her. He was terrified. Imagine, you're seven years old and you find your mother's bloody, lifeless body."

"What did he do?"

"He ran to a neighbor's for help. But when they got back, the body was gone. Only the blood remained. But even though they never found Mama's body, Ethan's story of seeing her with the bull's-eye on her forehead led the police to finally arrest my—to finally arrest Matthew Colton, one of the most infamous serial killers in Texas history. Arrested. Tried. Convicted."

Holly hadn't missed the slight catch in Chris's voice or the way he'd changed *my father* to *Matthew Colton*. This morning he'd said he needed to visit his father in prison. *What happened between this morning and now?* she wondered. But she wasn't going to ask. If Chris wanted to tell her…that was a different story. If Chris *wanted* to tell her…he would.

Wally leaped to his feet and let out one bark of welcome when Chris pulled his truck into the driveway and parked. Chris grabbed the pharmacy bag from the armrest once Holly exited, and shoved it into his front pocket so she couldn't see it. Wally was eagerly wagging his tail and standing right by the front gate when Chris unlatched it and held the gate open for Holly, then closed it behind him so Wally couldn't escape. "Down, boy," he said when Wally threatened to jump on Holly in his exuberance at seeing them, but he wasn't surprised when Holly merely ruffled Wally's fur and let him shadow her footsteps to the front door.

Chris paused and picked up Wally's food bowl and water dish. "Empty. Just what I was afraid of." He unlocked the door, reached in and punched in the alarm code, then turned on the hall light before he let Holly enter.

"Are you really worried someone might have broken in?"

"No, but I couldn't take my gun to the prison with me today, so…" He caught the expression on her face. "I'm careful about gun safety, Holly," he said levelly. "I would never leave my gun where the twins could reach it, I promise. But in my line of work…a gun is practically a necessity." He flashed a grin at her. "Besides, this is Texas."

He didn't wait for her answer, just trod down the hallway toward the kitchen, flicking on the lights as he went. He filled the water dish, then he found the scoop in the dog food bag, filled the bowl and placed it beside the water Wally was already furiously lapping at. "Sorry, boy," he murmured, patting the dog's side. "Didn't expect to be gone this long."

Holly had followed Chris into the kitchen, and now she said, "You never explained what happened. What I mean is, Peg told me you were taking your sister-in-law to the hospital because she was having a baby, but…"

"Let me get dinner started," he replied, "and then I'll tell you."

A guilty expression crossed Holly's face. "No, it's my turn to make dinner," she said. "I can't let you do all the cooking—that wouldn't be fair." She bustled toward the fridge. "You talk while I cook."

"Whatever it is, make it quick, okay? I missed lunch and I'm starved."

Twenty-five minutes later Chris sat back at the kitchen table, replete. Holly's omelet and toast hadn't been fancy, but it had been good. Best of all it had been quick.

"I was terrified Lizzie was going to have that baby right there in the front seat of my truck," he confessed, finishing up his story. "But it all worked out."

Holly shook her head, a smile curving her lips. "I doubt you were terrified." Her admiring eyes conveyed her conviction that whatever happened, Chris would deal with it competently. And his male ego responded. *So maybe you did okay*, his ego seemed to be saying, puffing out its chest a little. *Maybe you deserved to have baby James named for you after all.*

But his ego wasn't the only male part of him responding to Holly. And it wasn't only food he'd been hungering for. Now that one appetite had been satisfied...

But that wasn't fair to Holly, no matter what she'd told him last night. She deserved candlelight and romantic music, flowers and fine wine. She deserved gentle wooing. Not some guy with a box of condoms crammed into his pocket.

Which reminded him...he *did* have a box of condoms crammed into his pocket. A box he suddenly and desperately wanted to use.

Holly's smile faded. But before he could say anything, she jumped up from the table, cleared away the dishes, his included, and stacked them in the sink, saying, "Probably shouldn't use the dishwasher if it's only going to be the two of us, since it will take several days to fill, and—"

"Holly." That was all he said. Just her name. But she froze at the sink. He found himself standing behind her somehow. Just as last night he could have sworn he never moved, but there he was, sliding his hands down her arms, gently turning her unresisting body to face him. And he knew she could see the aching need in him he couldn't possibly hide.

"I want you," he admitted, as if it wasn't obvious. "God knows I want you. But not like this. Not if you're afraid of me."

"I'm not afraid of you," she said quickly. "It's me. I'm afraid of me." She must have read in his expression that he didn't follow her, because she added quietly, "I want you, too, Chris. In fact, that's pretty near all I can think about whenever you're around." Her voice dropped to little more than a whisper. "And even when you're not."

"Then why afraid?" he asked, one hand coming up to cup her cheek, to rub his thumb against her lips. This close he could feel the tremor that ran through her. "I won't hurt you, Holly, I promise. I'd never hurt you." Then it occurred to him maybe she was worried about—

"I haven't slept around, in case you're wondering." He brushed a strand of hair away from her face, tucking it behind her ear. "There hasn't been anyone since Laura." He hesitated, of two minds about revealing more. But then he figured she had a right to know. "And there wasn't anyone before her, either."

Something about the way his confession was made touched Holly so deeply she couldn't respond at first.

"Thank you for telling me," she whispered finally, cradling his face between her hands for a moment. She let her hands drop to her sides, wanting to be as honest with Chris as he'd been with her. "Grant was... I'd loved him all my life, so I never…" Her throat closed and she couldn't continue.

"Holly." The aching need embodied in that one word shook her to the core. Then he kissed her, and it was even better than it had been last night. Passion had exploded between them the night before, but tonight… tonight there was tenderness mixed in with the passion. And wonder. Chris kissed her as if he couldn't believe she was there in his arms, but at the same time as if he couldn't bear to let her go.

He whispered her name again, and Holly thought she'd never heard so many suppressed emotions in a man's voice. Want was there, and need. Overlaid with a cherishing tone that told her this would be more than just sex for Chris. If she hadn't already figured out from his confession that he only slept with women he cared for deeply, she would have known it by his voice.

And that made her decision easy. Here. Now. Tonight. It wasn't just that she wanted to know what it would be like with a man who hadn't grown up with her, who didn't see her as more of a friend than a lover. She wanted to know what it would be like with *Chris*, with this man who haunted her dreams and tugged at her heart in ways she'd never felt before. Ways she'd never realized she *could* feel. She wanted to know if the reality of making love with him came anywhere close to matching her dreams. Because if it did, that would reveal something about herself she was eager—and a little nervous—to learn.

Chris reluctantly withdrew his lips from Holly's and gazed down into her face. If she'd been wearing that "don't hurt me" expression, the one so like Jamie's, which appeared on occasion when she wasn't aware, he would have let her go. But she wasn't. Her expression said she wanted him...and she wasn't afraid anymore.

"I need a shower." He pulled away from her a little and coaxed. "Come with me."

"Okay." He loved the little catch in her voice, and the not-quite-shy way she agreed. Then she looked puzzled and reached down to his jeans pocket. "What's this?"

Crap. He'd forgotten. But he wasn't going to lie to her. "Condoms," he admitted. Then hurried to add, "I wasn't assuming... Okay, maybe I *was* assuming... but only if you... I wanted to be prepared, and I... Just in case..."

He was floundering—he knew that. But then Holly put her fingers over his lips to cut off his jumbled phrases and smiled. A womanly smile. "Thank you for thinking of it," she murmured, kissing the corner of his mouth. Then she took his hand and led him from the kitchen...down the long hallway...into the master bedroom.

They undressed in the master bathroom. Chris shucked off his clothes in no time. But after one moment staring at his naked body—a stare his body responded to noticeably—Holly stalled with only her jeans removed.

"Don't go shy on me now," he said, moving to stand in front of her and reaching for the buttons on her blouse.

"It's not that. Not exactly." She put her hands over his, stopping him from undoing the buttons. "It's just that...well...I've had a baby. *Two* babies. And...well..."

He got it. "You think I care about a few stretch marks?" He laughed softly. "Holly, Holly, Holly," he chided. "You must not have much of an opinion of me if you think that."

"I don't, but I…"

He was already undressing her. Parting the un-buttoned edges of her blouse, reaching back and un-erringly unclasping her bra, then helping her out of them both. Caressing the skin he'd bared. Including the ever-so-slight protrusion that was a reminder of the babies she'd carried, and the silvery, barely there stretch marks.

He slid his fingers beneath the elastic on her hips and slipped her underwear free, then down. When she was as completely naked as he was, he knelt and placed his unshaven cheek against her stomach, grasping her hips so she couldn't escape, rubbing until she shivered and her nipples tightened for him.

Then he stood. "Do you have any idea how beautiful you are?" he told her in his deepest voice, meaning every word. So she was obviously a mother. So what? So her body wasn't model perfect. Did she really think he cared? He wanted her like hell burning, and she was worried about these little imperfections? "So beautiful," he whispered, drawing her against his body and kissing her the way he'd dreamed of doing, with no barriers between them.

She was trembling all over when he finally let her go, and that turned him on big-time. But he needed that shower after the day he'd had. "Do you want to do something with your hair?" he asked. "So it doesn't get wet?"

She twisted her hair up, then used a clip to hold her hair in place.

Without another word he tugged her into the shower

with him. He soaped himself and rinsed off quickly but took his time washing her. Letting his fingers linger where he knew a woman loved to be touched. He'd made love to only one other woman in his life, but he knew the vulnerable places on a woman's body. Knew how to fulfill her, too—a man didn't have to be promiscuous to know that. All he needed was a little imagination and a strong desire to please.

He continued caressing her long after they were both clean, until she caught his hands and said, "Enough. I can't... I don't want..."

He captured her lips for a brief kiss. "Yeah," he growled when he let her go. "I don't want, either. I want to be inside you the first time. I want to feel you tight around me when you come." Primal, maybe. Direct. But the God's honest truth.

They barely managed to get the covers pulled down before they practically fell into bed together. Holly helped Chris roll on the condom—although *helped* wasn't quite the word that came to mind when her fingers touched his erection. But he held his breath and let her because she obviously wanted to. Because he knew it gave her pleasure to touch him this way.

That was his last coherent thought. As soon as the condom was in place he lost any claim to rationality he'd ever had. He felt like a heat-seeking missile, with Holly his only target. Despite the urge to thrust hard and deep, he eased into the damp warmth between her legs and she welcomed him with a soft moan of pleasure. Then another when he withdrew and returned. Again and again. Faster and faster. He pulled her thighs up around his hips to delve deeper, and she arched beneath him, gasping his name.

His lips found her nipples, first one, then the other, and she arched again and cried out, her fingernails digging into his shoulders as if she couldn't bear it. But he knew she could. "Yes," he groaned when she involuntarily tightened around him, and he knew she was close. So close. "Come for me, Holly. Yes, like that," he managed when he felt her internal throbbing, though he could barely breathe. Barely speak. "Like that. Oh, God, Holly, like that." Then with a flurry of thrusts he came, too.

In the few seconds before he lost consciousness, Chris tightened his arms around Holly, wanting to never let her go. *Needing* it. Needing her.

Chapter 13

Oh, my was all Holly could think of as she lay beneath Chris, both of them breathing heavily, his body still embedded in hers. *Oh, my. Oh. My.*

Her dreams hadn't even come close, because she'd had no idea. None. She gave a little hiccup that was half laughter, half tears, as she realized she and Grant hadn't… They'd never… Not even once. Not like this. For just a moment she grieved for Grant, because she wasn't sure she'd ever satisfied him the way she was absolutely certain she'd satisfied Chris. And she grieved for herself, too, for all the times she'd wondered what was wrong with her.

Chris grunted suddenly, as if he had temporarily blacked out and had just resurfaced. He tried to separate himself from her, but Holly tightened her legs, not wanting to lose this euphoric feeling, as if she was floating above herself.

"I'm too heavy," Chris muttered, but Holly's hands grasped his hips.

"Don't make me hurt you," she warned, only half kidding. "Move and die."

He laughed, a rumbling sound, then swiftly rolled them over so she was on top. "That's better," he said. "But, Holly…" His eyes teased hers. "You can't keep me prisoner forever."

"That's what you think." She deliberately contracted and relaxed her inner muscles around him. Once. Twice. Three times. And each time she felt him respond. "Have you ever heard of Kegel exercises?"

"What's that?"

"Something they teach women after they've had a baby. It helps restore pelvic floor muscle tone."

"Oh, great." He laughed under his breath. "I guess I really *am* your prisoner, 'cause I'm not risking damage down there." That made her laugh, too. "But, Holly, much as I'm enjoying this, I have to do something about the condom."

She'd forgotten about that, but he hadn't. She stopped Kegeling him, then squirmed until he was free. Chris jackknifed off the bed and disappeared into the bathroom. She heard the shower running for a minute, then he returned, a towel wrapped around his hips. His narrow hips. Above which his abs and chest muscles rippled in masculine perfection that until a few minutes ago she'd touched up close and personal.

Holly's fingers itched to touch him again, but instead she grabbed the top sheet and pulled it up to hide herself and her imperfections from his view. "Oh, hell no," he told her, throwing the towel on a chair and diving across the king-size bed. He wrestled the sheet away from her, then playfully held her down while he looked his fill.

Warmth in her cheeks informed her she was blushing, although she couldn't see it. But still he looked. And when his eyes finally connected with hers, he said softly, "Beautiful, Holly. You have absolutely nothing to be ashamed of."

She caught her breath at the very male, very intent expression on his face, and almost believed him. "I couldn't lose those last five pounds after the twins were born," she said faintly. "I tried so hard, too!"

"Where?" He settled between her legs, bearing most of his weight on his elbows. "Here?" He cupped her breasts, breasts that had never quite returned to their original size and shape after she'd breast-fed Ian and Jamie. His thumbs played over her nipples until they tightened unbearably. "You'll get no complaints from me here, Holly," he bantered. His big hands slid down to her waist, his thumbs stroking back and forth over her belly until she quivered. "Here? No, I don't think so." His husky voice, the look in his eyes, told her he wasn't kidding. Then those firm masculine hands curved over her hips. "Must be here, then," he suggested, as if he were serious, his long fingers lightly squeezing. He shook his head after a moment. "Wrong again."

She was melting and he knew it. That was all she could think of as his wicked blue eyes held hers. She'd just had the most incredible orgasm of her entire life, and already she wanted him again. And impossible as it seemed, he wanted her again, too—he was already hot and hard at the crux of her thighs, and she wiggled a little until she could feel him pressed up against exactly where she wanted him.

"Again?" he teased, emphasizing the last syllable.

She smiled at his playful tone and tried to make her tone just as light and playful. "Yes, please." She wasn't quite successful.

His eyes seemed to darken, and she shivered at the blatant desire that flared there. "Oh, I'm going to please you, Holly," he murmured, reaching for a condom on the nightstand, not waiting for her assistance. He fitted himself in place, then twined his fingers with hers. "I'm going to please you until you can't take any more," he whispered seductively. "And when I'm done, you'll know just how perfect you are." He smiled a very wolfish smile. "Hang on tight," he told her. "You may experience a little turbulence."

Holly's sudden laugh turned into a moan as he flexed his hips and thrust deep. Then withdrew and thrust again…slowly. Agonizingly slowly. Intense pleasure, sharp and urgent, knifed through her with each perfect thrust, until she clung to his hands and arched like a bow, crying his name.

"Still no word from Mr. Colton," Evalinda McCay reminded her husband as they dressed for bed…as if he needed the reminder.

"What do you expect me to do about it?"

The expression in her eyes bore no good for anyone. "How are we going to rid ourselves of Holly and get our hands on the twins and their trust fund if we can't locate her?"

"Mr. Colton promised us results," Angus protested weakly.

"One more day," she warned. "We'll give him one more day. Then I think we'll need to look for another detective."

"You really want to start all over? What if—"

"It was your idea to try to run her off the road the first two times," Evalinda reminded him contemptuously. "You were so sure that would work…but it didn't. Either time."

"Yes," he was quick to defend himself, "but at least Holly didn't suspect anything. It wasn't until you suggested running her down in the parking lot that she—"

Evalinda wouldn't let him finish. "Don't try to shift the blame for that fiasco onto me. *You* were the one who hired the men to kill her. If they hadn't been so incompetent…"

"You think it was easy finding someone who—"

"One more day," she repeated implacably, cutting him off, and he knew further argument was useless. Just as he'd fallen in with Evalinda's plans to murder Holly in the first place, he knew he would cave on this, too.

Chris woke at two in the morning when moonlight crept through the bedroom window. He thought about getting up and completely closing the top-down, bottom-up blinds that were lowered at the top. The way the blinds were drawn now gave the room's occupants privacy but still allowed them to see the night sky. That also meant, unfortunately, it let the moonlight in, and he'd always been a "pitch-black" sleeper. The blinds were completely drawn in the bedroom he was occupying. He just hadn't thought about it here in the master bedroom because he'd been too focused on the other things he was doing.

But he wasn't about to get up to close the blinds at this moment. Holly was sleeping cradled against him, her head pillowed on his shoulder. And he'd be damned before he woke her.

He and Holly had worn each other out earlier, but a certain part of his anatomy twitched to life at the reminder of everything they'd done tonight. Two spent condoms now resided in the wastebasket in the bathroom, but he hadn't been satisfied to leave it at that. They'd dozed after the second time but had woken before midnight. And as they'd cuddled and lazily caressed beneath the comforter, he'd told her in all seriousness, "I want to watch you come. Will you let me?"

She'd been adorable in her confusion, and he'd had a strong hunch no one had ever done that for her before. Holly had told Chris her husband was the only man she'd ever slept with, but that didn't mean other avenues had been completely closed. Apparently that had been the case, though. Equally apparent was the fact that Holly's husband had never put her needs first, which didn't surprise Chris. There were still a lot of men out there who never worried about pleasing a woman. Who thought she was responsible for her own orgasms, and if it happened, fine. If it didn't, oh well. He wasn't one of those men, but he knew some who were.

It had taken a little coaxing but eventually Holly had conceded. And then—*holy crap!*—her response had been off the charts. Hearing her…watching her… tasting her…had turned him on so hard he'd been tempted to use a third condom, but she'd pretty much passed out by then, so he'd refrained. But he'd promised himself next time they made love he'd start with that and see where it took them.

Next time? What makes you think there'll be a next time, hot shot? The thought hit him out of the blue, and he stopped to consider it. He'd come up with some ideas for trapping the McCays when he was at the hospital this afternoon waiting for Ethan and Lizzie's baby to be born, and they had to get going on that pretty damn quick. Now that Jim Murray had given them the go-ahead, he needed to coordinate with Annabel and Sam, who were supposed to stop by for breakfast tomorrow. If they were successful, in less than a week Holly wouldn't need his protection anymore. Which meant she'd be free to...return to her old life. Her old life outside Houston, more than three hundred miles away.

Devastation sliced through him—another shock. He didn't want Holly to leave; he wanted her to stay. And Ian and Jamie, too. He'd realized this afternoon that all three had crept under his emotional fences. He just hadn't recognized how firmly entrenched they already were in his life.

Not even a week, the rational side of him protested. *You haven't even known her a week.*

That didn't seem to matter—somehow he and Holly just clicked. Not only in bed, although he couldn't believe how perfectly matched they were, as if she were made for his earthy brand of loving. He had no doubt he'd pleased her, too—no way could she fake her response, especially the last time. But their sexual chemistry had its roots in something deeper. He wasn't sure what to call it, but a connection existed between them. An emotional connection.

He examined that word—*emotional*—and acknowledged that somehow it fit. Problem was, he wasn't sure exactly what it meant to him. Even worse, he wasn't sure what it meant to Holly.

The pealing of the doorbell woke them. Holly unwrapped herself from where she'd migrated in the night—splayed across Chris's chest—and pushed her tousled hair out of her eyes. She clutched the top sheet, wrapping it firmly around her. When she was finally able to focus, she glanced at the clock on the nightstand and realized it was already close to seven thirty.

She nudged Chris's shoulder—the one she'd been using as her personal pillow—and said urgently, "Wake up, Chris! Someone's at the door."

He awoke with a start, looking from Holly to the clock, and groaned. "It's Annabel and Sam," he informed her. He was out of bed in a flash, retrieving his jeans and shirt from where he'd left them hanging on the back of the bathroom door. "I forgot to tell you they're coming to breakfast," he said as he pulled his jeans on commando and zipped them up. His shirt was halfway on before he realized it was inside out. The doorbell pealed again and he ripped his shirt off, turned it right side out and tugged it on.

He ran a hand through his shaggy hair—and oh, how she hated that it fell right into place as if he'd brushed it—then added, "They're coming to have breakfast with you and me so we can make plans for catching the McCays in the act. I'll go let them in and take them into the kitchen. You can come in after you're dressed."

He was almost out the door when he turned back, snatched Holly up from the bed into his arms and kissed her senseless. He took his time about it, too. "Good morning," he whispered when he finally raised his head. His eyes were an intense blue, and Holly couldn't think of anything to compare them to. "Thank you for last night." Then his expression morphed from romantic hero to hard-as-nails PI. "And for God's sake, don't let Annabel see that satisfied look in your eyes—she's a bloodhound. Sam, too, but Annabel's a woman—she'll know exactly what put that look there." Then he was gone.

"About time," Annabel said when Chris finally opened the door barefoot. "I thought I was going to have to use my key."

Chris stared at her, perplexed. "When did I give you a key?"

"You didn't. I asked Peg, and she gave me a copy. She gave me the alarm code, too."

"What the—" He started to say *hell* but remembered just in time he was trying to break the swearing habit. He shepherded Sam and Annabel toward the kitchen while his guilty conscience gave him hell for all the times he'd said "crap" yesterday. *You're supposed to be cleaning up your language*, his conscience reminded him. Not just for Susan and Bobby, but for Ian and Jamie, too.

Annabel was still explaining about the key. "I asked Peg what her cleaning schedule was, what days of the week she came out here, and I told her I'd swing by regularly to check on her. I also told her I'd stop by every few days when she wasn't here, just to keep an eye on the place for you."

Chris was touched. "Thanks, Bella."

Annabel said gruffly, "Just part of my job—serve and protect," as if pretending she hadn't done anything out of the ordinary. When they walked into the kitchen, she glanced around, then said drily, "Nice breakfast."

"Coming right up," Chris told her. "You and Sam have a seat. I kind of overslept this morning." He quickly dumped food in the dog's dish and checked there was still water. Then he grabbed bowls from the cabinet, spoons from the drawer, and slapped them on the table. The gallon of milk from the fridge was followed by boxes of Cap'n Crunch and Cheerios from the pantry.

"Are you frigging kidding me?" Sam asked. "Cap'n Crunch?"

"Hey," Chris said, feigning hurt. "It's one of the basic food groups."

"I thought we'd at least be treated to your signature French toast," Annabel said.

"I was planning on it, but I told you, I overslept." Chris turned back to the counter to grab a couple of paper towels for napkins when he sensed rather than heard Holly walk into the kitchen. He swung around and barely managed to keep the betraying smile off his face. She was dressed as she normally was, in jeans and a cotton blouse—a deep, rich yellow this time. But now that he knew what she looked like *without* her clothes…

"Good morning," Holly said, smiling at Annabel. Then she turned to Sam. "I've already met Annabel, but you must be…Sam, right? Sam Colton?" She held out her hand. "Chris said you're a detective with the Granite Gulch Police Department. I'm Holly McCay."

As soon as Sam let her hand go, Holly glanced at

the table and said longingly, "Ooohhh, Cap'n Crunch. I haven't had Cap'n Crunch since I was little." Then she reached for the Cheerios box instead. "But I shouldn't."

Chris heard the regret in her voice. He poured Cap'n Crunch into a bowl and handed it to her. "Indulge. Once in a blue moon won't hurt you."

"Thanks." The smile she gave was one some women reserved for a gift of expensive jewelry, and Chris couldn't help returning her smile.

Out of the corner of Chris's eye he could see Annabel's head swivel from Holly to him and back again, and he could almost see her radar antenna quivering. *Crap!* He quickly amended the thought to *crud*, but it didn't come anywhere near expressing his fear that Annabel had somehow divined he and Holly had slept together. Just because he'd given her a bowl of Cap'n Crunch.

Chris tried to deflect Annabel's attention—and Sam's, too, for that matter, since Sam was giving him the once-over and doing the same to Holly—by saying, "Before I forget, I should tell you I went to the prison yesterday, and I got my clue." He snorted. "Biff."

"Biff?" Annabel measured Cheerios into a bowl and added milk. Then she handed the cereal box to Sam. "What's that supposed to mean?"

Chris turned the coffeemaker on, leaned back against the sink and crossed his arms. "Beats the heck out of me." He glanced at Sam. "Mean anything to you?"

His brother shook his head. "Doesn't seem to match the other clues. Texas. Hill. *B.* Peaches. Remember Trevor's theory that Matthew buried Mama on her parents' property in Bearson, Texas? That house sits on a hill, and there's a peach tree in the back yard. So all those clues fit. But Biff?"

"Sounds like a name," Holly volunteered.

"Yes, but…I can't think of anybody in the family by that name," Annabel replied. "Not even if it was a nickname." She turned to Chris. "Did you ask Trevor?"

He stiffened. He couldn't help it. "No," he said curtly. "Couldn't reach him yesterday. Left a message on his voice mail. And Ridge's, too." Annabel looked as if she were going to take him to task over his attitude toward Trevor, but he cut her off, warning, "Don't start, Bella. You can ask him if you want."

Which effectively ended that conversation. Chris's gaze moved from Annabel to Sam, who had his head down and his attention focused on his breakfast. Then Chris's gaze ended up on Holly. She was acting as if nothing was wrong, but she'd poured cereal into a bowl for him—his beloved Cap'n Crunch—and was adding milk. Just as if he were as young as her twins. Their eyes met, and for a moment they were alone in the room. "Eat your breakfast," she said eventually in a composed voice. Her "Mommy" voice, which she used with Ian and Jamie.

A smile tugged at the corners of his lips. "Yes, ma'am."

Sam and Annabel had left an hour ago, promising to start setting their end of things in motion. Holly was talking with her sons on the phone in the master bedroom. Wally at his feet, Chris was sitting in his office, brooding. Not over the plans they'd made about the McCays, but about his clue, Biff. And about Trevor.

A voice from the doorway said, "Want to tell me what that was all about?"

He swiveled around in his chair. He didn't ask "What do you mean?" because he knew. "Trevor and I have... issues."

"No! Really?" Holly said in a fake shocked tone. She moved into the room and took a seat on the sofa. Wally bounded over, tail wagging, and Holly scratched him behind his ears. "Want to talk about it?"

He did and he didn't. He knew what Holly would say. The same thing Annabel said—he wasn't being fair to Trevor. And he didn't want Holly to think he was holding on to a grudge like an eleven-year-old kid... although he was.

He sighed. "It's ancient history. And I know I should let it go. I *know* that. Annabel has told me often enough. But—"

"But you can't."

He shook his head.

"So what is it you can't let go?"

He didn't answer right away, tying to marshal his thoughts into some kind of order. Finally he said, "Trevor is three years older than me. I practically worshipped him as far back as I can remember. He could do anything in my eyes. And he was a great brother. I mean, he never seemed to mind when I tagged along after him, although three years is a pretty big gap in children's ages. He taught me to read when I was four. How to slide into second base when I was seven. How to throw a perfect spiral when I was nine, even though my hands weren't big enough to really hold the football right. He taught me so much..." The memories were all coming back to him, making his throat ache.

"So what happened?" The gentle, nonjudgmental way she asked the question told him she didn't want to know because she was curious. She wanted to give him the opportunity to talk about something he'd kept bottled up inside him for years.

"My father murdered my mother, that's what happened," he said flatly. "All seven of us were sent to separate foster homes. I was eleven. Trevor was fourteen." He swallowed the sudden lump in his throat that belonged to the eleven-year-old boy he'd been. "Trevor never made any attempt to stay in touch with me. I saw him a few times a year, but never at his instigation. Only during court-mandated visitation we all had with Josie at her foster parents' home. And when Josie decided she didn't want to see us anymore, that was it."

"Oh, Chris." Two little words that spoke volumes about Holly's tender heart.

"That's not all of it," he told her. "The story is that when Trevor turned eighteen he tried to get custody of Josie—the baby of our family. She was only seven at the time. But I always wondered just how hard he really tried before he headed off to college."

Holly's eyes closed as if she were holding back sudden tears, a conjecture that was confirmed when she opened her eyes again and they glistened. "What did Trevor say when you asked him?"

"I never asked him."

There was a long silence. Then softly, "Why not?"

Why hadn't he asked Trevor? When Chris had finally reconnected with all his brothers, why hadn't he asked Trevor why he'd abandoned him? Why hadn't he asked him about Josie?

"Because…" *Because why?* he asked himself. "Because a grown man doesn't ask another grown man those questions."

"Oh, Chris." The same two words she'd said before but this time was slightly different. Even though the maternal tenderness was there, even though he could hear how she ached for the lost and bewildered eleven-year-old boy he'd been as well as the man he was, there was also a note of something he couldn't quite put his finger on. Then it came to him. It was the same way all the women in his life had from time to time said, "Men!" As if the workings of the male mind were incomprehensible to women, and their feelings about it could be condensed down into one word that all other women automatically understood.

Despite the emotions churning inside him, something about it tickled his funny bone. "Stupid, huh?"

"Not stupid." She looked down at Wally at her feet and scratched his head again. "But if you never ask, you'll never know." She raised her eyes to his. "And I think you need to know, Chris, one way or the other. You need closure. Just like you need to know where your mother is so you can bring her home. So you can give her a decent burial. Just like you need to find out what happened to Josie. Closure. You'll never rest until you have it. One way or the other. Think about it."

She stood and snapped her fingers at Wally, who immediately rose. "Come on, boy," she said. "I think it's time to let you outside."

Chris stared at the door through which Holly had just left, thinking about what she'd said, and realized she was right in one way. But she was wrong, too. Because there was another reason he'd never asked his brother why he'd abandoned him—he was afraid to know the answer. Because the answer might be...that Chris hadn't been worth the effort.

Chapter 14

After lunch Chris told Holly, "I need to take a ride out to my grandparents' place to check on something. It's about an hour from here, in Bearson. Come with me?"

It was worded as a question, but Holly knew it wasn't really. Chris didn't want to leave her alone in the house, not even with an alarm system and Wally to protect her. Thinking of the dog made her ask, "What about Wally?"

"We'll take him with us. He can run free to his heart's content out there—the house sits on a hill overlooking several acres."

"Okay."

"Need to call Ian and Jamie before we go?"

Holly was touched Chris had asked, but she shook her head. "I called them right before lunch. They're having a blast. And besides, Peg has my cell phone number. I hardly ever use it—"

"I know."

He knew because he'd been hired to find her. The reminder made her shiver, wondering what would have happened if the McCays had hired a different private investigator, one without the strong moral conscience that was such a large part of Chris's makeup. She sent up a little prayer of thanks that Chris *had* been the one who'd found her and the twins. And that he'd taken them under his protection.

"Well…anyway," she said, "Peg has my number if anything comes up, and she knows to call me."

"And we won't be that far away," he reminded her.

"Right." She smiled. "When did you want to leave? And is what I'm wearing okay?"

The wicked gleam in his eye as he looked her over sent warmth surging through every part of Holly's body, reminding her of last night. The way he wouldn't let her be shy with him. Especially the last time, when he'd coaxed her into letting him do unspeakable things to her body. Unspeakable things she wished he would do again. And again. But all he said was "If you've got boots, wear them. Otherwise you're fine. Five minutes okay?"

Chris had laid a blanket down in the back of his truck and had fastened Wally's leash to the side when Holly came out of the house, tugging the door closed behind her. "You want to lock this, Chris? And I don't know how to set the alarm."

He quickly hooked Wally's collar to the leash, then jumped down and headed to the house. "You should have reminded me to explain about the alarm the first day. All you do is this," he said, showing her, then making her repeat the six-digit code after him. He locked the door and resettled his black Stetson on his head. "You ready?"

They drove west, picking up US-380 and crossing over the southern tip of Lake Bridgeport, then through Runaway Bay. At Jacksboro they switched to TX-114. The truck ate up the miles—Holly smiled a little to herself and didn't say a word about the speed-limit signs they passed. But she trusted Chris and his driving, so she wasn't unduly worried they were going a good ten miles per hour over the limit.

He slowed as they drove through the little town of Jermyn, then resumed his earlier speed. "You seem to know the way," she said for something to say.

"I've been here before. We visited my mother's parents every couple of months when I was a kid. But after Matthew mur—after we went into foster care, no. And my mother's death was the death knell for my grandparents. They went downhill quickly after that, is what I heard, and I never saw them again. I didn't even know they were ailing—but that's probably why we had to go into foster care permanently—they weren't able to take care of us. They passed away a month apart."

He was silent for a moment. "My brothers and sisters and me—we own the place now. No one wants to live there, but no one can bear to sell the place because it's where Mama grew up. We all chip in to pay the taxes and the upkeep—well, not Josie but the rest of us. And we rent out the acreage to the farmer across the road, who keeps an eye on the house for us—vacant houses are easy targets for vandals and migrants—we gave him a fair reduction on the rent to do that."

He drew a deep breath. "And I've been here a few

times since I graduated from college. Not a lot, maybe once every two years, because—"

"Because what?" she asked when he didn't continue.

"Don't get me wrong, I don't believe in ghosts. But every time I go there, I feel…I don't know…sad, I guess. Thinking about my mother as a little girl there. Remembering the whole family visiting my grandparents there. They were good people, Holly, and my mother was their only child. It killed them—literally killed them—when she was murdered. I don't know how anyone ever survives the loss of a—"

When he broke off this time Holly knew what he'd been going to say. *The loss of a child.* Chris had lost a child. Not a child he'd held in his arms, but still…

She tried to imagine losing Ian or Jamie, and couldn't. She just *couldn't*. Chris's baby had died unborn, but that didn't mean he hadn't already loved it. She remembered how she'd felt when she'd been four months pregnant, and how Grant had felt, too. They'd already loved their baby-to-be—before they'd known there were two—but that was nothing compared to now. So she knew how devastated Chris's grandparents had been at the loss of their only child.

She reached across and placed a comforting hand on Chris's arm, letting him know she understood. Not just how his grandparents had felt, but how he felt, too.

Just before Loving they turned south on TX-16—Loving Highway, the sign read. And Holly wondered where the name had come from. Loving Highway was obviously named after the town of Loving, but how had the town gotten its name? *Must have been named after someone*, she figured. She didn't imagine Texas cattle barons being the sentimental kind.

Her curiosity piqued, she asked Chris. "You're right," he said. "Nothing to do with loving." He glanced at her and all of a sudden she couldn't breathe. Couldn't think. Could only remember how Chris had made her body sing last night. Her nipples reacted as if he'd caressed them, tightening until they ached. She crossed one arm over her breasts to hide her reaction from Chris, because she didn't want him to know.

Then he turned his eyes back to the road and said, "The town was named Loving because it was built on part of the Lost Valley Loving Ranch. And *that* was founded by a famous north Texas cattle drover, Oliver Loving."

"Thanks." Her body still humming with need, Holly turned away and gazed out the window. Very, very sorry she'd asked.

Regina Willard surreptitiously slid the wallet she'd just stolen from a woman in the drugstore into her purse, then walked out as if she hadn't a care in the world. *Women are such fools*, she thought contemptuously. Carrying their wallets in purses so full they couldn't be zipped or snapped closed. Then placing their opened purses in the child seat of a shopping cart…and wandering away. *She deserves to have her wallet stolen*, Regina rationalized. She wasn't a thief. She would cut up and discard the credit cards. And she would drop the money in the wallet into the collection box of the first church she came to.

No, she wasn't a thief. But she needed the driver's license. Now that the FBI and the Granite Gulch Police Department had trumpeted her name and photo to the news media, she needed new identification so she could get a job. One middle-aged woman looked very like another in most people's minds. And besides, driver's license photos were notoriously bad, often looking nothing like the people they were supposed to represent. So she wasn't worried about bearing only a vague resemblance to the photo on the driver's license she'd just stolen. All she'd needed was new ID, so she was set now. Next step, finding a job…unless she spotted the woman who'd stolen her fiancé. Killing her would take precedence over anything else.

"This is it?" Holly asked as they drove up a long, winding drive to an older farmhouse perched on the top of a rise. "It's beautiful. Oh, I love those tall trees planted all around the house."

"Folks did that a lot in the old days. Windbreaks, they're called. Nowadays a lot of homeowners don't want to be bothered with trees—too many leaves to rake." He smiled as he parked the truck and they got out. "Back then the trees did more than act as windbreaks. They provided much-needed shade at a time when there was no air-conditioning. Which reminds me," he told her with a slight grimace. "There's no central air. My grandparents had window units installed, but…"

"I'll be fine. It's hot, but it's not that hot. When I was a little girl, before I started school, my parents used to take me on their missionary trips to South America. No AC in an Amazon rain-forest jungle hut. I think I'll survive."

They crossed the deep front porch, and Holly looked around curiously. Two wooden rockers resided on one side, a porch swing on the other. Chris saw where her attention was focused and said, "My grandparents called it a courting swing. But we kids didn't care about that." A reminiscent smile curved his lips. "We all tried to squeeze onto it when we younger—Trevor, me, Annabel, Ridge, Ethan and Sam. Five squirming boys and one long-legged girl with sharp elbows." He rubbed his ribs as if remembering all the times Annabel had dug her elbows into his ribs, but he was smiling, so Holly knew it was a good memory.

"No Josie?"

"She was just a baby." He laughed. "No way Mama would have trusted us with her on the porch swing." Then he seemed to recollect why he was here. He unlocked the door and pushed it open. "Come on. I want to see if I can find anything that might relate to Biff."

The curtains were drawn over all the windows in the front parlor, making the interior dim and gloomy even though the sun was shining brightly outside. So Chris flicked the switch, and the old-fashioned overhead light fixture came on. "We kept the electricity on," he explained. "The water, too. But we disconnected the propane and sold the stove and the refrigerator because we figured we didn't need them if no one was living here. Not that they were worth a lot—the fridge was almost twenty years old, and the stove was even older. But they were useful to someone, so…" He shrugged.

Holly looked around. "Who keeps the place clean?"

"The farmer who rents the land, his wife comes over once a month. She dusts—not that a lot of dust accumulates with no one living in the house—and she runs the vacuum over the floors. That's one of the reasons we kept the electricity on. We let her pick whatever she wants off the peach tree in the back, too, because otherwise it would just go to waste. She makes her own preserves and she bakes one heck of a peach cobbler."

He was silent for a moment. Then he admitted, "We probably should sell the place, but…as I told you, none of us can bear to let it go."

Holly was wandering around the room, picking up a knickknack here, a hand-crocheted doily there, then carefully replacing them. "I can understand in one way, but…someone put a lot of love into making this house a home with all these little personal touches. You shouldn't leave these things here where they can be stolen or vandalized."

Her eyes met his. "But it's not just that. You—I don't mean just you, but the rest of your family, too—should go through the furnishings and decide what you want for your own homes. These things should be used, Chris. Treasured…but used. Not left as some kind of shrine." She reverently touched the afghan folded and placed across the back of the sofa, crocheted in a light-ning pattern of royal blue and grass green, with a thin stripe of orange to add pizzazz. "If this were mine…"

She sighed, remembering her home in Clear Lake City, which had contained similar handmade treasures she'd inherited from both her grandmothers. Including three patchwork quilts and a yo-yo quilt. Not to men-tion the old-fashioned foot-pedal sewing machine she'd never used but had proudly displayed, which had come to her from her great-grandmother. When she'd run, she'd called a moving company to pack up everything and put it in storage, because even though shc'd been terrified, she couldn't just abandon her heritage. *Having money comes in handy*, she thought. What would she have done if she hadn't been able to afford to put her belongings in storage?

You still would have run, she acknowledged. *It might have broken your heart to abandon everything, but you still would have run.*

An hour later, while Chris was searching the bedrooms, Holly came across a stack of old photo albums on a bookshelf in the corner of what she insisted on calling the parlor. *Because that's what it is*, she'd stubbornly told Chris.

She knelt in front of the bookcase and pulled out a half-dozen velour-covered photo albums. The deep blue velour was faded, but the silver lettering was still visible, and she figured she'd just uncovered a gold mine. "Look at this, Chris," she called. When he joined her, she handed the photo albums to him and stood, wiping off the knees of her jeans even though the floor wasn't really dusty.

Chris was already sitting on the sofa, turning the leaves of the first album, when Holly sat next to him. "Look," she exclaimed. "There are captions on the photos!"

The books appeared to be in chronological order. They went through the first one, but it was mostly pictures of Chris's mother as a baby, then as a toddler, all of them neatly labeled. There were a few pictures of a man and a woman Chris identified as his grandparents—which matched the first names in the spidery handwriting beneath the pictures—and some of people he admitted he had no idea who they were. "Todd and Nora," he read. "Todd and Nora who?"

"Doesn't matter. Neither one is Biff."

Holly touched Chris's arm to get his attention. "Would you explain about the clues? You said your clue was Biff, and Sam mentioned other clues that seemed to point here to your grandparents' house. But why is your father doing this to you? Why won't he just come right out and say where he buried your mother?"

"Because he's a twisted son of a bitch," Chris said roughly. "I think he's getting a kick out of torturing us. Like 'Ha-ha-ha, you think you can find her?'" His right hand, the one he'd been using to turn the pages of the photo album, formed a fist.

She didn't know why she did it, but she curled her left hand around Chris's fist, her fingers stroking gently until he unclenched his hand and twined his fingers with hers. "It hurts," he whispered. "Not just that we can't find her, but that he won't tell us. Won't tell me."

"Why does it hurt so much?"

Chris released her hand abruptly, stood and strode restlessly around the room. "All these years I never wanted to see my—to see Matthew. Never visited him in prison the way Trevor did, even when he asked to see us. Not that Trevor was visiting because he wanted to," he explained, "but because it was his job as an FBI profiler. He's the only one who ever visited Matthew until Matthew began this…blackmail scheme."

He drew a ragged breath. "Until I went to see him yesterday, though, I always believed… I don't know… I always believed that somewhere inside him was the father I remembered. Strict. Stern. Okay, yeah, harsh, too, sometimes. But a man who loved his children as best he could."

"But you don't believe that anymore."

He shook his head. "Yesterday I realized the father I remember no longer exists. If he ever did."

Holly tried to think of something to say, but all she came up with was "No one is all good or all bad. Do I think he's a twisted son of a bitch, as you called him? Maybe. And maybe he's using these clues to torture you, the way you think. But you said he's dying, and he knows it. You also said he asked to see you before—but that none of you did, except Trevor…and then only because it was his job. Isn't it possible Matthew wanted to see all his children one last time before he died? And in his sick, twisted mind, this was the only way he could think of to compel you all to visit him?"

She rose and walked to where Chris was, looking up at him, beseeching him to understand there was always another side to a story. "If he gave you halfway decent clues," she said softly, "you might solve the riddle before he provides the last clue. Which means the children who haven't yet visited him probably wouldn't have to."

The arrested expression on Chris's face told her he'd never considered this as a possibility. "You really think…?" he began.

"I don't know. But neither do you. Not for sure. Don't assume you know his motive. And don't erase what few good memories of him you have. Is he a serial killer? Yes. Did he murder your mother, who loved him? Yes. Am I glad he's in prison and can't do to anyone else what he did twenty years ago to all those other people? Of course. I despise what he did. But I also pity him from the bottom of my heart."

"You feel *sorry* for him?"

Holly nodded slowly, hoping she could make Chris understand. "Because he'll never know how wonderfully his children turned out. He'll never see the man I see when I look at you."

Chris didn't know what to say. He never knew what to say when someone gave him a personal compliment. *And why is that?* he wondered now. Insecurity left over from his childhood?

He was a damned good private investigator, he knew that. And he'd built Colton Investigations from nothing into the hugely successful business it was today with only his determination and willingness to work harder than anyone who worked for him—sometimes twelve- to fourteen-hour days. A thriving business with three—soon to be four—offices.

Self-confidence in the business arena didn't always translate into self-confidence in the personal arena, however. And he'd never quite convinced himself that his older brother hadn't abandoned him...because he wasn't worth hanging on to.

Laura loved you, he reminded himself. But it had never erased that sliver of self-doubt from his psyche.

Not that he'd dwelled on it a lot—he wasn't the kind to waste time in fruitless self-analysis, as a general rule. But yesterday's meeting with his father, the heart-to-heart with Ethan at the hospital and the conversation with Holly this morning about his issues with Trevor had all forced him to consider how the man he was had been impacted by everything that had happened in his life. Losing his mother and his family, not to mention Bouncer, his constant companion for five years. Growing up in a town where he could never escape the notoriety of being a serial killer's son. Foster parents who'd never been invested in him, who'd taken him in not out of the goodness of their hearts but for the money. The deaths of his wife and unborn child.

Pity party, Colton? he jeered mentally. *Suck it up, old son, suck it up. Don't dump this crap on Holly—she's got enough to handle right now.*

So instead of (a) telling Holly how much it meant that she saw him as a wonderful man, (b) kissing her and telling her the same thing, (c) kissing her until the pleading expression in her eyes became a plea that he make love to her until neither of them could walk or (d) telling Holly what he was thinking, he settled for (e). "Let's finish going through those photo albums," he said curtly. "There's got to be a Biff in one of them."

It was in the second photo album, containing pictures of Chris's mother around the time she was starting kindergarten, with dark hair in two pigtails when she was wearing jeans, and hanging in loose curls when she was wearing her Sunday best, that they spotted it.

"'Saralee and Biff,'" Chris read, not quite believing what he was seeing. Then he said blankly, "Biff was her dog."

Chapter 15

"She looks to be about five, wouldn't you say?" Holly asked, a trace of excitement in her voice. "He's just a puppy, but he kind of looks like Wally. Biff must be a golden retriever, too."

Chris turned the page, and there were more photos of his mother as a child, and the dog—no longer a puppy—who appeared to be her best friend. There were photos of Saralee with other girls, too, but Biff seemed to feature in most of them. Chris flipped through all the way to the end, then quickly opened the third photo album. There were fewer photos of Saralee here, as if she'd become self-conscious about having her picture taken when she grew into her teens. But there were still photos of her with Biff, and Chris felt a sudden ache in the region of his heart, an unexpected kinship with his long-dead mother he'd never felt before. "I never realized..."

"Girls and dogs," Holly reminded him. "I told you a strong bond can exist between a girl and her dog." She went through several pages, one by one, Saralee maturing with each page. They were almost to the end before they realized there were no more photos of Biff. Holly turned back to the previous page, and there was a photo of Saralee all dressed up, with a young man at her side, obviously her date for the evening. There were other teenagers in the background, and the caption read "Saralee and Jeff—Sweet Sixteen Birthday Party." Captured in the bottom right corner of the photo was Biff. Just one ear and his muzzle, but it was definitely him.

But on the following page and all the subsequent pages, Biff was noticeably absent. One picture caught Chris's attention, titled "Saralee and Luke—Junior Prom." He touched it, thinking how much Annabel resembled their mother when they were both that age. Annabel was a blonde and Saralee was a brunette, but their faces were nearly identical.

"Junior prom," Holly said softly. "She would have been seventeen." She was silent for a moment. "Biff must have died sometime between her sixteenth birthday and her junior prom. Seventeen."

"Yeah." Chris carefully went back through everything between the Sweet Sixteen and Junior Prom photos, but there was no picture indicating exactly when Biff had died, or where he might be buried. *Mama would have buried him in a special place*, he told himself, knowing it for the truth. Just as he would have buried Bouncer in a special place...if Bouncer hadn't been euthanized at the pound. If Chris had been allowed to bury his dog.

He couldn't help but wonder—if his mother really *was* buried somewhere here on her parents' land— if his father had buried her near her beloved dog. It didn't sound like the father who'd blackmailed his children into visiting him in prison. The father who'd grudgingly doled out meager clues to his wife's burial place. But it *did* sound like a man who'd once been in love with his wife. Who hadn't meant to kill her...and then felt remorse when he saw what he'd done. Who'd wanted to make amends in some way...even in something as simple as this.

Holly was right, he realized suddenly. *You can never really know another man's motivations. You might think you do, but...*

Chris didn't subscribe to the theory that to know all was to forgive all. His father had killed ten people. Not surprising he'd gotten the death penalty in a state where the death penalty was often imposed in capital murder cases, but behind the scenes political machinations had gotten those death sentences commuted to sentences of life in prison without the possibility of parole—to be served consecutively. Matthew would never get out of prison—except in a box. And Chris couldn't be sorry. Maybe his father had been sick, but if so, it was a sickness that could never be cured. No one else's loved one would ever die at Matthew's hand, and Chris was fine with that. Matthew was in prison— exactly where he belonged.

But...

Holly was right about that, too, he acknowledged. *No one is all good or all bad. Mama wouldn't have loved him if he was purely evil. And she* did *love him—I know she did.*

Which meant that Holly could be right and he could be wrong. Maybe his father *had* just wanted to see all his children one last time before he died. No matter what he had to do to make it happen.

Holly swung on the front porch swing while Chris strode around the outside of the house and the barn with an exuberant Wally at his heels. He'd told her he really didn't expect to find anything—it was twenty years ago, he'd stated flatly—but he had to look anyway.

Holly watched Chris from afar, her thoughts in turmoil. Every so often she pushed the swing with one booted foot to keep it moving. The hinges squeaked—*needs oiling*, she told herself—but it was still soothing to swing. And she needed something to soothe and calm her, because she realized she was in over her head.

Whatever this was with Chris had gone from zero to sixty in nothing flat. Last night—she couldn't get last night out of her mind. She'd never looked on sex as a recreational pastime. Sex with Grant had been an extension of her love for him, and even though it hadn't been...well...hadn't been anything like sex with Chris, she'd never in a million years have imagined she could react that way with a man she didn't love.

Three times in one night. The thought chased around and around in her mind, three orgasms that had shattered her image of herself. She'd almost convinced herself the first time had been a fluke...until the second time. Until Chris's fingers had intertwined with hers and he'd whispered in her ear, *I'm going to please you until you can't take any more. And when I'm done, you'll know just how perfect you are.*

Her response the second time had been as cataclysmic as the first, and she'd thought nothing could ever surpass either of them. She'd been wrong. Because the third time, when he'd said, *I want to watch you come. Will you let me?* she hadn't been able to refuse—she'd melted just *thinking* about it. She'd always been curious, but Grant had never wanted to do it, and she'd never pressed.

But Chris seemed to have no inhibitions. And he hadn't let her have them, either—that was what she couldn't get over, how utterly different she was when Chris was in her bed.

Best time ever, she acknowledged now. All because of a man who tugged at her heartstrings on so many levels. A solitary man who should never have been allowed to be such a loner—he was made for laughter and sweet loving. For children's hands trustingly clutching his, and a woman's tender smiles.

And sex. Holy cow, was he made for sex. All six foot two, hundred seventy-five pounds of solid muscle and bone, with an unerring knowledge of her body, as if she was made for him. As if he was made for her.

That thought brought her up short, and she dragged one foot on the ground to stop the swing. It wasn't possible. She'd known him for less than a week. "Not even a week," she muttered under her breath. But if she were honest with herself—something she tried very hard to be, always—it felt as if she'd known him forever, because she could usually tell what he was thinking, the way long-married couples seemed to be able to do.

Long-married couples? *What made you think of that?*

And sleeping with him? What was *that* all about? Not something she'd ever done before, sleep with a man she barely knew. Which begged the question—why *had* she slept with Chris?

She shied away from answering, because the question alone scared the hell out of her...much less the answer.

The drive home seemed to take longer than the drive out to the farm in Bearson, mainly because Chris and Holly didn't talk much. He glanced at her from time to time as she gazed out the window at the passing scenery—scrubland that wasn't much to look at.

Finally he couldn't take it any longer. "What are you thinking about?"

She turned and resettled herself against the truck door. "Last night."

"Before, during or after?"

She laughed as if she couldn't help it. "Why is it," she asked him, trying to look stern but failing miserably, "that you can always make me laugh, even when I don't want to?"

"Answer my question first." He cast her a wicked look before firmly fixing his gaze on the road. "Then I'll answer yours."

Laughter pealed out of her, and she shook her head. "Mine was a rhetorical question. I'm not expecting an answer."

"I am." And just like that he wanted her. His voice dropped, the husky sound taking on sexual overtones that at one time had come as natural to him as breathing. "Before, during or after?" He stole a sideways glance at her, and loved the way her cheeks betrayed what she was thinking, and guessed, "During."

"Yes." It was just a thread of a sound.

"If we hadn't been interrupted this morning…"

"Yes?"

His answer mattered to her. He didn't know how he knew, just that it did. So instead of teasing her—his first inclination because it was such fun to tease her—he confessed, "I wanted to see you in the light of day. Not with the sheets pulled up under your chin like they were this morning. But in all your glory."

"You…you shouldn't say things like that to me," she said faintly.

"Why not?" When she couldn't come up with an answer, he said, "Tell me you don't regret last night."

"Oh, no!" Those little flags of color were back in her cheeks, but she leaned over and placed a hand on his arm as if she thought he needed reassurance. He did…but he wasn't about to admit it. "I could never regret last night."

His ego liked hearing that. A lot. That was something else he wasn't going to admit, though, so all he said was "Me, neither." But he couldn't keep the sudden, lighthearted grin off his face.

The first thing Holly did when she got back to Chris's house was call Ian and Jamie, talking with them for almost half an hour while they babbled in their childish way about everything they'd done that day. Then Peg had gotten on the phone, filling her in on how the twins were doing. "They're fine today. No issues. And I wasn't going to tell you," Peg admitted, "but…"

"But what?" Sudden concern made her voice sharp.

"We did have a teensy scene at bedtime last night. Jamie wanted you, and when I told him you weren't there and weren't *going* to be there, he dissolved into tears and sobbed, 'Call-her-on-the-phone.'"

"Oh, Peg, why didn't you call me?" Guilt speared through Holly that she'd been having the time of her life with Chris while her baby needed her.

"I would have, Holly...if he'd continued crying. But Susan gave him her teddy bear to sleep with—you know the one that's bigger than she is?—in addition to his bunny, and he calmed down after that. It only took three bedtime stories and four lullabies and he was out like a light. We haven't had any issues today, although when I asked Ian and Jamie what they wanted for breakfast, they both said, 'Waffos!' So I—"

"You had toaster waffles in your freezer."

"Well, no, I didn't, but no big deal. I dragged out the waffle iron, mixed up a batch of waffle batter, and they were happy as clams."

"Oh, Peg," Holly repeated, but this time it wasn't a reproach of her friend. This time it was said in gratitude that Peg was doing all this for her. "Thank you so much! I can never repay you for—"

Her response was typical Peg—she snorted a very unladylike snort. "Don't talk to me about repayment, missy," she told Holly. Then her tone changed. "Besides…"

"Besides what?"

"Our tenth wedding anniversary is coming up at the end of next month, Joe and me."

She didn't come right out and ask, but Holly quickly volunteered, "I'd love to keep Susan and Bobby for you and Joe. You could go somewhere nice and romantic."

Peg chuckled in a suggestive way. "Nice and romantic is how we ended up with two children barely a year apart."

Holly was forced to smile. "You know what I mean."

"Yes, and we'll be happy to take you up on your offer...as soon as your in-laws are in jail." That reminder drove the smile from Holly's face. "I know it's only the first day," Peg continued, "but are you making any progress?"

"Not on the McCays," she admitted. "Annabel and Sam have some things to do before we can get started on that. But we may have uncovered something more on where Chris's mother might be buried."

Chris was in his office. He considered calling Annabel and his brothers to tell them what he'd found out about Biff this afternoon, but then chose to shoot one email with the details to all of them instead, saving himself time.

He'd brought all the photo albums back with him, and now he pulled the fourth one out, wondering what else he might uncover. He and Holly hadn't reviewed the last two photo albums after they'd figured out Biff had died near the end of album number three.

But he regretted his decision to keep looking as soon as he opened the fourth album. Because there on the very first page was a professionally taken picture of his mother and father in their wedding finery. So young. So obviously in love.

Two pages later he came across another picture of his parents, both smiling, with an infant. The caption, in what by now he'd figured was his grandmother's handwriting, read "Saralee, Matthew and Trevor."

There were more pictures of Trevor—some with their parents and some by himself—from infant to toddler. Then Chris came upon another professionally shot photo, with three-year-old Trevor looking somewhat self-conscious in a tiny suit, propping up two babies—one in blue and one in pink. And underneath that photo it said "Trevor, Chris and Annabel—our first granddaughter."

Chris turned the pages slowly. Soon Ridge made an appearance, followed by Ethan, then Sam. Josie still hadn't shown up by the time Chris came to the end of album four, so he switched to number five. And there was Josie. Baby Josie as he vividly remembered her. He and Annabel had been closer than most brothers and sisters—that bond of twins—and he'd been protective of her...when she wasn't nudging him with those sharp elbows of hers or trying to wrestle him over something. But Josie had been his baby sister. So tiny, so beautiful, with dark, wispy hair and a baby smile that fascinated him. He'd been eight when Josie was born, and he and Annabel had tried to do whatever they could to help their mother—who'd never really seemed to recover completely after Josie's birth. "Why didn't I remember that?" he whispered as the memory came back to him now, crisp and sharp.

Pictures of all seven children now, some that Chris could have sworn were taken at his grandparents' farm, and— Yes! There was a picture of six of them wedged tightly in the front porch swing, with his parents standing behind them, Josie lying in the crook of his mother's arm.

Then all at once the photos stopped. Halfway down

a page, two-thirds of the way through, the photos stopped. And Chris knew why.

Holly, with Wally at her heels, found Chris standing at the window in his office, staring out at nothing. She'd intended to pretend to knock, then ask him what he wanted for dinner. But when she saw him, silhouetted by the dying sun's angled rays through the window, it flashed across her mind that Chris could be alone even in a crowd.

"Chris?"

He swung around sharply, his right hand reaching for the gun in his shoulder holster in what she could tell was an instinctive move. "Holly," he acknowledged a heartbeat later, his hand dropping to his side. "Sorry. You took me by surprise."

Wally bounded across the room toward Chris, tail wagging, tongue hanging out. Sure of his reception in a way Holly envied. She would have liked to run to Chris, wrap her arms around him and let him know he wasn't alone. But she couldn't do that. Could she?

Chris squatted on his haunches, stroking Wally's head with both his hands. Scratching behind the ears where the dog couldn't reach, eliciting the doggy equivalent of a satisfied whimper. And in her mind Holly heard her own whimpers last night as Chris had caressed her body with those big hands of his—not once, not twice, but three times—then made her cry his name, a sound that still echoed in her consciousness.

Her heart kicked into overdrive, and in that instant she would have given anything to have Chris touch her that way again. Make love to her again. But instead of saying what she wanted to say, she glanced at the schoolhouse clock on the wall, drawing his attention to the fact that it was long past dinnertime. "It's getting late," she announced. "You must be hungry. Did you want me to make dinner for us?"

He raised his gaze from Wally and gave her his full attention. "I can cook," he said. His smile was a little crooked. "Pepper steak okay? You can help me chop the vegetables."

In the middle of slicing and dicing, Holly asked quietly, "You want to talk about it?"

Chris narrowly avoided slicing his own thumb when the knife he was using in a semiprofessional manner on the onions threatened to break free. "Not much to talk about."

He turned to the stove and dumped the contents of his chopping board into the cast-iron skillet he'd already used to sear the steak strips. As the onions began sizzling, he took Holly's neatly sliced bell peppers and dumped them into the skillet, too. "It's just… looking at old photos brought back…memories," he volunteered finally.

"Good memories?"

He nodded slowly. "And bad ones. They're a reminder—as if I really needed one—that we don't know where Josie is. But it's not just that. She was three when…when she went into foster care, and we were only allowed to see her a few times a year. She turned Trevor down, she turned me down, when we tried to get custody of her."

"You mentioned that before."

He added a little water to the skillet using the lid, then stirred the onions and peppers, making sure they cooked evenly. "Yeah, but the hardest part is not knowing anything about *who* she is, not just where she is. I remember her when she was little—she was the happiest baby. And so precocious. She walked early. Talked early. She loved coloring and finger painting—" He chuckled suddenly at a memory. "And oh, how she loved to finger paint, but what a mess she always made. Mama used to say Josie got more paint on herself than on the paper."

"That's one of the good memories, then."

"Yeah." He smiled slowly at Holly. "I'd forgotten all about that. Guess sometimes it does pay to talk about what's on your mind."

They smiled at each other for a minute, until Chris suddenly realized the veggies for his pepper steak were in danger of scorching. He turned back to the stove and stirred furiously, then added in the steak strips he'd seared earlier. Finally he turned off the burner.

"Who taught you to cook?" Holly asked as she got the plates from the cabinet.

"Taught myself when I was in college. I lived off campus with three friends, none of whom could cook. I couldn't stand eating frozen cardboard-like food heated up in the microwave the way they did, and I certainly couldn't afford to eat out all the time. So I checked out a basic cookbook from the library and started messing around. I got to liking it—not just eating decent-tasting food, but the actual process of cooking from scratch. It's relaxing. Once I started Colton Investigations, though, I rarely had time to cook except on the occasional weekend."

"This is really good," Holly said as she dug in.

"Cooking must be like riding a bike. You never really forget how to do it."

Chris forked a bite and chewed thoughtfully. "Not too shabby, if I do say so myself. Meat could have used a little time to marinate—I should have planned ahead and done that."

Holly shook her head at him, smiling. "It's delicious and you know it."

"Well…" Once again he didn't know how to respond to a personal compliment. No one who knew him professionally would believe it, he acknowledged. He was supremely confident as a PI. Not so much in his personal life.

Holly changed the subject back to Josie. "So you've been searching for your baby sister for six years, that's what you said."

"Off and on. Whenever I can."

"But no luck."

He almost agreed, then realized that wasn't quite true. The whole Desmond Carlton thing was setting off alarm bells in his mind, telling him there *should* be a connection there…he just hadn't been able to figure it out. "There *is* something new on Josie—at least I think there is. Remember when I asked Annabel to look after you and the boys the other afternoon?" Holly nodded. "I needed to meet with a reporter in Dallas about an article he wrote."

He went on to give her all the details. If he'd stopped to think about it, he might not have. Holly wasn't a PI. She wasn't even family. But he suddenly wanted to share this with her, knowing instinctively she could be trusted to keep everything to herself. Including…

"So you're worried Josie might have killed Desmond Carlton," Holly stated, going right to the heart of the matter, "and that's why she disappeared."

Chapter 16

"I never said that," Chris was quick to point out.

"You didn't have to say it. But you *are* worried."

"Maybe. Okay, yeah. I am."

"If she did—and that's a big leap, Chris—but if she did, did it ever occur to you it was probably in self-defense?"

He took a deep breath, trying to dispel the tightness in his chest. "It occurred to me."

"Josie was seventeen," Holly said gently. "If she's anything like Annabel—I know Josie has dark hair and Annabel's hair is blond, so I'm not talking about that, I mean her features—but if she resembles Annabel, then she's extremely attractive. She wouldn't be the first seventeen-year-old to be accosted…possibly assaulted…by an older man. Especially if that man was a frequent visitor to her home. If Desmond Carlton was related to her foster parents…"

"Doesn't make it any easier for me to think she killed him in self-defense," he said grimly. "It just reminds me I failed to keep my baby sister safe."

"Oh, Chris…" The hint of gentle chiding in Holly's voice reminded him of the way she talked to the twins sometimes, when they did something she didn't approve of. "You can't blame yourself for *everything*."

"I'm not—" he began, then realized she was right. "Okay, maybe I am," he conceded. "But…"

"But nothing. You tried to get custody of her. You *tried*. She turned you down. You can't *make* other people do the things you want them to do, no matter how much you love them." A stricken expression slashed across Holly's face, and though they'd been discussing Josie, Chris knew instantly she wasn't talking about his sister anymore. "No," she whispered. "No matter how hard you try, you can't make someone choose you. You can't."

Regina Willard shuffled her way up the aisle with the rest of the crowd exiting the movie theater. Her prey was right behind her. Ingrid Iverson—the name the bitch went by these days—had no idea she was being stalked, of course. Inside Regina was cackling with glee. But outside she appeared no different from the other movie patrons who'd just spent an hour and fifty minutes in the darkened theater.

The bitch was with a friend, but Regina wasn't deterred. She slowly made her way to her car while the two women stood talking for a couple of minutes Then the women waved at each other, got into their own cars and pulled out of the parking lot, one turning left, the other turning right.

Regina turned right, following her prey from a safe

distance. The woman drove a few miles over the limit. *Breaking the law*, she thought self-righteously as her foot depressed the accelerator to keep pace. *But what do you expect from a loose woman like her?*

She'd first spotted Ingrid Iverson a few weeks back, at the Granite Gulch Bar and Saloon. Regina hadn't recognized her at the time, though. Hadn't realized Ingrid was the bitch in disguise. But she *had* seen what a loose woman Ingrid was. Flaunting herself to the men in the bar in a tight-fitting, low-cut blouse and jeans that appeared to be spray painted on. Accepting offers from three different men to buy her drinks. Then letting one of the men sweet-talk her into a booth, where the two sat canoodling until after midnight.

Disgusting, Regina had thought at the time. *No modesty. No morals.*

But she hadn't recognized Ingrid as the bitch who'd stolen her fiancé until she'd spotted her in the movie theater tonight just as the lights were dimming. Then she'd had an epiphany.

Regina had killed the bitch only three nights ago. What name had she been using then? Helena Tucker, that was it. But she was already back. The days between sightings of the bitch were getting fewer and fewer, forcing Regina to take shortcuts. Risks. But she didn't mind, because she was on a mission—making *sure* the bitch stayed dead.

So Ingrid Iverson had to die. And Regina could rest…for a few days, anyway.

Angus McCay propped the phone against his shoulder, writing furiously. Then he put the pen down and gripped the phone in his right hand. "Thank you *very* much, Mr. Colton," he said, waving the notepad on which he'd written an address and a phone number, trying to catch his wife's attention. "What's that?... Oh. Oh, yes, we'll see if we can get a flight up to DFW first thing tomorrow."

He listened intently to the man on the other end. "Hold on while I write that down. Bridgeport Municipal Airport, you said. Do I have that right?" He jotted the name down on his notepad. "Appreciate the suggestion, Mr. Colton. Not likely any plane out of Houston's international airport flies into there, but Houston Hobby might. We'll check."

He listened again, then said, "No, no, we don't need you to pick us up at the airport. We'll rent a car. We'll fly into whichever airport we can get the earliest flight to—we'll let you know. What's that?...Come to your office in Granite Gulch first?"

Angus glanced at his wife, who was nodding vigorously. "Of course, Mr. Colton. We'll call you once we have our flight, let you know when you can expect us tomorrow. And thank you for everything. My wife and I are thrilled we'll finally be able to see our grandsons after all this time."

He hung up. "Why did you say to tell him we'll go to his office?" His face displayed his surprise. "I don't think that's—"

"Of course we won't go to his office." Evalinda Mc-Cay's expression was the long-suffering one Angus had seen many times. "That was just a ruse. We aren't even going to book a flight. Call Leonard," she ordered, referring to Leonard Otis, the man who'd been behind the wheel during the last of the three attempts on Holly's life. "Tell him to drive up there tonight with his partner and take care of the problem. Permanently."

Holly was lying on top of the comforter on the king-size bed in her room, crying softly to herself because she didn't want Chris to hear her. She'd retreated to the bedroom after they'd done the dishes, and she'd been in here alone for the past two hours. Chris hadn't followed her. Hadn't sought her out. Had he sensed her need to be alone? Or was there another reason?

She'd almost blurted out her most closely guarded secret at the dinner table...but she hadn't. She'd managed to change the subject while they finished eating and had steadfastly refused to think about it until the kitchen was spotless. But then...then she'd escaped.

She'd called Ian and Jamie, needing to talk to them one last time before they went to bed. And when Peg had gotten on the phone, Holly had been secretly relieved the twins *were* missing her, although she would never have said that to Peg.

But that wasn't the only reason she'd called. She'd also needed to reassure herself she wasn't a bad person because of what she'd done. That the ends justified the means. And while she'd been talking with the twins, she'd believed it.

When she'd finally hung up, though, her thoughts had inevitably returned to her dinner conversation with Chris. She'd been trying so hard to convince him he shouldn't feel guilty over Josie...but she was just as bad. The guilt she was carrying...the guilt she would *always* carry...could never be forgotten. Pushed to the back of her mind much of the time, but...always there. Waiting to sabotage her happiness.

Her heart was breaking. Not for Chris and what he was going through—although she wished with all her heart she could take his pain and heal him. And not for herself—she'd long since acknowledged she couldn't undo what she'd done and she just had to live with it. No matter how often her conscience gave her hell, she deserved it.

No, her heart was breaking for Grant…and her boys. Knowing she could never tell Ian and Jamie. She *couldn't*. Knowing, too, that wherever Grant was, he knew. Had he forgiven her? She would never know. Not in this lifetime.

A knock on the closed bedroom door startled her, and Chris's deep voice sounded on the other side. "Holly?"

She dashed the tears from her eyes and realized there was no way she could disguise the fact that she'd been crying. She darted toward the master bathroom, grabbed a clean washcloth from the shelf and ran it under cold water. She wrung the washcloth out and placed it like a cold compress against her red and swollen eyes.

"Holly?" he called again. "Are you awake?"

"Just a minute! I'm in the bathroom." Which she was, but not for the reason Chris would think.

She repeated her actions twice, then checked her appearance in the mirror. Passable. Maybe. She clutched the washcloth as she opened the door and pretended to be scrubbing her face, hoping the pink in her cheeks would make Chris think the remaining pink around her eyes was due to the same thing. "What's up?"

Chris stood in the doorway with a partially drunk

bottle of beer in one hand, an unopened wine cooler in the other—the wine coolers he'd bought that first day over Holly's not-very-insistent protests. But the first words out of his mouth were "You've been crying."

And what do you say to that? she asked herself. "Yes," she finally admitted. "But nothing to do with you, so don't add it to the load of guilt you're already carrying." Her tone was wry. "That load is already stacked way too high."

The worry in Chris's face over Holly crying morphed into something else, and for just a moment she couldn't figure it out. Then she recognized it—an expression she'd begun wearing herself shortly after she and Grant were married, whenever she forgot to disguise it. Remorse was a big part of it. And something else—a lack of forgiveness...for oneself.

"Why do you look that way?" she whispered, wanting desperately to know. Wanting Chris to confide in her. Wanting him to *trust* her...the way she already trusted him.

"I should never have touched you..." Holly barely suppressed a gasp, but then he continued, "Without telling you..."

"Telling me what?"

Chris glanced at the king-size bed behind her. "Not here," he said curtly. "Not where I...where we..."

"Then where?" She wasn't about to let him get this far without telling her everything.

"Let's go into the family room. I have something to tell you anyway." He handed her the wine cooler and smiled faintly. "And you might want Wally for moral support."

* * *

"I called Angus McCay," Chris said without preamble as soon as Holly settled on the sofa, with Wally at her feet, her wine cooler sitting unopened on a coaster on the end table beside her. Chris perched on the arm of the recliner, a few feet away, one booted foot swinging. He took a sip of his beer. "I told you I was going to, but I wanted you to be aware I actually spoke with him. Starting now we both need to be on high alert. Annabel and Sam will join us for breakfast again—and will stay with us all day tomorrow. So whatever the McCays intend to try, we'll have plenty of witnesses, and plenty of firepower."

"What about tonight?"

"In addition to Wally, this house is as safe as I could make it," Chris explained. "You know the little tinkling sound whenever the front and back doors are opened from the inside?" She nodded. "All the doors and windows are wired. Anything opened from the inside just warns you—that tinkling sound is the interior parent alarm, so parents know if a child is opening a window or a door. But the exterior alarm system is something completely different—it will give us ample warning in case someone tries to break in. I built the house knowing that Laura—" He broke off for a moment, and that remorseful expression returned.

He stared at the beer in his hand, then continued. "I knew Laura might be here alone at times, so I built in every fail-safe I possibly could. If the phone signal is lost, the alarm company calls the police. If someone cuts the electricity, the alarm has a battery backup it can run on for up to eight hours. And if the alarm switches to battery power, it goes off immediately—loud enough to wake anyone—and the alarm company is notified. You can override the alarm, in case the electricity goes out because of a storm or something like that, but you have to have the alarm code. Same thing for letting the alarm company know. There are special codes that tell them if something's wrong and you can't discuss it with them."

Holly started to ask when the battery had last been checked, but Chris forestalled her. "I checked it the day I brought you and the boys here, Holly." A muscle twitched in his cheek. "You think I would have let you stay here a single night without that safety feature?"

In her mind she heard Chris saying the other day, *No one is dying on my watch ever again, you got that? I made myself responsible for you...*

That was when she made the connection. Annabel telling her Chris blamed himself for Laura's death. Peg telling her Chris needed to take care of her and the twins.

"That's what you meant when you said you should never have touched me without telling me," she whispered. "It's something to do with Laura, isn't it?"

Chris stiffened, but he didn't look away. "Yes."

"Not that Laura was the only woman you ever slept with before me, because you told me that up front. It's something to do with her death."

His face could have been chiseled from granite. "Yes."

"Then..." Her throat closed as her heartbeat picked up. Whatever Chris told her was going to take their relationship to an entirely new level. One she wanted. But she would have to be as open with him as she was asking him to be with her. And that would take all the courage she had. "Then tell me whatever it is. Because

I want you to touch me." She breathed deeply. "I want you to touch me again, and if you can't until you tell me…then tell me."

He contemplated his beer, then took a swig. And Holly knew whatever it was wasn't easy for Chris to talk about. He wasn't much of a drinker—this was the first beer she'd seen him with in all the time she'd spent in his company—but apparently he needed a little something to loosen his tongue.

Abruptly he said, "Do you know what it's like growing up in a town like Granite Gulch? Not many secrets remain secret for long. And of course, when something bad happens in your family, it's an albatross around your neck forever."

Holly nodded her understanding. "Your father was a serial killer *and* he murdered your mother. Granite Gulch never let any of you forget it."

"Yeah." His eyes met hers. "So I always felt I had something to prove. From that time on I was driven—to excel. Not just to succeed, but to succeed spectacularly. Does that make sense?" She nodded again.

"I met Laura sophomore year in high school. I took one look at her and I knew I was going to marry her—it was that simple. Through the rest of high school and four years of college, I never really looked at another woman."

Envy unlike anything she'd ever known stabbed through her. Envy of a dead woman who'd had the unswerving love and devotion of a man like Chris, while she… "You loved her," Holly managed. "I know. And she loved you."

"Yes, Laura loved me, and I loved her. But not enough to temper my ambition. Not enough to make her my first priority…as I should have." He was silent for a moment, then dropped the bombshell. "And when she told me she wanted a baby, the first thing I thought of was that would at least give her something to do so she wouldn't always expect me to be home. She never complained, but I knew. I just never…" The expression of savage self-recrimination on his face tore a hole in Holly's heart.

"When she got sick, I wasn't here. I was at work. I was always at work. One office wasn't enough for me. Not even two. I was spreading myself too thin—I knew that—but I was driven to succeed…spectacularly. I was going to prove to everyone in Granite Gulch that I wasn't my father's son. Living here in Granite Gulch but having offices in Fort Worth and Dallas meant I had a hell of a commute every day. Something had to give…and that something was Laura. I loved her, but I didn't make time for her. I gave her *things*," he said bitterly, waving his free hand to encompass the beautiful house around them, "but not the one thing she wanted the most. Me."

He tilted the beer in his hand and drained the dregs, setting the empty bottle on the chair behind him. Then he faced her again and said, "That's the kind of man I am, Holly. My father's son. A cold, uncaring bastard."

She couldn't bear it. She left the sofa and moved swiftly to stand in front of him, cradling his face in her hands. "You may be his son, but that's not the kind of man you are," she said softly. "You think you're the only one who makes mistakes? Mistakes you can't ever make up for, no matter how much you regret them?" She brushed her lips over his and blinked back tears.

"I never told Grant…never told anyone…but I…I

trapped him into marriage." She swallowed hard. "The McCays were right. I trapped him. I loved him so much, I thought that made it right. I thought I could make him love me."

Chris shook his head. "I don't follow you."

"I...seduced him one night when he'd had too much to drink, but not so drunk he couldn't...couldn't perform. I just wanted him to *see* me for once. Not as his best friend since forever, but as a woman. I thought..."

She gulped air. "I didn't... I wasn't deliberately trying to get pregnant... We did take...precautions. But I was overjoyed when it happened. I thought...it's a sign this was meant to be. That we were meant to be together. I knew Grant would do the honorable thing when I told him—that's the kind of man he was."

Her tears spilled over, trickling down her cheeks. "Long before Ian and Jamie were born, I knew I'd made a mistake. But I couldn't undo it. I couldn't even tell Grant what I'd done. He went to his grave thinking it was *his* mistake, thinking *he'd* taken advantage of *me*."

She bent her head and covered her face with her hands, sobbing uncontrollably as remorse and regret swirled through her. Then strong arms closed around her, pulling her against a hard, male chest. "Every time I look at Ian and Jamie," she choked out, her tears staining Chris's shirt, "every time I see Grant in them...I think of how they were conceived. And I know I can never make it up to them. No matter how good a mother I am, I can never make it up to them."

"Shh," he soothed, his hand stroking her back in a comforting fashion. "It's okay, Holly. You're human. You made a mistake." She couldn't have spoken right then even if she'd wanted to. "You love those boys,"

Chris continued as his arms tightened around her. "Anyone can see that. That's all that matters."

Her fingers clutched his arm, needing something solid to hold on to. Needing the human connection as she cried out her grief over what she'd done to one man in another man's arms. When her tears finally abated, she raised her face to his. "I didn't tell you that for me," she whispered, catching her breath on a sob. "I just wanted you to know you're not alone. Just wanted you to know you're not a cold, uncaring bastard. It's not your fault you didn't love Laura the way she wanted. The way she needed. Just as it wasn't Grant's fault he wasn't in love with me the way I was in love with him." Her eyes squeezed shut for a moment, then opened to face him honestly. "You're human, too, Chris. You made a mistake, just like me. But that doesn't mean you need to live in purgatory the rest of your life to atone for it."

They ended up back in the master bedroom. A part of Chris knew he'd kissed Holly as if his life depended on it, and she'd kissed him back. Then he'd swung her into his arms and carried her in here. But another part of him was taken completely by surprise. He wasn't the romantic kind. He was earthy. Direct. And his love-making had always reflected it. But somehow, Holly brought out the romantic in him, and at the moment he'd done it, carrying her into the bedroom had seemed like a good idea.

But he wasn't the only one having romantic ideas, and Holly surprised him. She dragged him into the master bathroom but prevented him from stepping into the shower when he stripped. "Uh-uh," she said, tugging his hand. "Whirlpool tub. When I was giving Ian and Jamie a bath in this tub, I couldn't help thinking it's big enough for two adults." She was already running the water, and when it was six inches deep, she asked, "How do you turn the jets on?"

He showed her, and with the water still running Holly put his hands on the top button of her blouse. Her suggestive "Help me" sent blood pulsing through his body—and one body part in particular.

When she was as naked as he was, he turned the water off, climbed into the whirlpool and helped her in after him. But when Chris would have sat down with his back to the tub, Holly stopped him. "I have this fantasy," she told him, a tiny smile on her lips. "Do you mind?"

Mind? He had no mind when she looked at him that way, when her voice curled through him as tangible as a caress. And the fantasies that came to Chris made his voice husky when he asked, "What did you have in mind?"

Chapter 17

Chris lay half-submerged in the whirlpool, his head pillowed on Holly's breasts, the water swirling around him. Holly's fantasy hadn't involved kinky sex—but then, neither had his. Her fantasy had turned out to be relatively tame compared to some he'd thought of. But how could he complain about fulfilling a fantasy that had him cradled in Holly's arms? A fantasy that involved breasts as tantalizing soft and smooth as hers beneath his head?

And oh, yeah, let's not forget what her hands are doing, he reminded himself blissfully. *Not to mention her legs.* Holly was amazingly limber.

Eventually, though, he couldn't take any more. "Holly," he warned.

"Me, too," she whispered.

They dried themselves quickly, and Chris was glad

to note Holly no longer seemed shy about letting him
see her body. He looked his fill, which took his body
from low gear to full throttle in less than a minute.

He knocked the box of condoms off the nightstand
next to the bed in his haste. "Leave them," he told
Holly when she made a move to retrieve the spilled
contents. "I have enough for now." He opened his fist
and let the handful he'd grabbed fall onto the nightstand. All except for one.

She gasped and he sucked in his breath when
his fingers stroked over her tender flesh and found
her ready. His voice was guttural when he said, "So
damned ready for me, Holly. Do you know how much
that turns me on?"

He captured her right hand and wrapped her fingers
around his erection. "Take what you want." He almost
went ballistic when she squeezed, then seated him in
place, raising her hips as if to envelop him. She couldn't
quite accomplish it—but he wasn't going to deny her
or himself. His lips found hers as he slid into her tight
sheath, swallowing her moan of pleasure. Her hips rose
to meet his, taking him so deep he again experienced
that sense of coming home he'd felt last night.

He soon found a rhythm that pleased Holly—if her
little gasps meant anything. As for him, he loved riding her soft and slow, holding back and building her
excitement to fever pitch. "Wait for it," he panted when
her breathing quickened too soon. "Wait for it."

"Can't."

"Yes, you can." He slowed and she whimpered in
frustration. He knew she'd been close, but that orgasm
would have been a prairie grass fire—easily started,

quickly over. He was aiming for an all-out conflagration, and he wouldn't be satisfied until she achieved it.

Deep and slow, deep and slow. Her fingernails digging into his shoulders, urging him to go faster. Sharp little fingernails that would have hurt—if he could feel anything other than Holly tight and wet around him, and oh so perfect. *Made for you*, he thought with that fraction of his brain that could still think.

But eventually his control cracked. His thrusts quickened. And Holly's body arched as she cried out his name and came. And came. And came. Her orgasm triggered his, and he let go with one last thrust and her name on his lips.

Wally's howl woke them both from a profound sleep. Holly was dazed and disoriented for a moment, but Chris wasn't. He was in and out of the bathroom before she knew it, tugging on his jeans and zipping them carefully. Wally's howls changed into urgent yips, as if he was trying to get at something. Chris's hands clasped Holly's arms and he pulled her close in the darkness to whisper in her ear, "Get dressed, but stay here. I'm going to check it out." Then he was gone.

"Oh, heck no," she muttered, scrambling into her clothes and tugging her boots on. "What kind of a wuss do you think I am?" She grabbed the first thing she could find that was big and could be used as a weapon. Then she ran after Chris.

She made it into the living room just in time to hear an engine roar as a car or truck accelerated away from the house down the long, winding driveway. A bare-chested Chris was crouched at one of the front windows, peering through the curtains. One hand was tightly clutching Wally's collar, holding him back. The other hand held a gun.

"Chris?" she hissed, and he whirled around.

"Damn it, I told you to stay in the bedroom."

"You're not the boss of me," she shot back without thinking. Then could have smacked herself for the less-than-adult response. She and Grant had used that phrase when they were kids, and it had become something of an inside joke when they were older. But Chris wasn't to know that.

The tense, worried expression on Chris's face rapidly changed to amusement. "I'm not the boss of you? What are we, in grade school?"

"Okay, that came out wrong. What I meant to say is you can't expect me to just obey you blindly."

"And what's that in your hand?"

Holly glanced down. "Oh. Well. I thought I might need a weapon."

"You were going to take on intruders with a Wiffle bat?"

"It belongs to the boys. I couldn't find anything else." She quickly put it down. "Forget about that." She pointed to the front door. "Was someone trying to break in? Is that why Wally was barking?"

Chris's expression went from amused to grim in a heartbeat. "Apparently so." He opened the front door, then turned on the porch light to see better before stepping outside. But there was nothing to see; whoever had been there was long gone.

"Burglars? Or do you think the McCays…?"

"Could have been your garden-variety burglar, but I doubt it. Too coincidental. But the two figures I saw moved way too quickly to be the McCays—late twenties, early thirties, I'd say." He turned to look at her, his face half in light, half in shadow. "You said the McCays tried to have you killed. Could have been the same goons. If it was them, they probably drove up from Houston—they had enough time."

"It probably *was* them." Holly shivered even though the evening was warm. "I know this is going to sound funny coming from their intended victim, but…they didn't seem all that competent when they tried to kill me before. What I mean is—"

"If they were halfway good, you'd already be dead?"

She laughed a little. "Something like that." Then another thought occurred to her. "The alarm didn't go off."

Chris came inside, closed the door and locked it with the two dead bolts. "They never got close enough to try the door or attempt to pick the lock. They took off as soon as Wally started howling."

He did something with his gun—*putting the safety on?* Holly wondered—then slid the weapon into the shoulder holster she hadn't noticed before was sitting on the floor by the window. He must have drawn his gun right away, as soon as he retrieved it from his bedroom, she reasoned, but he needed the other hand to hold on to Wally.

"Be right back," Chris told her, disappearing down the hallway. When he returned, his hands were empty.

He crouched down and scratched Wally's ears. "Good boy!" He praised the dog for several more seconds, getting his face washed in the process by an adoring Wally, then stood. "Let's continue this discussion in the kitchen. I want to give Wally a treat."

* * *

The clock in the kitchen said it was a quarter to four. Holly watched Wally gobble down the treat Chris gave him in one gulp, then plead for another. "Oh, hell, why not?" Chris said, suiting his actions to his words. "You deserve it." Then he glanced up sharply at Holly and stood. "Sorry."

"Sorry?" She wrinkled her brow in a question.

"I shouldn't have said *hell*. I should have said *heck*."

A smile slowly dawned along with understanding. "You're trying to clean up your language." Chris looked abashed, and she knew she was right. "I noticed it before, but I didn't really focus on it, if you know what I mean."

"Yeah." He put the bag of doggy treats back into the cabinet. "Peg mentioned the other day that Susan understands a lot of what she hears now. Peg also said she told Joe he needed to watch his language. She didn't say *I* did, too, but…"

The backs of Holly's eyes prickled suddenly, and she knew tears weren't far away. "You're such a good man, Chris," she whispered, moved by his attempt to do the right thing, to set a good example for the children around him, even in something as simple as this. "*Such* a good man."

That was the moment she fell in love with him.

No, that's not true, her inner self argued. *You've been falling in love with him since the first day. You're just now acknowledging it, that's all.*

She walked toward him, then placed her hands on his bare chest. She didn't realize her tears had overflowed their banks until Chris said, "You're crying again." Bewildered. His right hand came up to cup her cheek, his thumb brushing her tears away. "And this time I think it *does* have something to do with me. I just don't know why."

Holly choked back her tears as the laughter Chris could always evoke came to the fore. "Because..." She wasn't about to tell him her sudden revelation that she was in love with him, so she settled for "Because you're such a good man. The kind of man I want Ian and Jamie to grow to be someday."

Chris shook his head. "I'm no role model, Holly."

She cradled his hand against her cheek, smiling through the tears. "Think again."

Chris and Holly decided to try for a couple more hours of sleep before morning, although Holly made a sound of dismay when Chris brought his gun into the bedroom with them. "Just to be on the safe side," he assured her. "I don't think those men will be back. Not without a better plan." He placed the holstered gun on the nightstand...right next to the box of condoms she'd picked up and returned there last night.

He drew her into the curve of his shoulder. "You're safe here, Holly. I won't let anything happen to you."

"But what if the McCays don't fall for the trap we've set? What then?"

He smiled in the darkness. A grim smile he didn't let Holly see. "Those goons they sent? I'll call Angus McCay first thing in the morning, let him know they failed to kill you."

"How will you do that? You're not supposed to be staying here with me—at least that's what the McCays believe—so how would you know? And besides," she added, "you're not supposed to know the McCays want me dead, remember? So even if you know someone tried to break in, you wouldn't know they were anything other than burglars."

"Trust me, I'll come up with something believable." He laughed, but the humor was missing. "The McCays thought I was stupid enough to fall for their original story and not do a little digging on them. I won't do anything to disabuse their minds of that belief. But I'll get them up here in person." He kissed her temple, his voice softening. "See if I don't."

This time when Annabel and Sam arrived, Holly and Chris were dressed and ready for them. Chris was in the kitchen, putting together the fixings for his "signature French toast," as Annabel called it, and Holly was setting the table.

"I'll get it," she said when the doorbell rang.

Chris glanced at the clock as he whisked eggs in a bowl. "They're late." He looked at Holly. "Make sure it's them before you open the door."

Holly cast him an "are you kidding me, you think I need to be told that?" expression, but didn't say anything.

She glanced through the peephole and saw Chris's sister and brother on the porch. She swung the door open. "Hi, Annabel. Hi, Sam." Sam was in plainclothes; Annabel was in uniform. But they both looked...exhausted. Neither returned her cheerful greeting. And there was no answering smile on either face. "What's wrong?"

"Where's Chris?" Sam asked.

"He's in the kitchen making breakfast for you. French toast?" she faltered.

Sam headed straight for the kitchen, Annabel right

behind him. Holly clutched at Annabel's arm. "What's wrong?"

Annabel didn't stop, but she did say over her shoulder, "We found another woman murdered last night. Another copycat serial killing, with the red bull's-eye on her forehead."

"Oh, my God!" Holly covered her mouth with her hand, then quickly followed Chris's twin into the kitchen.

Sam was already telling Chris, "...and her name was Ingrid Iverson. Did you know her?"

Chris put down the bowl he was holding, turned off the fire beneath the skillet and shook his head. "Name doesn't ring a bell. But then the last few years new people have been moving into Granite Gulch. It's not like when we were kids."

Annabel said bluntly, "We're here, Chris, because we promised we would be. But we've been up all night." She glanced at her younger brother. "Sam won't admit it, but he's dead on his feet. I am, too."

"I'm okay," Sam insisted, but Holly saw the smudge-like circles of total exhaustion beneath his eyes. Beneath Annabel's, too.

"No, you're not." Chris's voice had that big-brother quality to it, mixed in with concern. And love. The kind of emotions most men hated to admit they felt toward a brother...even if they did.

Holly would have smiled if this wasn't so serious. Annabel and Sam were supposed to help them spring the trap for the McCays today. That was why they were here. And Chris had already set the plan in motion last night—the attempted break-in early this morning was proof the McCays were already taking the bait.

"I'm not letting either of you participate in this sting in the condition you're in now," Chris said unequivocally. "You're practically weaving on your feet." He thought for a moment. "The McCays sent men to kill Holly early this morning. Yeah," he confirmed when his siblings cast him alert looks that contradicted their exhausted faces.

Chris gave them a brief rundown of what had happened. "Their goons were here, but the McCays are still in Houston, so—"

Annabel interrupted him. "How do you know that?"

Chris smiled faintly. "Trust me, I have my sources. If they're coming in person—and I have a plan to get them here—they can't possibly arrive for a few hours. If they fly, we're talking three to four with all the hassle of flying nowadays. If they drive, at least four hours, maybe five or six even, depending on traffic. Either way, there's time for the two of you to get a few hours of shut-eye." He gestured toward the stove. "How about I make breakfast, then you can sack out." Chris was already heading out of the kitchen and down the hallway toward the bedrooms, Sam and Annabel following him. Holly brought up the rear.

"You can take my bedroom," Chris told Sam, opening a door. "And, Bella, you can have the other bedroom." Thinking she was being helpful, Holly opened the door to the bedroom across from the master bedroom. "Not that room!" Chris warned…too late.

A baby's room confronted Holly's eyes. Pale green with yellow-and-white trim, colorful decals decorating the walls. A baby crib held pride of place in the center of the room, a darling mobile of butterflies and flowers dangling above it. Exactly the kind of bedroom she'd decorated for the twins—times two—back in Clear Lake City.

Tears sprang to Holly's eyes as she realized this room had been lovingly created by Laura in joyous anticipation of her baby…her baby and Chris's. How much Laura had wanted her baby was clearly evident, even though she'd been only four months pregnant when she…

Holly blinked rapidly to hold back her tears and closed the door as quickly as she could. She turned, and when her eyes met Chris's across the hallway, she mouthed, *I'm sorry.* He shook his head slightly, as if telling her it was okay, he didn't want her to feel bad about her honest mistake. And though she knew he meant it, she hated seeing the shadow of sorrow cross his face.

"Must be this one," Annabel said in her calm voice, as if she hadn't witnessed the interchange between her brother and Holly—something Holly was sure Annabel had seen. "And you're right, Chris. I'm wiped out. A good breakfast and a couple hours of sleep, though, and I'll be good."

"Okay, okay," Sam finally conceded. "You've made your point. But I want a hot breakfast and a warm shower before I hit the hay."

Angus McCay hadn't had a decent night's sleep in months, and last night had been no exception. He'd managed to stave off his creditors, but robbing Peter to pay Paul only worked in the short run, and now the vultures were circling. If he and Evalinda didn't get their hands on the income from the trust Grant had set up for Ian and Jamie—and soon—the house of cards Angus had built would come crashing down. The fallout from that would be disastrous. Not to mention Evalinda would hold him personally responsible.

He and Evalinda had tried to overturn Grant's will legally…to no avail. They'd tried to gain custody of the twins legally, by painting Holly as an abusive mother… but that had gone nowhere. Angus hadn't wanted to resort to murder, he really hadn't. But Evalinda had convinced him it was the only way.

The problem was, as Evalinda had been quick to point out at four this morning, the men he could afford to hire weren't all that bright. Thugs willing to commit murder, yes. But easily stymied. They'd called him shortly after they'd been scared away—by a damn dog—from the house where Chris Colton had told him Holly was staying. But instead of lying in wait for Holly to come out of the house in the daytime and killing her then, they'd been spooked. They hadn't turned tail and run all the way back to Houston—not yet—but they'd called Angus in a panic, looking for direction.

"Lie low," he'd instructed them. "I'll come up there."

He didn't want to. As Evalinda had stated last night, it was far better for the two of them to stay in Houston, establish an alibi there, than to head to Granite Gulch to take care of Holly themselves. But it was beginning to look as if they had no other choice.

And that was another thing. He wasn't sure he could actually pull the trigger. *Squeamish*, Evalinda had called him in that despising way she had when he'd balked at killing Holly, back when Evalinda had first raised the possibility. Eventually he'd caved…as he always caved when Evalinda had her heart set on something. This huge house in the best neighborhood, which they really couldn't afford. The luxury cars that screamed "money," money they didn't really have. The expensive jewelry Evalinda just had to have, *because I deserve it*, she'd insisted.

This time, though, he wasn't going to cave. If Evalinda wanted Holly dead, she was going to have to do it herself. Sure, he'd help. But he wouldn't pull the trigger, and that was that.

Chapter 18

"Give me your keys," Chris told Sam as soon as breakfast was over. "I'll park your truck in the garage—make it look as if Holly's alone in the house." He glanced at Holly. "And as soon as I make one phone call, I'm driving over to the Merrills' to swap my truck for your SUV, so we can set the stage. I'll park your SUV right out front, so anyone who knows what you drive will know you're here."

Holly looked hopeful. "I can go with you and see Ian and Jamie?"

He shook his head and said gently, "Probably not a good idea. You wouldn't be able to stay long, and it might upset your sons more to have you come and go quickly than if you don't show up at all."

At her crestfallen expression he said even more gently, "Why don't you go call them now? I'll clean up in here."

He could tell she was disappointed, but she was putting a good face on it. "You cooked, I'll clean," she insisted. "Besides, it's still early. They might not be awake yet."

Chris was going to argue but thought better of it, since he was anxious to call Angus McCay. So while Sam and Annabel went to get some much-needed sleep, he moved Sam's truck, then headed for his office.

He hooked a recording device to his phone and dialed Angus McCay's home phone number. It rang five times before it was answered, and by the third ring he was saying, "Come on, be home!" under his breath.

"Hello?" A man answered and Chris had no difficulty recognizing Angus McCay's gruff voice.

"Mr. McCay? Chris Colton here."

"Oh. Oh, yes, Mr. Colton. I…I haven't had a chance to book a flight yet, so I can't tell you when my wife and I will be there. But soon, as soon as we can, because we can't wait to see our grandsons now that you've found them for us."

"About that," Chris said, smiling to himself. "I thought you should know your daughter-in-law called the police early this morning. Apparently someone tried to break into the house where she's staying. The police took her report, of course, but they have more important things to worry about than a break-in that never actually happened. You've probably seen the news by now—the Alphabet Killer claimed another victim last night. The FBI and the Granite Gulch police are all focused on that investigation."

"Sorry to hear—another victim, you say? No, I haven't read my newspaper yet this morning, so I didn't know." Angus cleared his throat. "Of course, it's terrible two men tried to break into Holly's house. Good thing her dog scared them off."

Bingo, Chris exulted inside. *Got you on tape, too.*

Angus kept talking. "If Holly was back home where she belonged, and Ian and Jamie, too, she wouldn't be alone at a time like this."

Chris rolled his eyes at the fake concern, but all he said was "Yes, sir. I totally agree with you. Holly and her sons need the kind of protection and support only a family can give." Spreading it on thick. "So when do you think you might get here? The thing is, an emergency cropped up in my Dallas office, and I'm going to have to drive over there—it'll probably take me all day to resolve. So I won't be able to meet you at my office in Granite Gulch today after all."

"Don't worry about a thing," Angus McCay reassured Chris. "You gave us the address last night. If we can get a flight, I'm sure we can find the place. As for your bill—"

"Not an issue. I can mail the bill to you after your daughter-in-law and your grandsons are safely back in Houston. Good luck convincing her that's where she belongs."

Chris hung up, laughing softly to himself. He disconnected the recording device and played back the conversation, nodding to himself as Angus McCay revealed three things that could be crucial at trial. First, Chris had never mentioned any details about the attempted break-in. But Angus McCay had revealed without prompting he knew it was two men. Second, he knew the men had been scared off by a dog. A dog he had no idea Holly had. Third, Angus McCay had admitted Chris had given him Holly's address last night. So he couldn't claim he didn't know where she was staying.

"What's so funny?" Holly asked from the doorway.

"Your father-in-law makes a lousy criminal," Chris joked. "Almost as bad as you."

Holly's face turned solemn, and Chris realized too late it wasn't a joke to her. "I had more difficulty accepting he was trying to kill me than I did about my mother-in-law," she said quietly. "She never liked me. Not when Grant and I were little, and not when we got married. But I never got that impression from my father-in-law. He...he's weak, though. His wife rules him. So if she decided I had to die, he'd go along."

She breathed deeply, letting the air out long and slow. "My parents were so different. Theirs was an equal partnership as far back as I can remember. Neither tried to dominate the other. Doesn't mean they didn't have their ups and downs. Doesn't mean they never argued. But the few times they couldn't reach an agreement, they agreed to disagree and left it at that. I promised myself that when I grew up I'd have a marriage like theirs."

He had to ask. "And did you? Was that what your marriage to Grant was like?"

She nodded slowly. "In a way. It wasn't like my parents' marriage, because Grant never— I mean, he loved me, but he was never *in* love with me. And that made things difficult at times."

She sighed softly. "But it wasn't like Grant's parents' marriage, either, thank God. I'm not a doormat kind of woman," she said, as if she were revealing a closely held secret. "Maybe you can't see that in me because you've only known me on the run. Terrified something will happen to me, but more because if something did, Ian and Jamie wouldn't have a mother. They've already lost their father. I can't let them lose their mother, too. If I didn't have them, I don't think I would have run. I would have stayed and fought it out with the McCays."

One corner of his mouth turned up in a half smile. "I know you're not a doormat kind of woman. Would a doormat have told me I'm not the boss of her?"

She smiled, but there was a touch of sadness to it. "That was an inside joke between Grant and me. If one of us tried to—oh, you know what I mean—the other would say that as a joking reminder. Then we'd laugh and things would be okay between us. But that was before we were married. When we were just friends."

More than anything in the world, he wanted to erase that sadness from her face. Wanted to banish it forever. Wanted to tell her how sweet she was, without being *too* sweet. Wanted to confess what a difference she and her sons had made in his life. Wanted her to know he couldn't imagine a more responsive lover—not just in the heat of passion, but the before and after, too. The way she fit so perfectly in his arms. The way she touched him so tenderly. The way she looked at him at times as if all light and hope in life emanated from him.

The way she loved him.

The realization hit him and knocked him for a loop. *She loves you.*

Hard on the heels of that thought came another, just as much of a body blow as the first. *And you love her.*

He opened his mouth to tell her, but the words wouldn't come. And before he could stop her, she turned away, saying, "I'm going to call Peg, see if Ian and Jamie are awake now." Then she was gone.

Chris stared at the doorway where Holly had stood, calling himself all kinds of a fool for not grabbing the chance to tell her how much he loved her. He started after her and was halfway across the office when his cell phone rang. He was going to ignore it at first, but when he glanced at the touch screen, he recognized the caller and cursed softly because he knew he had to take the call.

"Hey, Brad," he said when he answered his phone. "What's up?"

"Hey yourself. Just wanted to touch base with you about those names you asked me to track down. Desmond Carlton and Roy and Rhonda Carlton."

Chris quickly sat at his desk and pulled a pen and a pad of paper in front of him. "Okay, yeah, what have you got?"

"You were right. There's no mention of Desmond Carlton on any search engine I could find. Not that I didn't trust you, Chris, but it never hurts to double-check, you know? Desmond Carlton is a zero in cyberspace. A cipher. You'd think the guy didn't exist, unless..."

"Unless what?"

"Unless you peruse old police blotters and dig out old copies of newspapers. That's where I hit pay dirt. Desmond Carlton *was* a drug lord who was murdered six years ago—I located an article from that time. And get this—the obit on the guy lists he was survived by his brother and sister-in-law—"

"Roy and Rhonda Carlton?"

"Give the man a cigar. Also mentioned was a daughter, Julia. I haven't been able to track her down, but what I *could* find is that she was eighteen when her father bought the big one."

"She could have moved away. Gotten married. Changed her name some other way."

"Gee, thanks, why didn't I think of that?" Brad asked drily.

Chris chuckled. "Sorry. What else have you got?"

"Roy and Rhonda died five years ago in a car crash, just as you said."

"Was it really an accident?"

"Sure looks that way. Particularly gruesome one, but there never seemed to be a question it was anything other than an accident." Brad hesitated. "You know, when I dug into Roy and Rhonda, I came across a couple of names that—"

"Let me guess," Chris said laconically. "Josie Colton and Lizzie Connor, now Lizzie Colton. Right?"

"Yeah." Brad seemed relieved this wasn't news to Chris. "Lizzie's older than Josie, but both fostered with the Carltons from an early age. Josie until she was seventeen—when she up and vanished—Lizzie until the car accident. Apparently the Carltons considered her like their own daughter, and she was still with them even after the state was no longer paying for her foster care."

"Anything tying Desmond and Roy together other than they were brothers?"

"Nada. Roy was a straight arrow, and so was his wife. But Desmond?" Brad snorted his disgust. "Desmond had a rap sheet as long as my arm," he said. "But get this, Chris—no convictions. A dozen arrests, not a single conviction."

"That's got to be a mistake. A major drug dealer with no convictions?"

"No mistake. Not even a misdemeanor." Brad's

voice took on a cynical tone. "One thing after another. Problem with the chain of custody of the evidence? Case tossed out. Witness against him fails to show up at trial? Case tossed out. Oh, and I love this one. Evidence mysteriously disappears from the police lockup? Cased tossed out. The prosecutors were fit to be tied."

Chris cursed under his breath. "Either this guy was the luckiest SOB on the planet, or—"

"Or someone on the police force—maybe more than one—was helping him out."

"Right." Chris thought for a moment, trying to put all the puzzle pieces together. "Anything else?"

"Desmond Carlton's name came up in a murder investigation eleven years ago. He was never arrested, but he was brought in for questioning. A small-time drug dealer was murdered and word on the street was that Carlton had something to do with it. You know how that goes. But the police could never pin it conclusively on him, and the case went cold."

Eleven years ago. Something about that niggled at the corners of Chris's memory, as if it should mean something. *I was twenty,* he mused. *I'd just finished my sophomore year in college, but Laura and I weren't engaged yet. That was in the fall. So what happened eleven years ago?*

Try as he might he couldn't pull a thread loose, so he shelved the question, knowing that forcing your brain to remember rarely worked. But if you put it aside, the answer usually came when you least expected it.

"Is that all?" Chris asked.

"Pretty much."

"This is terrific stuff, Brad. No kidding. I knew you

were the right guy to put on this case, and you really came through for me. I won't forget it."

Chris took a moment to ask about Brad's wife and his three daughters, who were all in college and grad school. Then he disconnected and sat there, staring at the notes he'd jotted down on the pad of paper. "Eleven years," he'd written near the bottom, and circled it twice. It meant something. He didn't know what, but he knew it did.

The more he stared, the more convinced he became. Then he did something he would never have done a week ago…before Holly entered his life. He picked up his cell phone and hit speed dial. When the phone was answered, he said, "Trev? It's Chris. I know you're busy, but I need to ask you a quick question."

The urge to see her sons was so strong when Holly hung up the phone, she acknowledged Chris had been right. If she'd had her SUV, she wouldn't have been able to resist driving over to Peg's, even if only for a few minutes. And that could have been fatal. Not just for her, but for Ian and Jamie, too. Whoever had tried to break in during the wee hours of the morning could be lying in wait somewhere, watching for her SUV. She could be followed to Peg's house, and…

Chris had also been right about not going with him when he went to pick up her SUV. Ian and Jamie were doing okay. They missed her, but they were okay because Peg was making sure of it. It wouldn't be fair to Peg to flit in and out, getting the twins all wound up when their mother left.

One more day, she reminded herself. *Only one more day away from my babies.*

Holly wandered into the bathroom to brush her teeth, which she'd forgotten to do after breakfast. Her gaze fell on the whirlpool tub, and her memories of last night came rushing back. Not just what she and Chris had done in the tub. Not even what they'd done in the bed, although that qualified as one of those "just once in my life I want to" occasions she'd never forget. No, it was the moment they'd stood together in the kitchen, when she'd fallen in love with Chris, that she was thinking of now.

She stared at the mirror, but she wasn't seeing herself, she was seeing Chris in her mind's eye. So many different aspects of his character, but none more lovable than the "born to be a father" persona that came so naturally to him.

She wasn't looking for a father for her sons. She could never fall in love with a man who *wouldn't* be a good father, but that wasn't why she loved Chris. She loved him for the gentle, caring way he had, for the tenderness not far beneath the surface. She loved him for his straightforward approach to sex, and how he made her believe physical perfection was highly overrated. She loved him for the protectiveness he displayed, not just to her and her sons, but toward his sister and brother—his love for them ran so deep, but she wasn't sure he knew how deep it ran. She even loved him for his insecurities, for his self-doubt.

But most of all she loved Chris because he made her laugh. Despite the threat hanging over her head, despite her fear for herself and the twins, he made her laugh—she'd forgotten how much *fun* life could be. Nothing could ever be so bad that Chris couldn't find some humor in it, and she loved that about him. Gallows humor, maybe, but humor nevertheless.

"Now all you have to do is make Chris fall in love with you," she murmured to her reflection, "and you'll be in high cotton."

That was the problem in a nutshell. Holly had tried to make a man love her once and had failed spectacularly—she wasn't going down that road ever again. She'd even done something of which she would forever be ashamed in her quest for her love to be returned. Never again would she marry a man who didn't love her, heart and soul, unreservedly. No matter how much she loved him. No matter how tempted she might be.

"But if Chris *grows* to love you," Holly whispered to herself, "then…"

He was attracted to her. Okay, *more* than attracted. She was the first person he'd made love to since Laura, and that said a lot about how much he wanted her for herself. The question was, did he want her permanently? With all the baggage she brought with her?

"Not that Ian and Jamie are baggage," she corrected. "But we *are* a package deal."

She wouldn't use her sons, though. She wouldn't hold them out as an inducement to Chris to replace the child he'd lost—Chris had to love her for herself alone.

But if he did…she and the twins could make him so happy. Ian and Jamie were already attached to Chris—they could easily grow to love him, just as she did. They could be a family here. So much love had gone into this house—Holly could feel it. Not just the love Laura had for Chris, wanting to make a happy home for him and their baby. But the love Chris had for Laura, too. All the safety features he'd built in, to make his wife and child as safe as he could when he wasn't there.

Holly wouldn't be taking anything away from Laura—a part of Chris would always love Laura, just as a part of Holly would always love Grant. Holly didn't want to *replace* Laura in Chris's heart, she wanted to build her own place there...if he wanted it, too.

Love wasn't linear, it was exponential. And there was room in Holly's heart for the man she'd once loved...and the man she loved now.

She just prayed Chris would come to feel the same way.

"Eleven years ago?" Trevor asked Chris. "All I can think of is Josie telling the social worker she didn't want to see us anymore. I was a year out of college, just starting my career with the FBI. It was a knife to the gut, but Josie was adamant."

Chris snapped his fingers. "That's right. I'd forgotten exactly when that happened, but you're right."

"Is there anything else you needed?" Chris heard the exhaustion in Trevor's voice and figured he'd been up all night with the latest Alphabet Killer murder, same as Annabel and Sam. He'd been tempted to do as Holly had suggested—ask Trevor point-blank why he'd abandoned him when they all went into foster care. But his brother had enough to deal with right now. "Nothing urgent," Chris said. "Thanks for reminding me about Josie. Good luck on the case."

"Same to you."

"How'd you know I—"

Trevor cut him off. "I hadn't seen you around for a few days, so I asked Annabel. If anyone knew what was going on with you, it'd be her. She mentioned she and Sam were helping you set a trap to catch a couple of attempted murderers in the act. I wish *we* were that fortunate—catching our serial killer in the act," he added drily. "So good luck."

"Thanks." Chris disconnected, then sat there for a moment, mulling over what Trevor had said, carefully fitting one more puzzle piece in place. Then he saw it, the whole picture. And he could have kicked himself it had taken him this long.

Chapter 19

"You had it all wrong," Chris murmured to himself. "Josie didn't kill Desmond Carlton, not even in self-defense. That's not what this was all about." Pieces of the puzzle were still missing—pieces only Josie could fill in—but he was pretty sure he knew the basic outline of what had happened.

Josie's strange behavior eleven years ago...at the same time that small-time drug dealer was murdered. She'd only been twelve—she couldn't possibly have had anything to do with it. And word on the street was that Desmond Carlton had killed the other man. What if Josie had witnessed the murder? Carlton had probably been a visitor in his brother's house—heck, the murder could even have taken place there for all he knew. And what if Carlton had threatened Josie somehow? Carlton could have killed her, but...he had a daughter himself, just a year older than Josie. What if he couldn't bring himself to kill Josie because of that, but had threatened her instead? *Keep quiet or I'll kill everyone you love.*

That made a heck of a lot of sense. Lizzie had given them all a clue back in February, when Josie had still been a suspect in the Alphabet Killer murders, but none of them had made the connection because they hadn't known about Desmond Carlton. Chris couldn't recall Lizzie's exact words, but the gist was that Lizzie and Josie had been extremely close, like sisters. Right up until Josie suddenly became distant and guarded at age twelve…eleven years ago.

Josie had never given Lizzie an explanation, Lizzie had told them, no matter how hard Lizzie had pressed Josie to open up to her. But Lizzie had also been adamant back in February that Josie wasn't the serial killer, long before there was concrete proof. That Josie didn't have it in her to kill at all.

Someone had killed Desmond Carlton six years ago, but not Josie. And someone—or some *organization*—had done their best to erase Carlton's name from existence. "Should have focused on that before," he berated himself. "Only one entity has that kind of power. That kind of clout." Conspiracy theories be damned, in this case there was only one answer—the federal government. That led directly to federal agencies that might have reason for secrecy of this nature, and only one came to mind. Witness Security, run by the US Marshals Service.

Which would mean Josie was in Witness Security, commonly known as Witness Protection by the general public. Which would also mean she hadn't run six years ago because she was guilty of something. And she hadn't cut off communication with her family when she was twelve because she no longer loved them, either. She'd been *afraid* for them...*because* she loved them. Carlton's threat wouldn't have worked otherwise.

Now Chris's mind was flowing freely from one conjecture to another, but conjectures that fit all the facts. What if six years ago Josie decided she was tired of living in fear, tired of living under Desmond Carlton's threats? What if she went to the police and told them what she'd witnessed? And what if they'd set up a sting to trap Carlton...a sting that went horribly wrong?

That matched what the reporter had said about Carlton's death. *There were no shell casings and someone even dug the bullets out of him, so there was very little to go on...* A botched sting would explain it. Or even a *deliberately* botched sting. Either way, they'd whisk Josie away into Witness Security afterward. Give her a new identity, just in case any of Desmond Carlton's associates decided they wanted revenge.

The more he thought about it, the stronger Chris's hunch became that Carlton's death might somehow be connected to why he had no convictions after twelve arrests. Why his murder had never been solved. Because someone didn't *want* it solved?

Maybe. But that wasn't the most important thing right now. Because all of Desmond Carlton's known associates were either dead or in prison. And if Chris's conjectures were true, Josie no longer needed to fear reprisals. Which meant...if she really *was* in Witness Security...she could finally come home to her family.

Annabel had told Chris where the man from the FBI's Ten Most Wanted list was currently incarcerated—the man who'd once run with Carlton. After this whole thing with the McCays was wrapped up, Chris was going to rope Trevor into paying the guy a visit with him. And get some answers.

Chris left, but not without telling Holly he was leaving. "I already took Wally outside, so he's good," Chris told her. "I'll be back long before the McCays can get here, but don't answer the door, just in case last night's goons return. Sam and Annabel are here—if Wally starts barking or the alarm goes off, they'll know what to do—so you don't need to worry about that. If the phone rings—"

"Don't answer it. Got it."

He shook his head. "*Do* answer it. We *want* the McCays to know you're here because we want to draw them here." He grinned suddenly. "Gotta bait the trap with something irresistible, and..." He looked her up and down, sending her pulse racing when he waggled his eyebrows at her and said in his most suggestive voice, "I can't think of anything more irresistible than you."

Then he kissed her as if he meant it, and her racing pulse went into overdrive. He muttered something Holly couldn't catch and reluctantly let her go, then grabbed his black Stetson from the hook by the front door and settled it firmly on his head. He turned with his hand on the door handle and said, "And stay away from the windows. I mean it, Holly," he added implacably when she started to speak. "You trusted me to keep you safe, and I will. I'm not chancing a marksman taking you out with a high-powered rifle."

He grinned again. "And before you say it, I *am* the boss of you when it comes to this."

* * *

The morning dragged for Holly. "Stay away from the windows," she grumbled under her breath. Problem was, there wasn't a single room in the house that didn't have at least one window, not even the bathrooms. She made the rounds of the house, Wally at her heels, and confirmed she was right.

The drapes were drawn in the living room and formal dining room—neither had been used since she'd been here—but could someone see her shadow if she got too near those large windows? The kitchen windows only had café curtains—they let in the sunlight beautifully, but she would be a sitting duck if someone took aim at her while she was in there. The family room wasn't any better than the living room, unless she crouched in the corner—something she wasn't about to do.

There were no drapes in the master bedroom, only those top-down, bottom-up shades, with a valance across the top and floor-length swags on either side. But those swags were decorative only—they wouldn't close. They looked pretty, but they wouldn't provide any additional coverage. The two guest bedrooms were occupied. And no way was she going into the baby's room, not for any money—she'd probably start crying for Chris and everything he'd lost.

Which left Chris's office. It had a window, but only one. And it was L-shaped. If she sat at his desk, no one would be able to see her.

She fetched a book from her bedroom, then settled down in Chris's desk chair to read. But for some reason the book couldn't hold her interest, so she glanced around the room. For the first time she realized that of all the rooms in the house, this was the only room that reflected Chris's personality. The rest of the house—even the master bedroom—had been furnished to a woman's taste. Laura's taste.

But this room was different. There were none of the little decorative touches here that were in the other rooms. Chris's office was beautifully furnished—desk, bookcases and credenza were all honey oak—but there was a solidity to the furniture and a lack of feminine knickknacks that bespoke a man's occupancy.

Holly nodded to herself, smiling a little. If she never saw Chris again after this was all over, if she returned to her life in Clear Lake City with Ian and Jamie, she would always remember Chris in this room. Sitting on the floor with Wally draped across his legs, Ian on one side, Jamie on the other, as he read them their bedtime stories. Sitting at this very desk, concentrating on his work. Standing in front of this desk and kissing her as if his life depended on it—their first kiss that had devastated her with how much she wanted him, and—oh, God—how much he'd wanted her. *Go to bed, Holly*, he'd told her in that deep rasp his voice made when he was hurting. *This isn't what you want.* Thinking of what was best for her and the hell with what he wanted.

"How could I not love him?" she asked herself.

Still smiling, but just a tad misty-eyed, Holly glanced down at the notepad sitting in the center of the desk. Cryptic notes jotted down in a distinctive scrawl that had to be Chris's—who else could it be? But she couldn't make heads or tails of it, although she was sure it meant something to Chris. Especially the two words circled near the bottom—*eleven years*.

She realized with a sudden start of guilt she had no

business reading anything on Chris's desk, and she hurriedly put the notepad down. She turned away, and that was when she saw the silver-framed photograph standing in a secluded corner of the desk. Not large—four by six, maybe—but the face, surrounded by wavy light brown hair parted on one side, was immediately recognizable. The resemblance to Peg was obvious, but even if it wasn't Holly would have known who this woman had to be. Annabel had described Laura to a T—sweet, pretty, with a gentle, almost shy smile.

Curious, even though Holly told herself not to be, she reached over and picked up the photograph, studying it minutely. Peg's features were here, but nowhere did she see what Peg had an abundance of. Grit. Determination. Character. Not Wonder Woman, but a woman who did what she had to do without complaint. Her love for those around her flowed from strength.

What had Annabel said about Laura? *Chris was her world, and whatever he did was right. Good in some ways, not so good in others.*

If this photograph was anything to go by, Laura wasn't much like her older sister. Not that sweetness and gentleness were traits to scoff at. And Laura was far prettier than Holly could ever hope to be. But there was something lacking in Laura's face Holly couldn't quite make out. Then it dawned on her—Laura wasn't a fighter. In Holly's place she could never have stood up to the McCays.

Maybe that was what Annabel had been trying to tell Holly the other day, that what Chris really needed was a strong woman. An independent woman. A woman who wouldn't always agree with him, who wouldn't let him immerse himself in his work, body and soul. Who would force him to have some balance in his life.

A woman like me.

The phone shrilled suddenly, and Holly almost dropped the framed photograph. Remembering that Chris had said to answer the phone if it rang, she snatched up the receiver. "Hello?" Nothing but dead air answered her. "Hello?"

Whoever it was disconnected without saying a word, and Holly shivered. Could it have been one of her in-laws? One of their henchmen? Or just a wrong number?

She hung up and carefully replaced the photo of Laura exactly where she'd found it. Then whirled and caught her breath when the bell-like alarm went off, indicating a door or window had been opened somewhere in the house.

"Holly?"

She breathed sharply when Chris called her name, only then realizing she'd been holding her breath until she knew who it was. She shook her head, impatient with herself because she should have known by the tinkling sound it wasn't someone trying to break into the house. "In here," she called back. "Your office."

Chris appeared in the doorway, so reassuringly big and male. "Hey," he said, juggling her keys in one hand. "Anything happen when I was gone?"

"Someone called just now. I answered, but they didn't say anything."

He smiled and nodded with satisfaction, as if this was just what he expected. "The McCays checking to make sure you're here."

"It could have been a wrong number, but—"

"But probably not," he finished for her. "I parked your SUV out front. They can't possibly miss it."

"So what do we do now?" she asked.

"We wait."

"What if they don't show up?"

He leaned his weight on one hip, his eyes narrowing as if debating whether or not to tell her something. Then he said, "They're already on their way. Driving, not flying."

"How do you know that?"

A faint smile touched his lips. "Because I sent a couple of men down there yesterday to shadow them."

She stared at him. "You did?"

"You think I'd have told the McCays yesterday where you were if I didn't have eyes on them? You think I'd have left you here today—even with Annabel and Sam—if I didn't know exactly where the McCays were at all times?" He laughed under his breath. "What kind of PI do you take me for, Holly?" He held up one hand when she started to speak, and joked, "No, don't answer that."

Holly's lips curved in a smile as she walked toward Chris. "But I want to answer the question," she said when she was close enough to touch him. Her fingers brushed a lock of hair from his forehead, then trailed lightly down, coming to rest on his shoulder. "I think you're incredible. Amazing. There aren't words to describe you. I thank my lucky stars the McCays hired you to find me, because I'd be in a world of hurt if it had been anyone else."

His slow smile rewarded her. "You'd have managed somehow," he said. "You're a fighter—no way would you ever surrender. I knew that from the minute I entered your room in the rooming house. That's what I lo—"

Chris stopped midsentence when the sound of bedroom doors opening down the hallway and questions asked and answered between Sam and Annabel suddenly intruded on their conversation.

Holly rarely cursed—it hadn't been acceptable in her home growing up as the daughter of missionaries. But if she *did* curse, she would have just then. She would have given anything to know what Chris had intended to say. Love? As in, "that's what I love most about you"?

But she couldn't bring herself to ask, especially since Chris had already turned toward his sister and brother. "Well, if it isn't Beauty and the Beast, finally awake," he drawled.

"Bite me." Sam obviously wasn't of a sunny disposition when he first woke up.

Annabel elbowed Sam. "What makes you think *you're* the Beast?"

Chris turned his head and his eyes met Holly's, a glint of humor in them. "And there you see why Ridge is a better choice than 'don't you dare call me beautiful' Annabel and 'don't call me a beast even though I am' Sam."

"I think I'm missing something here," Sam growled.

Holly laughed. "Let's have lunch and I'll explain."

Holly went to her bedroom after lunch to call her sons—"Keep away from the windows," Chris told her in no uncertain terms.

"I will."

Chris watched her go. Part of him wished they

hadn't been interrupted earlier, but another part was glad. He hadn't intended to say anything to Holly yet— not while she still needed his protection. He'd already had one tussle with his conscience over making love to Holly while he was guarding her—he didn't want her to think there was some kind of quid pro quo going on, that he expected sex in exchange for looking after her and her sons. And he'd had no intention of telling her how much he loved her until she was free to make a decision without the threat of murder hanging over her head.

But somehow, when Holly had smiled at him, when she'd touched him and told him he was incredible and, oh yeah, amazing, the words of love had almost come tumbling out despite his best efforts.

Annabel jabbed Chris in the ribs to get his attention, her tone caustic. "Wake up there."

"Ouch!" Chris rubbed his ribs. "Darn it, Bella," he complained. "You still have the sharpest elbows of anyone I've ever known, even if you *are* my favorite sister over thirty."

"I'm your *only* sister over thirty," she retorted.

"*Darn* it?" Sam raised his eyebrows in a question Chris wasn't about to answer.

He headed for his office, with Annabel and Sam right behind him. "Before we get caught up in the sting," he said as soon as they sat down, "I want to run something by you two."

He recounted his conversations with Trevor, Brad and the reporter for the *Dallas Morning News*. He reminded them of what Lizzie had said about Josie back in February. Then he gave them the conclusions he'd drawn. "Am I way off base here?" he asked. "Or does my theory fit all the facts as we know them?"

Sam glanced at Annabel, who nodded. "Your logic is sound," he told Chris. "But the only way to know for certain is to track Josie down and see what she says."

"Trevor might be able to help there," Annabel said. "If Josie really *is* in the Witness Security Program, the FBI is in a better position to approach the US Marshals Service. Let's see what he can shake loose."

Chris ruthlessly suppressed the tiny flare of jealousy triggered by Trevor's name. Annabel was right—Trevor was in a better position than Chris to take the investigation into Josie's disappearance to the next level. Yeah, Chris had been searching for his baby sister for years, but it really didn't matter who ultimately solved the mystery. Bringing Josie safely home was more important than his ego. "You're right," he told Annabel. "As soon as we wrap up this case, I'll talk to Trevor."

Holly walked into the office with a smile on her face, and Chris couldn't help it—his eyes softened at the sight of her. Then he caught Annabel watching him, and he quickly schooled his expression into one of pure professionalism. "Everything okay with the twins?"

"Fine, but Peg says they're starting to fret over the least little thing. Which means—"

"They're missing you something fierce." He and Holly shared a private smile.

"I shouldn't want them to," she confessed. "But I do. I want them to miss me." She glanced at Annabel. "Does that make me a bad mother?"

Annabel chuckled. "No, it makes you a perfectly normal mother."

Chris brought his mind back with an effort to the

reason they were all here, and said, "Let's get every-thing nailed down—who's going to do what. Planning ahead is half the battle."

Fifteen minutes later Chris had laid out his plan in detail. "Any questions?"

He glanced from Sam, who shook his head, to An-nabel, who did the same, and finally to Holly. "Got it," she said.

"My men tracking the McCays already called from the road. We'll know in advance almost to the minute when they'll arrive, so no worries there. My men will turn off before they get here—we don't want to spook the McCays, let them know they're being followed. I'll have them double back afterward, although I don't think we'll need them. But just in case…"

Just like the morning had, the afternoon dragged. Holly just wanted it *over*—she was unexpectedly calm about the upcoming confrontation with her in-laws, but she wanted it to be past tense.

Everyone, it seemed, had something to keep their minds distracted—except her. Sam read the morning newspaper he'd brought with him. Annabel had another police procedural textbook she soon became engrossed in. And Chris worked on his computer, answering a string of emails. Holly felt a twinge of guilt. Chris had a business to run after all. He'd made her case his top priority, but that didn't mean everything else came to a screeching halt. She wanted to ask him about the notes he'd left in the middle of the desk, but she didn't—for two reasons. She didn't want to interrupt him, and she didn't want him to think she'd been snooping. She wasn't sure which reason reigned supreme.

Holly sat on the floor stroking Wally, who lay in a contented heap at her side. And she wondered if Chris would let her take Wally back with her to Clear Lake City…assuming she went back. Assuming something didn't go wrong this afternoon. Assuming Chris didn't love her.

Chapter 20

At six minutes past three, Chris's cell phone rang, and he closed his laptop. He answered his cell phone, listened for several seconds, then said, "Thanks, Matt. Tell Andy the same from me…No, I think we've got it covered, but just in case, have Andy double back and park about a quarter mile before the driveway leading to the house. You can't see that part of the road from the house, so the McCays won't know you're there. If you don't hear from me in…oh…fifteen minutes, assume the worst and come to our rescue. But be careful—"

He broke off sharply, and Holly knew he could hear the same thing she did—the sound of a car pulling up in front of the house. "They're here. Gotta go."

Holly scrambled to her feet and wiped her suddenly sweaty palms on the sides of her jeans. Annabel and Sam were already moving purposefully to their assigned places—Sam to the coat closet near the front door and Annabel secreted behind the door in the kitchen.

The doorbell rang a minute later. Chris grabbed Holly's arm, pulling her back as she started to leave the office to answer the door. "We're right here," he reminded her." But worry etched furrows in his face. "If there was any other way, I—"

She put her fingers on his lips to stop him from completing that sentence. "I know," she said, her earlier calm returning. "But there isn't another way. And I won't let them get away with it this time."

The doorbell rang again, sounding somehow impatient, and Holly looked Chris directly in the face. "I love you," she said quietly. "If anything happens— I know you'll do your best, but… Anyway, I wanted you to know." She turned and walked out without waiting for a response, Wally at her heels.

Chris swore under his breath. Damn Holly for choosing that moment to tell him she loved him, when he couldn't do a thing about it. And damn her for walking out before he could tell her he loved her, too. That he couldn't imagine life without her. That there was no way—*no way*—she was dying on his watch.

Gun drawn, he double-checked the switches on the two hidden cameras in the living room, making sure the cameras were rolling—the different angles would ensure at least one would capture whatever the McCays tried to do. Then he did the same for the voice-activated recorder. The wireless microphones were already set up, just waiting to record every word the McCays said.

He pulled the door to the office nearly shut, listening intently. Time seemed to stretch out, and he could hear

Holly clearly as she opened the door and exclaimed, "Angus! Evalinda! How did you find— I mean, how lovely to see you."

Chris smiled grimly. Holly was playing it perfectly— acting surprised to see the McCays, but also acting as if she had no idea they were there to kill her. If the McCays were innocent, the first thing they'd ask was why Holly had run away with her sons six months ago. But they never asked...because they already knew the answer.

"Come into the living room," Holly invited.

This was the most dangerous moment, Chris knew. He'd theorized earlier that the McCays wouldn't just open fire the minute they saw Holly. That they'd make *sure* she was alone in the house before they started blasting. But theories were one thing. The woman he loved turning her back on her murderous in-laws as she led them into the living room was another thing entirely. He took comfort in the fact that Sam should be able to see everything from his vantage point in the closet, which was cracked open. And if one or both of the McCays reached for a gun...

"Where are the boys?" Angus asked.

Chris shifted slightly for a better viewing angle. *Nice job!* he told Holly in his mind as she seated the McCays on the living room sofa, directly in his line of sight—and right in the field of vision of each camera. She disappeared from his view, and he knew she was sitting in one of the armchairs across from her in-laws, exactly as planned.

"They're not here right now," Holly replied. "They have a playdate with friends—Susan and Bobby. Their mom and I take turns having playdates for the children." She laughed easily, as if she didn't have a care in the world. "It gives both of us a little free time to ourselves. And you know how it is with small children, Evalinda. Much as you love your children, sometimes you just need to be alone."

"So you're alone in the house?" Evalinda McCay asked sharply. Chris saw Mrs. McCay's hand reaching into her capacious purse, and he readied himself to launch.

"Yes, I'm alone. Except for Wally here." Chris couldn't see Holly, but he imagined she was patting the dog's head. "Why do you ask?"

Even if Chris hadn't seen the gun come out, Wally's sudden growl would have warned him.

"You should never have opposed us," Evalinda McCay said, as matter-of-factly as if she were discussing the weather.

"What are you— No, Wally," Holly said when Wally's growls deepened. "What do you think you're doing, Evalinda? I'm your daughter-in-law. The mother of your grandchildren. Why are you—"

Regret was evident in Angus McCay's voice when he explained, "I'm sorry, Holly. We didn't want to do this, but you left us no choice."

"Is it money? Do you need money?" Holly's voice held just the right panicked note. "I have Grant's insurance money. I'll be happy to share it with you, if you—"

Evalinda McCay laughed, but it was an ugly sound. "That pittance?"

"Not a pittance," Holly insisted. "Half a million dollars. If you had told me, I—"

"We want the money Grant put into a trust for Ian and Jamie," Evalinda McCay stated viciously. "That damned unbreakable trust. The only way to get our hands on that money is to get custody of the twins. And the only way *that's* going to happen is if you're out of the picture."

"You'd kill me for money?" Holly's disbelief sounded like the real thing.

"You turned Grant against us. You convinced him to leave us out of his will." Chris saw the evil smile that tugged at the corners of Mrs. McCay's mouth. "So killing you will be a pleasure, not just a necessity."

"I didn't!" Holly insisted. "Grant did that all on his own, I swear!"

Wally's growls were nearly ferocious now, and Chris imagined Holly was having difficulty holding the dog back. *Good boy!* he thought. *Protect Holly!*

"It doesn't matter either way," Evalinda McCay said. "But don't worry. We'll take good care of Ian and Jamie…for now. Everyone will be convinced—just as that stupid private investigator was convinced—that we're loving grandparents who only have our grandsons' best interests at heart." She sighed with mock regret. "You'll be the victim of a terrible home invasion. Thank goodness the twins weren't here when it happened! We'll play the grieving grandparents to the hilt, stepping in to care for our orphaned grandchildren." Evalinda McCay was obviously already getting into the role.

She stood suddenly. "Now get up. Slowly. I can make this easy, or hard. If you try to run…I'll have to shoot you quickly. The first bullet might not be fatal." The evil smile was back. "But I'll make sure you're dead before I leave, Holly. Count on it."

"Police! Freeze!" Annabel and Sam's voices rang out almost simultaneously, using the exact same words.

Chris burst through the library door, his one thought to get to Holly before Evalinda McCay fired. But Wally was there before him. With one last growl the dog pulled away from Holly's restraining hold and leaped for the hand holding the gun. His jaws closed on Evalinda McCay's wrist and jerked, so the bullet went wide.

"On the ground!" Sam ordered, wrestling a shocked Angus McCay down, then cuffing him with his hands behind his back.

Annabel was doing the same to Evalinda McCay, who was moaning in agony. She'd already dropped the gun and was holding her bleeding wrist, where Wally's teeth had broken the skin and nearly broken her bones.

"You're under arrest for attempted murder," Annabel intoned, then began reciting the Miranda warning to both McCays. "You have the right to remain silent. Anything you say can and will be used against you in a court of law…"

She reached the end and said, "Do you wish to talk to us now?"

"Go to hell!" snapped Evalinda McCay. "This is entrapment! And police brutality. My wrist is broken, and these cuffs are making it worse."

Annabel listened politely, then said, "We'll stop off at the hospital to have your wrist x-rayed. But you're still under arrest."

Long before the McCays had been cuffed, Chris had enfolded Holly in his arms, his gun still drawn. She was trembling—aftereffect, he knew—and his arms tightened. "It's okay," he told her.

"She was really going to kill me," Holly whispered as Annabel and Sam led the McCays away in handcuffs.

"Yeah, but you already knew that." Chris pulled back just long enough to holster his weapon, then his arms closed around her again.

Wally was bounding around the room in excitement, following the prisoners and, when the front door closed behind them, snuffling enthusiastically around Holly's and Chris's legs.

Holly extricated herself from Chris's arms and knelt to embrace the dog. "Good boy, Wally!" she praised. "I knew I could count on you."

Chris crouched down to ruffle Wally's fur in silent affirmation of the dog's heroic actions. "What about me?" he asked Holly.

Her unexpected smile warmed his heart. "I knew I could count on you, too."

He could have stayed like that forever, except he suddenly remembered something. "Oh, cra—crud," he amended, rising to his feet and whipping out his cell phone. He clicked quickly between screens and hit the callback button. "Matt? We're good here. Sam and Annabel put the McCays under arrest for attempted murder and are taking them to jail with a short detour to the hospital. You and Andy are done for the day, and there'll be a special bonus in your next paycheck— you've earned it. I'll talk to you both tomorrow."

Holly was still kneeling beside Wally, and after Chris disconnected, he helped her to her feet. "You and I have some talking to do," he told her.

"I still can't believe she was really going to kill me herself. I mean…it's one thing to want someone dead. Hiring someone to do it—that's worse. But killing someone yourself…looking them in the face and pulling the trigger…" She shivered. "That's so cold. I can't imagine hating someone enough to do that."

Chris drew Holly into his arms again, staring down into her face. "Forget that," he told her dismissively. "I have a bone to pick with you, and I'm not deferring this conversation until you have time to come to terms with what Mrs. McCay was going to do to you."

Holly shook her head, puzzled for a minute. Then her eyes widened in understanding. "You mean…?"

"Yes, I mean…" he replied. "You sure can pick your times, Miss Holly," he teased. "Dropping a bombshell on me, then walking out cool as you please to face down murderers."

Warm color rose in her cheeks. "I didn't mean to tell you— Well, yes, I did, but not— And anyway… You see, the thing is…"

"The thing is you love me."

It wasn't a question, but she answered it anyway. "Yes."

"If you'd waited half a second instead of rushing out, you'd have heard me say the same thing."

If anything her eyes grew even bigger. "You mean it?" she whispered. She clutched his arms. "Don't say it if you don't mean it. Please don't."

He tightened his hold on her. "I never say what I don't mean, Holly." He drew a deep breath. "I don't know how it happened, honest to God I don't, because I was determined it wouldn't. But it *did* happen. And now…"

A hint of a smile appeared in her eyes. "Is this where I say I love you and you say 'ditto'?" she teased, referring to an incredibly romantic movie more than twenty-five years old she'd seen on cable. "Because if that's the best you can do…" Her smile melted away, replaced by a touch of uncertainty. "I need the words, Chris—I think you understand why. So please…*please*…"

He tilted her face up to his with one hand and, with heartfelt conviction, said, "I love you. I need you. I can't live without you." He'd mocked Ethan—not once, but twice—with those same words the day Ethan and Lizzie's baby was born. But he'd never been more serious in his life. "If any of those statements match how you feel, Holly…please tell me. Because I'm dying here."

"I can't believe you even need to ask." She touched his lips. "I already told you in the office earlier."

"Tell me again."

She smiled tenderly. "I love you, Chris. I need you in my life. And I don't think I can live without you anymore, either."

He grinned as a weight lifted from his shoulders… and his heart. Even though he'd already figured it out on his own, even though she'd told him right before the McCays had arrived, he'd needed those words from her, too, and not uttered in the heat of the moment.

Then his grin faded and he said, "I don't just want you, Holly. I want Ian and Jamie, too. I want to be their father. Not that I want to replace their real father. From everything you've told me about Grant, he was a decent man and the twins are his legacy—I would never want them to forget him. But I love your sons, and I want the chance to be the kind of father I never had."

How was it possible to love Chris even more than she already loved him? Holly didn't know, but when he said things like this, she didn't have much choice. "The other day you said you were no role model. And I told you to think again. I knew then that I loved you. And I knew there couldn't possibly be a better role model for Ian and Jamie than you. You want to be their father? You can't want that more than I do—I would be honored to share them with you."

They kissed then. Not a passionate kiss, but a sacred pledge for the future.

"You don't read poetry, do you?" Holly asked when their lips finally parted.

"Not unless country-and-western lyrics count."

She laughed softly. "That wasn't exactly what I was referring to, but I'll keep it in mind." She cupped his cheek and said, "Robert Herrick wrote a sonnet hundreds of years ago that begins, 'How Love came in, I do not know.' That's how I feel. I don't know how it happened, just that it did. And I wouldn't change it for anything."

He chuckled. "Okay, so *now's* the time I say *ditto*."

"Chris…" she warned, but in teasing fashion so he'd know she wasn't serious. Much.

He shook his head at her. "I already told you I have no idea how it happened for me, but I wouldn't change it for anything, either." He drew a deep breath. "So, Miss Holly. If I were to get down on one knee and ask you to marry me, what would you say?"

Her heart sped up, then slowed down, but not back to normal. Not by a long shot. "Ask me and see," she murmured.

She thought he'd been joking, but when he gently pushed her into the armchair and knelt on one knee, she realized he was dead serious. *Yes, yes, yes!* her heart was already answering, but she waited.

"I know you loved Grant," he began. "But I also know you love me. I don't want to replace him in your heart, Holly. But I *do* want to build my own place there. Will you marry me?"

She was barely able to contain her gasp, because Chris was saying almost exactly the same thing she'd told herself yesterday. She didn't want to *replace* Laura, she just wanted to be the woman he loved *now.* Now…and in the future.

"I would be honored," she answered softly. She framed his face with her hands, the face that had become so incredibly dear to her in such a short time. "I would be honored to be your wife."

Chapter 21

Two weeks later the doorbell of Holly's Clear Lake City house rang at a quarter past six in the morning, waking her from a not-very-sound sleep. A jumble of dreams centering around Chris had woken her every few hours, and she was just dozing off again when she heard the chime.

She grabbed her robe and scrambled into it as she hurried to the front door, her only thought being *Please don't wake the twins!* Ian and Jamie had been fractious ever since the three of them had returned to Clear Lake City—apparently they were missing their life in Granite Gulch as much as she was—and she didn't want them to start off the day short of sleep.

The chime sounded again just as she reached the door, and she glanced through the peephole, intending to give whoever it was a piece of her mind for ringing the bell this early. Then she gasped and fumbled with the locks in her haste.

"Chris!" Holly threw herself at him, and his arms closed around her. "Oh, my God, what are you *doing* here?"

"I couldn't bear it without you a minute longer," he said when his lips finally let hers go. "I couldn't sleep because I was thinking of you, so I threw a few things in a bag, jumped in my truck and hit the road. Made good time, too."

"No speeding tickets?"

He grinned at her. "Not even one." His eyes softened as he gazed at her. "But if I *had* gotten one, it would have been worth it."

Two weeks' worth of yearning was obliterated in less than fifteen minutes. They snuggled in the aftermath, their hearts racing, both still having difficulty breathing.

"Wow," Holly said. Then, "Do that again."

Chris started laughing so hard he wheezed. "Give me five minutes—ten max—to recover, and you've got yourself a deal."

She joined Chris laughing helplessly. "I didn't mean *now*. Just *sometime*. Sometime soon."

He rolled her beneath him before she could protest. Then stroked his fingers over her still-hypersensitized flesh, making her breath catch in her throat. "Sometime soon can be now, Holly," he whispered seductively. "Just wait. I'll prove it to you."

And he did. All she could think of as her body took flight was that Chris was a man of his word. Then she couldn't think at all.

* * *

"When are you coming back to Granite Gulch?" Chris asked over the breakfast table an hour later. "I'm not trying to rush you—okay, yes, I am. The house just isn't the same without you and the twins."

"You're living in the house?"

He nodded. "I moved all my things out of my apartment the day you left. I also talked to Annabel and my brothers about the farmhouse in Bearson—what you said about not leaving it as some sort of shrine. So whenever you're ready, you can go through the farmhouse and pick out what you want for our home." A slow smile spread over her face, and Chris asked again, "So when are you moving back?"

"I've already listed this house for sale," she temporized.

"Yeah, I saw the sign on the front lawn."

"But I can't just move in with you," she began.

"The heck you can't." His voice was pure steel, his expression obdurate, but then he grinned suddenly. "Hey, did you hear that? I didn't even have to think about it, I just said *heck* instead of—" He broke off suddenly, glancing at Ian and Jamie, who weren't paying the least bit of attention to the conversation—they were eating their Cheerios with complete unconcern.

A lump came into Holly's throat. *How* she loved this man, especially at moments like this. But… "I can't just move in with you," she repeated. She tore her gaze away from Chris and looked at her boys, then back at him, praying he'd see what the problem was. "I don't want people to think—"

"That you're living in sin?" Chris waggled his eyebrows at her.

She flushed. "I know it's old-fashioned. And if it was just me, I wouldn't care, honest. But I don't want anything said that the twins might hear. They understand a lot more about what's going on around them, and I—"

Chris put his hand on hers. "You don't have to justify it to me, Holly. I told you two weeks ago, I love you. I need you. I can't live without you. I wasn't kidding. I asked you to marry me, and you said you would. So in my mind we were officially engaged the minute you consented to be my wife."

"Mine, too," Holly said softly.

"If it was up to me, we'd find a justice of the peace and make 'engagement' a thing of the past." She started to speak but he stopped her. "No, let me finish. I know weddings mean a lot to women. And I know you were denied a fancy wedding when you married Grant. I intend for this to be the last chance you have for the kind of wedding women dream of—so we'll do it right. Formal engagement party, formal wedding, and everything that entails."

Holly smiled at Chris through sudden tears. "Thank you for understanding."

"But once we're formally engaged, you're moving back to Granite Gulch, right?" The eagerness in his voice touched something deep inside her. She'd sworn she'd never again marry a man who didn't love her, heart and soul, but that would never be an issue with Chris. "I need you, Holly," he added in a low tone. "These past two weeks without you—life's too short. We both know that. So please don't—"

"I won't," she assured him. "They say suffering is

good for the soul. I don't know about you, but my soul has suffered enough."

He laughed softly. "Mine, too."

They stared at each other for endless seconds, then Holly cleared her throat. "So regarding an engagement party—would you believe I was going to call you about this today?—I was thinking next week would be good."

"We always go to Ethan and Lizzie's ranch for family celebrations now. I'd have to check with them."

Holly gave Chris her best "are you kidding me?" look.

"What?" he asked, obviously clueless.

"Lizzie just had a baby. Do you have any idea of the kind of work involved in a party like this? Even if it's potluck, the hostess—and the host, too—have a mountain of work both before and after. No way are we having our engagement party at their ranch."

"Then what do you suggest?"

"Peg offered to have it at her house, but I don't want to put that responsibility on her, either, any more than I want to do it to Lizzie. What about renting out the Granite Gulch Bar and Saloon for the afternoon? It's plenty big enough, it's right there on Main Street in the center of town and everyone would be free to enjoy themselves—no one would have to worry about the food or drinks or anything. And before you ask," she told him, "I already inquired. It wouldn't cost an arm and a leg, and besides, I have the money." She flushed a little. "My money, not money from the twins' trust."

Chris shook his head, a stubborn expression on his face. "We haven't talked about money, Holly, but I guess now's as good a time as any. I'm not a millionaire—not yet—but I'm not hurting, either. Your money is yours.

Whatever our family needs I'll provide. You want to be a stay-at-home mom until the twins are in school? Fine. I can afford it, no problem. I can afford to pay for our engagement party, too."

Holly lifted her chin, her eyes narrowing as she prepared to do battle. While she understood Chris's desire to provide for his family, to feel that he was taking care of them, there were a few things he needed to get straight before they went any further. She loved him with all her heart, but she couldn't be anything other than the independent woman she was. Not even for him.

She almost retorted that their marriage was going to be an equal partnership, with each of them pulling their own weight and all decisions made jointly, or else no deal. But then an idea occurred to her. "You're not the boss of me," she said softly. Hoping Chris would get the message.

The stubborn expression vanished and a lighthearted grin replaced it, followed by a reluctant chuckle. "Okay," he said after a minute. "We'll split the cost of the party fifty-fifty. But *I'm* buying the engagement ring. That's *not* up for negotiation."

In that moment Holly knew everything was going to be all right. Chris could always make her laugh… but she could always make him laugh, too. And that was just as important as love in building a relationship that would last a lifetime. There would be arguments in the future—of course there would be—but neither of them would ever go to bed angry with the other, because one of them would always make sure of it…with humor.

Epilogue

The engagement party was in full swing when Chris wandered over to one of the large coolers packed with ice and cold bottles of beer and cans of soft drinks. He helped himself, removed the bottle cap and let the ice-cold brew slide down his throat. It was only the end of May, but the day was hot and humid—typical north Texas weather—and even though the room was air-conditioned, the beer hit the spot.

Chris turned and watched Holly for a moment, the center of a small gaggle of women across the room, Annabel and Peg among them. Holly's dress was golden yellow—God, he loved her in yellow. Loved her in anything, really. But he loved her best when she was wearing nothing at all except the tender look of love she reserved for him alone. Their eyes met across the room, and there it was again—the expression that melted his heart every time he saw it.

"How did I ever get so lucky?" he asked himself quietly.

The rowdy song the band was playing came to an end, and the strains of a popular ballad soon filled the air. As Chris watched, Jesse Willard, Annabel's fiancé, walked up to her and touched her on the shoulder. The loving face Annabel turned to him was matched by the expression on Jesse's face, and a wave of happiness for his twin washed through him as the couple began to slow dance. All he and his brothers had ever wanted for Annabel was for her to find a good man to love her. She had that in Jesse. But Annabel was her own woman, the consummate professional police officer, finally doing the work she loved. Chris could understand that—he loved his work, too.

Peg was soon claimed by Joe for a dance, and Chris smiled. Peg and Joe were the best friends a man could ever have. Peg could have resented Holly on her sister's behalf—and he wouldn't have blamed her. But there was too much love in Peg for her to wish unhappiness on someone else. She deserved a steady-as-a-rock man like Joe to make her happy. And Joe, Chris knew, was counting his blessings, too.

Chris glanced away, and his gaze fell on his younger brothers. Ridge dancing with his high school sweetheart, Darcy, whom he'd finally reconnected with after all these years. Sam with Zoe, who was the best thing that had ever happened to him. And Ethan, with his arms wrapped tight around Lizzie, not really dancing, but swaying back and forth to the music.

"How did we all get so lucky?" Chris asked himself now.

Only Trevor was alone, and Chris's heart went out

to his older brother. At the same time he promised himself, *Soon. Holly's right. I have to ask Trevor why.*

Suddenly Holly was standing right in front of him. "Howdy, cowboy," she murmured. "You look familiar. Do I know you?"

Conscious that eyes were on them, Chris tamped down the urgent desire to kiss her until she was too dazed to tease him. Instead, he raised her left hand to his lips—the hand wearing the engagement ring that was his pledge to her—and kissed it. A romantic gesture he would have felt foolish making a few weeks ago. Before he'd known Holly.

"Okay, cowboy," she drawled, "you've made your point. I don't know who you are after all."

Chris laughed and feigned hurt. "And here I thought you'd be impressed with how romantic I could be."

Holly's soft brown eyes turned misty, and she whispered, "You're romantic enough for me, Chris, just the way you are. Every single day."

That deserved a kiss, and he didn't care how many people saw him do it. When he finally raised his head and took in the dazed expression in Holly's eyes, he couldn't help it—primitive masculine pride surged through him...particularly a certain body part.

"Don't you dare move," he warned Holly.

She laughed deep in her throat, but she knew what he was talking about so she stayed right where she was for a minute. Eventually he was able to release her without being too embarrassed, but he tugged her hand. "Come on," he told her roughly. "Let's go outside where no one can—"

That was when he spotted the dark-haired woman standing in the shadows across the room from them, near the door to the bar. A stranger, yet not a stranger. Incredulous, he whispered, "Josie?"

He dropped Holly's hand as if in a dream and took two steps toward the woman he instinctively knew was his baby sister. But when the woman saw him move toward her, she darted from the room like a frightened colt.

Chris gave chase. "Josie!" he called to the fleeing woman, who had already escaped through the front door. "Josie, wait! Don't run, Josie. You're safe, damn it! You're safe! It's all over!"

She must have heard him, because she stopped suddenly on the sidewalk, turned around and stared at him. But she was still poised to run. "It's over?"

Chris didn't stop running until he reached his sister, until he was sure he could prevent her from fleeing if she tried to take off again. "Josie," he whispered, still not quite believing she was really here. Then she was in his arms. "My God, it's really you."

Brother and sister finally stepped back, and all at once Holly was at Chris's side, her breath coming quickly. Then the rest of the family appeared—all crowding around Josie, hugging her repeatedly, exclaiming over her—their joy at finally being reunited with their baby sister mirroring Chris's.

Questions peppered the air. "Oh, Josie, we've been searching for you ever since you vanished."

"Where have you been? We've been worried sick."

"Why didn't you let us know you were alive?"

Chris held up his hands. "Hold it, everybody! One at a time."

Before anyone could ask a question, Josie looked at Chris, regret in her eyes. "I heard about Laura," she blurted out. "I wanted to call you when it happened and tell you how sorry I was. I really did, Chris. But I couldn't. I just *couldn't*. 'No phone calls,' they said. 'Let them think you're dead,' they said."

"Who said?" Trevor asked, getting his question in first. "Where have you been?"

"Witness Security. Six years. Ever since—"

"Desmond Carlton was killed," Chris said, cutting Josie off. When her eyes widened that he knew, he nodded, saying, "Yeah, I think I have most everything figured out." For the benefit of the rest of the family, he said, "Here's what I think happened. Correct me if I'm wrong, Josie." He laid out his theory of what had occurred eleven years ago, and then six years ago.

Josie interrupted him a couple of times to clarify a point, but when he was done, she said, "I can't believe you pieced that all together from what little you knew." Her eyes held admiration.

"Thank Lizzie and Trevor," he told Josie. "They're the ones who gave me the clues I needed." His gaze met Lizzie's, then Trevor's. Lizzie's eyes held nothing but joy, because she finally knew what had caused Josie to turn away from her friendship; Trevor's eyes held joy that Josie was found, tinged with…redemption? *Thanks, Trev*, Chris mouthed and knew Trevor had seen it by the slight nod he gave. Chris still didn't know why Trevor had abandoned him. But he no longer believed Trevor hadn't tried his damnedest to get custody of Josie when he turned eighteen. And that was a tremendous load off Chris's mind.

He turned back to Josie. "The most important thing in all of this is, everyone who was associated with Carlton six years ago is either dead or in prison—and will stay in prison for a long time. Which means it's all over as far as you're concerned. You don't have to hide anymore."

"You really mean it?" Josie couldn't seem to take it in at first.

Chris nodded. "And you're just in time. Holly and I are celebrating our engagement." He caught Holly's hand and raised it so Josie could see the ring.

"I know. That's why I came, because I...I wanted to be here with the family, even if I couldn't join in the celebration. Even if it meant risking being seen."

"You were spotted before," Chris told her. He glanced around the circle of his family. "Ridge saw you. So did Lizzie. And Annabel—"

"You left a gold heart charm in my house, didn't you?" Annabel interjected. "The one Mama gave you that's just like mine." When Josie nodded, Annabel asked, "Did you leave it on purpose?"

Josie nodded again. "I couldn't bear having you all think I was dead. No matter what my handlers in Witness Security told me."

Another flurry of questions ensued, and this time Holly intervened. "Let's take this back inside." She smiled at Josie and held out her hand, saying softly, "I'm Holly McCay, Chris's fiancée. I'm so glad you came to our engagement party. I can't think of anything that would make Chris happier than having you here. It's been tearing him up not knowing where you were. Not knowing if you were safe. Now he can really celebrate."

Chris disconnected and slid his smartphone into his pocket. He jumped guiltily, then whirled around when

Holly said behind him, "How are the boys doing with the babysitter?"

"How'd you know I was checking on them?"

She smiled the tender smile he loved. "Because I know *you*. Because that's the kind of man you are." She came to stand right in front of him and deliberately placed her hand on his heart, which immediately kicked up a notch at her touch. "You made yourself responsible for us that very first day," she said. "And thank God you did, because if you hadn't I never would have known you. Never would have loved you." Her voice dropped to a whisper. "And I never would have known what it was like to be loved the way you love me."

A lump came into his throat, and he wished he had Holly's way with words. Wished he could express what her love meant to him. But all he could do was touch her cheek with a hand that wasn't quite steady and say, "I don't want to lose you, Holly. Tell me that will never happen."

What you don't love you can't lose. He'd told himself that in the hospital right after Ethan and Lizzie's baby had been born. He'd lost so much in his life—Mama, Trevor, Josie, Laura, their baby—he hadn't wanted to risk loving again. Mama was dead, and so were Laura and their baby—he wouldn't see them again in this lifetime. But Josie had been miraculously restored to them. And if Chris ever got up the courage to ask Trevor one all-important question, maybe he'd finally find the older brother he'd once loved unreservedly—the brother who could do no wrong—in the man Trevor was now. Which meant it was still possible to find his mother and lay her to rest, the one remaining thing he desperately wanted to accomplish.

Holly seemed to understand what he meant when he said he didn't want to lose her, seemed to understand the lurking fear he refused to name but couldn't completely banish. "I can't promise not to die," she told him solemnly. "No one can promise that. But I *can* promise I'll love you, now and forever. Because love…enduring love…is a choice. And I choose you, Chris. I will always choose you."

The lump in his throat was back, but all he could think of to say was "Does this mean I get to be the boss of you sometimes?"

Her gurgle of laughter warmed the lonely place in his heart the way it had from the first time he'd heard it. The way it always would. "If I get to be the boss of you sometimes, too," she told him, her soft brown eyes alight with the laughter they would always bring to each other.

"Then I have nothing to worry about," he assured her, "because you already are that. Sometimes," he hastened to add, needing to be completely honest with her.

She laughed again, her twinkling eyes telling him she knew exactly the kind of man he was, flaws and all…and she loved him anyway. Then she kissed him, and in that instant he knew he was going to be all right. *They* were going to be all right.

Ethan had said it best. *I thought I could cut myself off from life.* Chris had thought that, too, but Holly had proved him wrong. You couldn't play it safe where life was concerned. Where love was concerned. You had to risk it all. You had to put your heart out there where it could get trampled, hoping and praying it wouldn't.

His heart *had* been trampled. There was no denying that. But Holly had healed him. She'd seen something in him worth loving, so she'd somehow mended the cracks. His heart wasn't good as new, it was *better*—because loving and losing and loving again had taught him never to take anything for granted, and he never would again. The really important things in life didn't entail proving a darn thing to anyone—except proving his love to those he cared about. It was a long list—something he finally acknowledged—and getting longer every day. Heading that list was Holly.

"Life is good," he murmured, drawing Holly back against him so they could look out at all his brothers and sisters together again…finally. And all his and Holly's friends also in attendance at their engagement party. Family. Good friends. Almost everything a man needed to make life worth living. Almost. Only one thing was missing from the picture—the one thing that was no longer missing from his life.

He curved his arms around Holly's waist, holding his future securely. "Life is good."

* * * * *

MILLS & BOON®

Mills & Boon have been at the heart of romance since 1908… and while the fashions may have changed, one thing remains the same: from pulse-pounding passion to the gentlest caress, we're always known how to bring romance alive.

Now, we're delighted to present you with these irresistible illustrations, inspired by the vintage glamour of our covers. So indulge your wildest dreams and unleash your imagination as we present the most iconic Mills & Boon moments of the last century.

Visit **www.millsandboon.co.uk/ArtofRomance** to order yours!

MILLS & BOON®

Why shop at millsandboon.co.uk?

Each year, thousands of romance readers find their perfect read at millsandboon.co.uk. That's because we're passionate about bringing you the very best romantic fiction. Here are some of the advantages of shopping at www.millsandboon.co.uk:

* **Get new books first**—you'll be able to buy your favourite books one month before they hit the shops

* **Get exclusive discounts**—you'll also be able to buy our specially created monthly collections, with up to 50% off the RRP

* **Find your favourite authors**—latest news, interviews and new releases for all your favourite authors and series on our website, plus ideas for what to try next

* **Join in**—once you've bought your favourite books, don't forget to register with us to rate, review and join in the discussions

Visit **www.millsandboon.co.uk**
for all this and more today!